The Still Point

Amy Sackville

W F HOWES LTD

This large print edition published in 2011 by
W F Howes Ltd
Unit 4, Rearsby Business Park, Gaddesby Lane,
Rearsby, Leicester LE7 4YH

1 3 5 7 9 10 8 6 4 2

First published in the United Kingdom in 2010
by Portobello Books

A CIP catalogue record for this book is available
from the British Library

ISBN 978 1 40749 111 0

Typeset by Palimpsest Book Production Limited,
Falkirk, Stirlingshire
Printed and bound in Great Britain
by MPG Books Ltd, Bodmin, Cornwall

To Alistair

At the still point of the turning world.
  Neither flesh nor fleshless;
Neither from nor towards; at the still
  point, there the dance is,
But neither arrest nor movement. And do
  not call it fixity,
Where past and future are gathered.
                    T. S. Eliot, 'Burnt Norton'

PART I

Wait:

. . .

There. A little ellipsis, the smallest pause, opening for him to slide into. Then withdrawal and a full stop.

Then they are unsticking from each other and, unstuck, are two separate bodies again in a too-hot room together. The bed creaks as he sits heavily on the side and gets up to wrench at the window, swollen in an old frame, letting in night noises without relieving the heat. A car passes unseen and she imagines the face within, pale in the dashboard glow, driving late and alone through the quiet town. Turning onto her back (creak), she lets a hand rest on the bone between her breasts; her skin is slick, still sticky, clamming to the sheet. Turning again to rest her head upon him, feeling the new but not fresh air across her thighs, this is the memory that her mind spirals into as she slips under:

When I was a girl, we cut holes in the world. My sister took a pair of scissors and cut two lines in the air in parallel, horizontal, and then cut down between them to make invisible curtains which she took carefully between finger and thumb and, drawing them back, invited me to put my hand through the gap. The air beyond was a different air, we'd have sworn it. Cleaner, I called it. Cool, unused. I'd wriggle my fingers, circle my wrist and then pull it out again. In time, my sister forgot the game but I tried that little magic again, alone, again and again, even after I was caught and scolded for playing with scissors. But I never cut a hole that was large enough to step through, for fear of being stranded in that other air.

I think now that perhaps I slipped through one of those holes without noticing, after all.

DAWN

Some hours pass without event. They shift a little. The nascent day will soon begin; have patience. We are watching them in the time most often lost to us, well into the night, but before the threat of dawn – that space in time when, if we wake, we are unsure if there are hours of sleep ahead or if we will be shaken seconds later by whatever it is that usually signals the day: music or the shrill beep of an alarm; a persistent bird at the window; a lover; dread.

You can draw a little nearer, if you're very quiet. Put your face close to his, close enough to feel the gentle rumble and stink of his breath; feel the damp warmth of hers on your own cheek. They fall asleep, as many couples do, first twined and then detached; as we rejoin them they have long since undergone this last conscious act, this delicate separation on the very brink of dreaming.

His posture is awkward, his arm at a sharp angle with his fist by his ear, so that there is a risk he will elbow her in the face as he has done sometimes in the past. His right knee, bent out to the side, is almost, almost touching her thigh. At this one point, between knee and thigh, this little heated space that's moist with their sweat, you couldn't fit your finger between them. They both sleep above the covers, he fully, she in part. There is, now the night has deepened, the softest of breezes from the open window which makes their sleep delicious, although they sense this only when they drift close to waking.

Look: he is skimming the surface now. His arm stretches a little, his elbow dangerously close to her cheekbone, but then he pulls it around as he turns away from her, drawing it over and down so it is snug against his belly. His breathing quietens, and with a long dreaming sigh, she curls a little closer in upon herself. Settled, they do not stir.

In a few hours they will rise and pass through this door to the adjoining bathroom, to rinse themselves of the night's residue. It is even hotter here, airless; there is no window and it is very dark without the benefit of streetlight, which seeps through their bedroom blind. They are not the kind of couple to share their ablutions, one in the shower while the other brushes teeth, and so forth. They are both quite private people, and whilst they have struggled to open their hearts as wide as they can to each other, the secrets of their bodies have remained their own. She would hate for him to watch her shaving her underarms, for example, or picking at her toenails as she relieves herself, pulling them short where necessary. He, on the other hand, might well be embarrassed if she were to see him cleaning the dirt from between his toes in the same posture. But they will in all likelihood never know of these similar habits. He will never watch her and tut – his own nails are carefully kept, on toes and fingers alike – but she in turn will never see him and smile as he scrubs with the nailbrush, seven times on each hand. We might observe as they perform these rites, if we stood here before the sink and waited a little longer; but it is hot and stuffy, smells a little of damp, and besides there is something unnerving, is there not, about a mirror in darkness. And perhaps we would rather not strip them entirely of mystique, not yet. Let us return instead to their bedside.

She too has turned, in our absence, emerging fully from the covers so that now they form the uneven outline of an urn: wide at the opening, their heads far apart, and narrowing to their bottoms, less than a foot between them; their bent knees make the swell of the bowl, tapering again to their feet. The zigzag of his body is sharper than hers, so that although he is much taller, if they were each to move their feet directly backwards their soles would touch. It is almost tempting to tickle them, both pairs so neatly stacked; she would pull hers away violently from our mischievous fingers, whereas he would barely stir, being more ticklish in the region of the torso.

Closer inspection of their eyelids will reveal that she is dreaming. Behind the skin you will just discern, in the violet dimness, the raised circles of her pupils scud and jitter as the eyes roll in their sockets. You would like to know the hidden colour of the irises. Very well, then: hers are brown, his are also brown, but darker. And if it were possible to ask what she is dreaming:

North, north, blue and white; silent, still. Beyond the world in a clean air. Unused, I am bare skin, against the snow. Laid out on bearskins, waiting. I am waiting. It is night now as it has been for a long time, a blue and white night. Always night here, or always day, and the long twilight between; time, limbs, stretching into the palest ache. There is no dirty city stain in the sky, which is depthless and goes on possibly for ever. Heavens above. It is not heaven, it is just air, deep, blue, indigo air, smattered silver. There is sometimes jade, rose and gold across it. Stretch the word out: cor-us-cating. The beat of my heart, high and skating. I wait. All my skin, immersed in air. Here there is no one to see and I am heedless.

She rolls just a little in her sleep. Her husband, who is now awake, thinks: I never knew a woman to fall asleep so easily, and to sleep so deep. Perhaps it is time to reveal his name: Simon.

Simon, too, has been far north in his sleep, and is still emerging from the frozen sea that he dreamed of, a sea churning with chunks of sea-ice. His north, too, is dark and silent, but it is jagged, bitter, hard. In Simon's dream he was sailing a gully that narrowed until his ship was gripped on both sides. It groaned; he woke, chilled, to air so hot that moving feels like swimming. And now he lies, stuck to the bed by his back in the brown night, beside his murmuring wife. He is listening to his wife's murmur, and thinking: Julia is talking in her sleep again. Unknown words. Julia, he knows, is the sort of person who dreams, and remembers her dreams, and sets store by them. Simon is one of those who profess not to dream, but in the fuddle of this disturbed night he will admit it, or lacks the will to deny it. How many hours have passed since he lay down beside and made love to his wife and listened as she slipped into sleep, and slept perhaps himself for a time; how many hours? Three and a half, approximately. Just over three more before he must rise. The red digits of the alarm clock state 03:42. The hands of his watch, laid out neatly beside it, also show forty-two minutes past the hour. It is dark and still and the too-few hours until dawn yawn before him.

There were corpses in the sea, afloat among the ice. The carcasses of whales which, when flensed – stripped of blubber and skin – are called *crangs*. It is a very loud word for something so vast and silent, for something so irrefutably dead. And rank, he's heard, or read. The hardiest of seamen quailed at the stench, their hot vomit hissing as it hit the water. In the dream the smell was formaldehyde, for he has never smelled flesh decaying.

In a waking doze, letting his hand rest on exposed skin, he thinks, Julia is very soft beside me. In her own Arctic, she is still dreaming, this:

Ice deep blue, smooth like skin, soft, like skin, rounding and dipping. I can see by the moon to the edge of land and beyond it, and no one comes. I stretch my arms to the edge and no one comes. No sunlight for months now but the moon is bright enough, the snow pale below it. No edges to the world or myself. No distance that I'd care to measure. All distance can be crossed. It is all one, everything is equidistant, equally far from me, as he is far from me. I am stranded here in this air, this ice, this indigo. But I do not weep. I am peaceful. My tears would freeze. Gold and rose across the sky. He does not come.

While Julia lies outstretched across the still point of the turning world, sleepless Simon, by what may be a rare coincidence, is thinking of that same pole that we dance around. Men of action have suffered to attain it. Julia's Great-great-uncle Edward, struggling through the snow towards it. It is something sacrosanct, a constant to believe in. Simon imagines himself standing upon it, exalted as Edward might have been. Proud, at peace, knowing he has reached the pinnacle and the centre,

10

thrusting the flag in. Thrusting a flag into ice? Expecting it to stay there?

The truth, he knows, is endurance and farce. Once within range, the crazed compass uselessly struggling for a different north (a point several hundred confusing kilometres south by now), the exhausted and intrepid explorer must pace the area around and over so that, upon returning, he might say, 'I must have crossed it.' There is nothing but one's own doggedness to believe in – nothing but dogs to eat, either, or so it was in the days when Julia's beloved ancestor trod those hopeless paths. There is no knowing which footstep is the true one, the moment when the whole earth turns below. You cannot pause upon it. You move, oblivious, over the still point.

The poets can't be blamed for this. The world is built around it. The grid is traced from this fixed point. So-called; a necessary, a useful fiction, but – and this, since he is unwilling to turn his thoughts inwards, is what is keeping Simon awake – it is not fixed, it isn't still at all. This is what incenses him: the still point wobbles. Yes, wobbles, an absurd and undignified word for the truth. The Earth is not constant on her axis. There is no great rod in space, holding her steady through the middle. She rolls, just a little, as the years roll on.

These thoughts continue to arch and slide in and out of coherence until, exhausted by his anger at the earth's inconstancy, Simon at last sleeps. According to the digital clock it is 04:29, and you can be assured that the time displayed at this particular bedside, on Simon's side of the bed, is accurate. The hands of his wristwatch concur.

A little later, in the creeping brightness, the heat of tomorrow already hovering in the clear air, Julia wakes. Abruptly, she flings off the covers (which at some point in the intervening hours she has pulled over herself) and swings out of bed. Toes deep in thick white fur, a little unwelcome luxury for her hot feet. Stepping with automatic care over the rug's massive head, her soles touch wood and she pads out of the room.

That is the word she thinks of as she walks, of the hard cushioned pads of her feet. She pads upstairs to the second floor, keeping close to the wall to avoid squeaks, makes her way along the corridor and turns up another crooked flight without once missing her footing, knowing her way through the dark at the centre of the house. She carefully pushes open the narrow door at the top.

This long attic room, which runs the length of the front, is stacked literally to the rafters with books, papers, letters, chests, boots and sealskins, skis and ski poles, instruments of navigation – all the saved scraps of Edward's legacy. In the corners, dust has been dredging for decades. Near the door, a heap of black canvas suitcases sits incongruous, only just beginning to fluff. Odd items of furniture, last pieces of once-grand suites, fade and tatter here; a chaise longue lolls invitingly, despite the wear at its edges. Someone has spent months procrastinating upon it: close by, a drift of magazines litters the floor – winter-warming casserole recipes, spring fashions, this year's best beach reads – three seasons' worth of newspaper supplements. A small kneehole desk has been set against a wall, a pile of black leather notebooks, seemingly little used, arranged neatly upon its green leather top, which is otherwise cluttered with framed photographs, pots, pens, paperweights and other oddments.

There is also, you will no doubt have noticed, a polar bear towering over you, her head grazing the beams. She roars protective over the cub crouched beside her. There is, in fact, a whole menagerie, all trophies from a hundred years ago, all, of course, long since stuffed. Simon would frown – the preferred term is 'mounted'. Technically they belong to Julia, but it is he who tends the animals. He has become adept in the care of fur, feathers and hide, although his own mounts are smaller, stickily furred and dusted, and kept elsewhere, carefully pinned wide in drawers.

Why has she come here at this dark lilac hour, Julia alone with the animals, the inherited relics and dead things from a century before? Certainly it is not her habit to rise so early, but she is not much a creature of habit. She woke and crept here under half-conscious compulsion; perhaps she is seeking the stillness of her sleep, seeking Arctic

13

blue in a summer dawn. The gazelle at the window watches her doe-eyed and hopeful – she hasn't gone so far as to imagine what it hopes for. She strokes its pelt and guiltily brushes the fine hairs from her palm. Maria is her private name for it, which she does not share with Simon for fear of being sneered at (and her fear might be well founded, but she does not see how lovingly her husband writes their Latin names on labels).

Like the bedroom, the attic faces the almost-rising sun, and a curious brightness fills the air, gilding Julia's naked skin and the glass eyes that gaze upon it. Opening a gabled window, she leans out into the approach of dawn. The heaviness of the day before has been refreshed by a moist coolness, a green-hazed promise of brilliance which will burn off in the morning sun. She closes her eyes and relishes it, elixir on her eyelids: Julia enchanted. If we were to transfer ourselves to the window opposite, so that we could look upon her and into the room beyond – but wait. We have been gazumped, for here, hidden, someone is watching. A woman in a towelling dressing gown, risen for the day, is curling her hair lock by patient lock, and all the while she is watching. From here, we cannot see the polar bear and her doleful cub, the albatross which soars on his wires above, the ill-stuffed silver leopard with his too-long face. The woman watching does not look beyond Julia anyway, she is too much absorbed in admiring bitterly the shining hair, loose about fine-boned shoulders; her breasts, squashed by her clasped arms, for warmth and comfort, not modesty. Bitterly? Too late – with a cloud of hairspray and a puff of perfume, the watcher is gone.

Julia remains, oblivious, apparently entranced, until her closed eyes flood apricot and she opens them to see the sun breach the rooftops opposite; she inhales, deeply, the grapefruit freshness of the sky before turning and padding out of the room. Only the anxious little white bear glances after her – a glance, if it can be so called, which is for ever fixed in glazed arrest upon the door.

She lies down as lightly as possible on top of the covers so as not to disturb Simon, but he is nonetheless disturbed. She falls immediately asleep and is woken twenty minutes later by the radio alarm, which is very loud and which he does not reach to turn off. Simon, whose night has churned past too quickly, is taking a small revenge for having the last twenty minutes of it snatched from him. He lies for a while tracing the horrible familiar fussy curls in the ceiling's plaster, knowing he has to get up; the skin around his eyes feels swollen by tiredness. In truth, as we know, he lost less than an hour to his own peculiar preoccupations. But he is a fastidious sleeper, and is not, to repeat, much in favour of dreaming; he is not looking forward to the day and would rather not face it exhausted, and they retired later than usual last night after an evening not in keeping with routine; and, to top it all, the act of love. When he turns his head he is surprised to see his wife curled towards him, smiling, not angered by his thought-lessness (his thought-out thoughtlessness; he is never unknowingly thoughtless). A smile not quite so radiant as the morning, perhaps, but possibly pleased to see him.

'I like this tune,' she says, as if to annoy him, to make the point that his plan has backfired and nothing can spoil her perfect day, her perfect summer day doing nothing apparently, while he has to be at work in – damn – an hour and twenty-five minutes, he's lost five minutes just lying here, will he have time to shower and have breakfast as well? He is about to say, 'Do you even know what it is?' when she asks:

'Did you sleep okay? Shall I make you break-fast while you have a shower?' and he is suddenly rather ashamed, and decides instead to tell her:

'It's Rachmaninov.'

'Oh, is it?' (she yawns, dozy, contented, not bored, not yet bored by the day) 'I like it.'

'I have it downstairs, on CD. Hm. I must say I've never thought of it as music to herald the dawn,' he opines. And seeing her face fall just a little, and hating himself just a little for it, he adds, 'I like it too, though. Gets the blood going, I suppose. Eggs would be nice – if you're getting up.'

Julia smiles again; Simon graciously allows a last tragic chord to fade to the point when it is almost certainly silent and switches off the radio just before the presenter starts speaking. Julia gets off the bed

16

in that peculiar way she has, looking until the last second as if she intends to simply roll off the edge to the floor. She puts on a jade-green silky gown, a gift from him and far more glamorous than that of her neighbour, that towelling misery she failed to witness. She hums to herself, 'How do you like your eggs in the morning?', but she knows his answer already, and although it is not that which the song prescribes, although he fails to join the duet, 'I like mine with a kiss . . .', she applies it anyway – to his further surprise – on his forehead on her way out of the room. He likes his eggs in the morning poached until the white has just set.

So begins the day. There is no reason that this particular Thursday should be anything other than ordinary; but already, as they surface into it, it is proving unusual. What has happened to so transform Simon and Julia's morning? This affection on her part, this talk of concertos? This request for cooked breakfast when, but moments before, he was huffily contemplating a hasty bowl of bran, standing at the kitchen counter, every scratchy woodchip spoonful somehow blamed on her? Any number of things have added up to this anomaly: a dinner; a little death; infidelity. These lazy high-summer days are long, and anything might quietly happen before night falls.

EGGS AND PHEASANT

Julia and Simon live in a Victorian house which, like almost everything in this very pretty market town, is listed. There is the attic, the master suite, several other bedrooms of various proportions, another bathroom, a basement kitchen, a small but much-loved wine cellar, an elegant reception room, a grand dining room, a cosy squashy much less tidy sitting room, other rooms that we probably won't have a use for. This is a house full of books, of prints and paintings and photographs on the walls and pottery and glass, and dark, weighty furniture; there are rugs and heavy curtains, there's a piano that Simon could but doesn't play, there are stuffed animals. Mounted, we should say, animals.

This house groans in the night, freighted with memories. They are stashed in every cupboard, they lurk in every corner, they gleam in the eyes of the albatross in the attic . . . Listen, and you will catch the echoes. Attend to the vanishing glint at the corner of your eye: great men have talked, slept, drunk and dined here, under a different, richer yellow light. History took its course here, and might yet be coursing through the corridors, to be caught at. Julia and Simon have lived here less than a year, but she has known these rooms for as long as she can remember, and a part of her has always been wandering through them.

Julia is descended from an important man. A hero even. Julia's father was the son of Edward Mackley, whose father was John, whose brother was also an Edward – the famous Edward Mackley, the explorer. John Mackley was himself a man not lacking in distinction, a prominent member of the Royal Geographical Society, a respected academic and physician. This is John's house; it is John's menagerie in the attic. But while the elder brother stayed at home carefully emptying and refilling animals for posterity, it was Edward and his like who brought home the spoils. It was John who inherited their father's home and practice, but it is Edward, the second son who had to make his own path, Edward – young, dashing, dead – that history remembers. And it is Edward who occupies Julia's days, to whom she has turned her archivist's ear, tracing the story that rimed the edges of their dreams with ice, honing the myth long since fixed and frozen. Edward, who was drawn to the Pole like a flake of iron to a magnet, who was lost in the snow.

It is Julia's task, since she has left her job in the city, to sort the orts and fragments of her inheritance, and to somehow extract and assemble them into Edward Mackley's legacy. His body remains half preserved in the ice; his Life is in her indolent hands.

For now, Julia is in the kitchen. She will not find Edward here, but she is otherwise occupied with poaching eggs for her husband's breakfast – her famous ancestor, who has been buried in the hard Arctic ground for more than a century, can remain on ice a little longer.

She negotiates her way around the table, plates, chairs, pans, hob, with a lazy shuffle. She is enjoying the sleepiness of her limbs and the mess she knows her hair is, and the blankness of being alone here while the water boils, the shower running upstairs. She will wait until she hears it stop, and then depress the toaster's lever, and then wait a further minute, and then she will carefully lower the eggs into the pan and the toast will pop and she will spread both slices with butter, not too much but all the way to the edges, by which time precisely the whites of the eggs will be just set and she will lift them out on to a plate and place the triangled toast alongside, because the eggs on top make it soggy. And she will set it down next to a cup of tea just as Simon comes into the room. It isn't like her, this precision on Julia's part, but this morning she is eager to please, and nothing pleases Simon like precision. For now, though, she is shuffling sleepily, aimless, and peering into the pan.

★   ★   ★

20

Snow; I was dreaming about the sky, snow, something blue, something . . . the pale blue sunrise this morning, so perfect. Like Scotland that time, where was it? Scotland. Yes, but where was it? A hill? A house? The sun, the sea. Water's boiling, let it boil, turn it down when the toast goes in. Sun, sea and sand . . . no, it was a pebble beach, a grey pebble beach and there was a stone I found that I kept which had magic in it because it was so smooth and oval white with the magic dark grey line across the centre, a dark blue line, indigo, the richest word in the rainbow.

Hearing the shower stop she thinks, It will be good to make him happy. The eggs will make him happy. Because last night she almost hated him and that won't do at all. *Pedant, pheasant . . .* her irritation twists around a half-rhyme.

Simon arrives in the kitchen, clean and stubble-free, to find that Julia's egg and toast plan has been successfully executed; he takes a seat at the solid old oak table and the plate is set, hot, before him. He makes a small incision in the top of each egg, then pours salt into the palm of his hand, pinching it with finger and thumb and circling above each one in turn, three times clockwise and finishing with a flourishing flick. Julia, sitting opposite, notices that one of the yolks is much more yellow than the other, a deep full yellow like the sound 'yolk'. The other is insipid, a perfect yellow for a lemon, but it's not a lemon, and it's not what a yolk should be. She wonders which he

21

will eat first and guesses, correctly, the paler. Each egg white carefully sliced away from the yolk's periphery, laid on top of a neat piece of toast, then dipped. Was the darker one fresher? Or was it fertilized, and the other not? Or both, but the pale one more recently? Why should proximity to chickenhood make a difference? He is now beginning the second egg. She would like to watch that lovely yellowness bulge before bursting under a crisp corner, and spill unctuous on to the plate, but Simon's egg yolk somehow stays contained within its circle, becomes its own little dipping pot.

Last night he drove them home from the Watsons'. He calls them the Watsons, which she finds sometimes merely anachronistic, sometimes actually annoying, as if she is a housewife in the 1950s or the 1970s or she's not sure when exactly. A time when middle-class people called their friends 'the Watsons' instead of James and Michelle, their names, by which they've always known them. In fact Julia has no real recollection of when she learned that surname in connection with this couple, perhaps when they were engaged or married but it doesn't really matter. What matters is that there is no reason now to say, 'Don't forget dinner tonight with the Watsons,' as if they were going to be greeted by glasses of sherry and a horrid bowl of bright green olives fished out of a jar of brine, and some waxy cheese on sticks and pickles, most likely, as they would be in the vaguely located but vivid time in which Julia imagines people saying such things.

Simon, too, carefully mopping his plate with a last piece of toast reserved for the purpose, is thinking of the drive home from dinner. He had driven because he'd wanted to be at work early in the morning and had decided not to drink. Julia had no such qualms; and James has very good taste in wine, as Simon knows. Had he not known it, then Julia's enthusiasm for every sip would soon have impressed it upon him. James is the kind of man who is allowed, encouraged even, to dominate social gatherings. Simon is willing to concede that he is witty, clever, attractive perhaps, although he is growing louder as the years go on and all that good wine might just be going to his paunch.

Michelle still works in arts heritage, as Julia did before she took up her inheritance. She is reasonably successful, somewhat rounded, wears high heels, the swell of her calves showing off very fine ankles, an alluring firmness to her buttocks. He dwells again upon these plump charms, as he did while driving, Julia beside him in a wine-red snooze. He appears so prim, so lacking in ardour as he sits at the table; it seems we have some things to learn about Simon.

The last trace of yellow is gone, and he lays his knife and then his fork across the plate, at a perfect

23

right angle to himself, and rises. Julia has her elbows on the table on either side of her mug, resting her face in her hands and staring down into it, so that her cheeks are pulled back and her lips are stretched long. She looks up, slightly out of focus, and he places a kiss on the top of her head and thanks her for breakfast before glancing at his watch and pulling on his jacket. Julia wonders, watching him, whether he will be too hot but decides not to say anything. Perhaps she is a little annoyed by him, a man who puts a suit jacket on to drive to the station on a summer's day, perhaps this is her little revenge in turn; but she is rarely so calculating or malicious, certainly not before breakfast. It is more a drift across the surface:

Warm, to wear a suit, won't you be too . . . too hot for eggs. I don't want that cloy. Back of the throat. Yellow yolk yellowyolkyellow. I'll just have toast.

When she hears the door slam – it has to be slammed to properly close – she stands and wanders to the kitchen counter. It is only a few steps but Julia can incorporate a wander into any journey when the mood takes her. She boils the kettle for more tea, puts a slice of bread in the toaster. While she's waiting for the toast she peers into the pan again, now cold and grimed with greyish albumen, and briefly enjoys the word *albumen*, and decides to wash it up later. She

24

spreads her toast thickly, with real butter, and then with real plum jam that she's still amazed she made herself, and thinks that indolence will make the perfect housewife of her yet.

The night before: Simon, impatient, driving a little too fast. The roads between their home and the Watsons' – it's catching – have no lines down the centre as there is room for only one car comfortably. In the rear-view mirror his eyes are shadowed, glancing at the dark behind and the empty back seat, the cat's eyes as they flare and stretch out to dimness, the same, the same, the same in soporific rhythm all down the road. Julia in the morning, over her slice of toast and second mug of tea, lulled by the wet rumble of the washing machine, is remembering:

Slash of bright before the sound, light is faster than sound; travelling too fast. Out of black, smack against the glass. Sound without a word for it, not bang or crunch, Simon shouting 'Fuck', half asleep himself (she smiles) *otherwise he wouldn't swear, not while I was there, maybe when I'm not too I don't know I'm not there. Thud two thuds off the bonnet. Please not the pheasant fact, don't say it don't or I'll hate you . . .*

'Pheasant. Sorry, darling.'

Don't say it

'Whoever's behind us can pick it up for dinner.'

25

'If someone finds it, they can pick it up. It's illegal to pick up a pheasant you've hit yourself, you know. There's a law, to stop people trying to hit them on purpose.'

She thinks of saying: 'Hunting with cars,' but doesn't because it's not very funny and it's what she said last time, or 'Yum, roadkill,' but she's sure she's used that at least twice.

Simon likes to impart this information upon passing any poor corpse in the road – not just pheasants, but foxes, pigeons, even moles if he spots them, however smeared, mangled or crushed, however sad and tiny. But this is, in fact, the first time their own car has hit a pheasant or any other bright streak in the night, and when it really happened, she so much wanted him to not say it. She can't think of anything to say in response, can't bring herself to respond, and realizes when minutes have passed that it's too late to say anything at all, and says anyway, 'Maybe it isn't . . .' but can't manage the word 'dead' and then notices that she feels sick, is trembling. Hearing again the crack of the beak against the glass, imagining she caught for an instant its frightened black eye before the impact. A terrible empty hollow where moments before she felt well fed and full. He almost but doesn't say, 'If not, it soon will be.' She opens the window and faces away from him, eyes dry and wide; he looks across and sees her pale face quite without colour, quite bloodless. He begins to reach for her, finds that his hand, too, is unsteady, and returns it to the wheel. She shakes, all the way home, in a small way she hopes he won't notice. He doesn't speak as he opens the door, as he turns to take her coat from her he doesn't speak. And she hands him her coat and bursts into rare tears, and he folds his arms around her then, and she remembers how tall he is, remembers the place for her head beside his breastbone, which has been there ten years, was there always, waiting for her, and he still doesn't speak, but places his mouth against her hair gently. He knows how close she is always to mourning and wishes he could make this count for all of it. But she is grateful to him, for his silence; she could not begin to find words for grief.

When he gets into bed ten minutes later, he finds her limbs cold and still trembling a little . . . and there it is again, that little ellipsis, and we've caught up with ourselves. On a Wednesday, of all nights of the week, and almost midnight, is his last thought before sleeping. But he is glad that she is warm now, and had need of him.

THE GARDEN

It is ten o'clock, or thereabouts – Julia is in the garden, and has left her watch indoors. Two and a half hours have passed since Simon's departure on the dot of half-past seven. After the toast, Julia realized that the dull pressure at the back of her head and the mild disgust of the egg pan were only red-wine remnants, now staining the creases of her brain brown. She took a painkiller and went back to bed, until woken an hour later by a pheasant falling out of the night and smack into her eyes. The bedroom was bright and harmless, but hot; she had left the blind open.

The shower helped to rinse away dreams and headache alike, cool water on a blank mind. Best not to try to plan the day, or to think that the day should be planned. She closed her eyes and tilted up her face and imagined rain, heavy warm summer rain upon her eyelids like the time that . . . When?

Running down the street in shorts in a hot city on holiday, not caring, Rome, it was Rome. Brown dust, deep pink evening and the bold red burst of tomatoes for dinner, and eating an artichoke, pulling it to pieces and sucking the pulp, and my sister laughing at polipo meaning octopus which I'd also never eaten, but when I chewed it I couldn't get the word out of my mouth, pulpy between the teeth until I had to spit it out. The rain, yes, the rain was in Rome. The man was Italian. The first man that watched me, dark eyes he had, he was short I suppose, his hair shining and my bra showing through the shirt I wore clinging, water running down my face and my thighs, and he watched me and for the first time I thought, I like that man watching me, caught in this torrent.

In the shower two hours before this, while Julia poached his eggs, Simon planned his day with care. He went over appointments and projects in process. He made a mental note to remind his personal assistant to rearrange a meeting next Thursday, and to book him a table for lunch. He thought about the menu and decided to have steak. He had a taste for simple, good red meat; the Watsons last night served some elaborate, spiny little birds that he couldn't bring himself to pick up and eat with his fingers. He turned his face up to the water and splashed off this prickle of irritation. He would start the morning with a fresh look at a set of plans that had been troubling him, and a fresh cup of black coffee; he would find Joanne making one when he arrived and she'd offer, as she did every morning. It was a routine. He would sharpen his pencils and begin.

As he shaved, a trickle of music interrupted the order of his mind, unbidden. He was a boy, fluff appearing in patches quite dark already on his chin, sitting down all awkward skinny and long at the piano and playing out, hesitant, a few first bars of the concerto that woke them this morning. Wondering and hoping that he might one day perfect them. And splashing his clean face, grown handsome perhaps, grown older, he thought, Where are wonder and hope? Not in so many words; he is not a man to despair; it is a cloud that passes. Moments later he couldn't recall what he was thinking, which annoyed him; he caught back at the notes as they faded, remembered Rachmaninov and thought he should find the CD for Julia before he left. He is not without kindness. But by the time he'd sat down to his eggs, the tune had again eluded him, and he forgot.

Now it is ten o'clock, or thereabouts. There is work to be done but no reason to forgo the sun – Julia's research, such as it is, can be conducted just as well in the garden. To this end, she's brought out a blanket to lie on and a book, which she isn't reading; instead, she is stroking the sun-warmed fur of a purring tabby named Tess. She has pegged the washing out on the line, so that the sheets billow fresh white at the edge of her vision like the sails of a ship; she is afloat in the summer morning. She has an appointment in the afternoon, but there are hours to pass before she has to make herself presentable for this rare break to the day, which is otherwise stretching out in the sun just as lazy as her own limbs. Any revelations can wait; she is, anyway, quite unwitting of whatever the approaching visitor may bring, and does not know that there is a revelation to come.

As she's laid out here, so well lit and lethargic, we might take a closer look. She is quite small, really. She looks quite small and slight lying there. Her skin is pale gold, and shiny with sun cream. She has lots of hair; we saw it loose about her shoulders at the window but it's pinned up now and still damp from the shower, and when she moves the coconut smell of her shampoo catches the air. Her face is placid and clear – she will most likely put make-up on later, and then she will look a little older. Her features might then strike her visitor as verging on the beautiful, but she will be perhaps a little less lovely than she is now, stroking Tess with her hair falling free of its knot. She is wearing an old, favourite summer dress, with fading printed flowers; she lies on her belly and her ankles are crossed in the air like a girl's. It is possible that here, now, in the garden, in the green, she is as lovely as she ever will be. The sun falls thick around her, lighting up golden the laburnum she lies under. There are fruit trees in the garden, there are dark cherries ripening in the heat, sweetness, fullness, leaves hot and glossy; there are tiny flowers dense as stars, pale blue, there are tall

31

stems, violet, pink and cream, heart's-ease and phlox, gentle lupin, tall hollyhocks. Julia isn't sure what phlox is. An English country garden; as a child she heard 'heart cease' in the song. But a heart is eased, surely, when at last it ceases to beat? She stretches out a hand to take the bud of a brilliant fuchsia between two fingers to pop it. The air, heavy and scented, sings of roses, fox-gloves. Forget-me-nots.

She is old enough that we might expect her to have children, but she does not. She has Tess, who is looking up through pale brown slits only slightly yellower than Julia's own eyes. She strokes her; is there sadness? Perhaps it is just the last of the red wine. The little girl next door is laughing and screaming in the garden; the chains that hold her swing clank and pull alarmingly at the frame, so that Julia looking up wants to call out, 'Careful! Be careful . . .' because she knows that she would fear for her own daughter to swing so high. Back and forth, little feet in sweet blue shoes poke over the top of the fence with a giggle and a 'Wheee!'

Wheee! When I was a girl there was a swing at the end of this garden. Two ropes tied to that apple tree, with a stick lashed to the bottom. Miranda would insist that Jumbles had a turn. Jumbles? Mumbles? Gumbles it was, the imaginary badger. She'd push the swing as hard as she could and catch it and push again and I'd hop up and down beside her squealing because it wasn't fair. Then she'd swing herself, and when she wanted to

32

get off she just let go, right at the top of her swing, just let go and landed eight feet away like some circus artist. I came outside one evening alone, I watched my white shoes among the daisies, both brilliant against the deep blue grass, deep blue evening, bewitched. The night soft, and anything possible. Alone, I swung higher than ever, than anyone ever, whee . . . and when I came to the top of my biggest swing I jumped, I flew through the air like my soaring extraordinary sister. I flew, I flew, silent like a night bird, and landed with a thump. Face down, hands out, dazed until my heart slowed and I felt the pain and I cried very quietly, but when I felt the scrape on my face I bawled.

On a day like this, these little nostalgias float in the air like so many seed pods and pollens and spiders. Julia has known and loved this garden since she was a little girl. It is the garden that appears in her mind when a garden is required as the setting for a story or a dream. It is narrow and long, it is far from neat. The apple tree at the end has, in its time, let its white blossom fall upon a fairytale giant. High walls have built themselves so that only Julia can enter through a little hidden door. There have been many mad tea parties on the lawn – in fact, it is true that Julia's Aunt Helen knew a great many eccentrics, and artists have stretched out with their bare-breasted girlfriends in this very spot. A lean, dark adventurer has strolled here by moonlight with the woman who would be his wife. He asks for her hand and places his heart in it; she promises to hold it until he returns. Edward and his Emily. Julia has played the part countless times in her mind.

Tess purrs under stroking fingers. The book lies open: it is close to the end of the tale, although there are many blank pages remaining. Even on a day such as this, you will still feel the frost on them if you touch lightly; the chill of resignation, of despair, of regret for a story untold. A man, fallen through the ice, is dying. Julia stares at the handwritten page without reading a word.

Edward Mackley's diary was found in an aluminium case in a frozen grave in Franz Josef Land, still clutched in his blackened hand along with a picture of his wife and a pocket watch, in the spring of 1959. His last days were spent in the endless dark on a small northern island, hoping for a sunrise he didn't live to see, squinting to see his own scrawl by dim greasy lamplight so that the world might know what had befallen them, should the truth ever be brought into the flawless Arctic light. After years of mystery, the *Persephone* expedition of 1899 was at last revealed to have been a valiant failure; he came painfully, dismally close, hopelessly far from triumph, and turned back too late to save them. 'I cannot go on with it, I fear,' he wrote; 'I cannot go on.' His wife Emily, an old woman now who had waited sixty years for news of her vanished husband, wept with pride and the pity of it and died that same summer.

34

GLASS

Far to the north, over the Pole, the sun reaches the apex of a day that will last until the next one, so that the dazzle of this shadowless noon is only a little brighter than midnight. But here in England, too, the midday sun is brilliant and the afternoon it slips into will stretch well into the evening. Askance, the sky is blue, but let the zenith fill your vision and you will fall into a blue-black depth more endless than an ocean.

Julia is no longer in the garden. The cries of little Jenny next door have been quieted; she is indoors, devouring ham sandwiches. Tess is still recumbent in the sun, relishing the tranquillity. She has forgotten already the giggles and squeals that earlier disturbed her and is quite at peace, the sun bright on her tabby back. The flowers bloom and burst a little more every minute. Snuff the air and you will smell the sheets that are hanging bright white on the line, barely stirred by the breeze; the peaches ripening, the crisp apple skins, the deep yellow odour of floating pollen. Bees are fussing about the delphinium, stripping each column busily one blue blossom at a time, rolling in the

35

powder like addicts. Painted Ladies and Peacocks strut upon the buddleia, crowding the purple with umber, gold, amethyst and white, sucking at nectar greedy and deep. In the shade of this frenzy, there are nettles growing, an acrid spike in the scent of the bush and the earth. And upon one particular nettle leaf, something is feasting. It is ragged-edged, burnished orange and oak; it folds its wings graciously to show an extraordinary patchwork of blue, grey and violet on the underside, then opens out to rest full-spread. Stay for just a moment to watch me, says the Comma butterfly. But it will not remain, it will be gone by the time Simon, who has long been waiting for just this brief pause, returns home. A pity for Simon, but he will never know, and a lucky escape for the Comma, who will live to see tomorrow, and maybe even another day, poor short-lived beauty.

The butterflies, then, heave and clamber; the bees bustle and hum; Tess is up and prowling, licking the last of a juicy bluebottle from her teeth with luxuriant tongue. Everywhere the creak and sigh of growing things, of life, but there is only a rumpled blanket, a discarded book, where we left Julia. The air stirs, lifting the pages until they hesitantly turn; the words grow faint until there is only regret remaining, 'I cannot go on' whispering across the garden, and then the merciful breeze turns on to the ending, where there is only unfilled white.

★   ★   ★

36

She is not in the conservatory either, which is unsurprising as it is unbearably hot; the palms flourish in the humidity, but we shall wilt. Let us pass through the doors to the dining room it leads on to, before we give up and collapse on the wicker divan, fanning ourselves with a hopeless paperback that we are too warm to persevere with. It is cooler here, and as the eye recovers from the brightness it becomes clear that the room is unoccupied; no one dines at the long table, which has stood for a hundred years here, more. If we were to lift it the squares of the rug flattened by its legs would reveal a brilliant crimson, faded and dirtied by years. There is a sideboard stretching along one wall (pull it away to reveal the true pattern of the damask); upon it are china tureens, an etched crystal fruit bowl, a silver serving dish – and a vase, unadorned, elongated, out of keeping with the period, incongruous on its crochet round. All over the house, Julia has placed her precious things beside what belongs here. She can't bring herself to sell anything, to move anything even. Surfaces are crowded with keepsakes, her own, her family's, piling up over the years so that a thick layer of memory blankets all alike. It is sometimes hard to move in a house like this.

The vase has an azure glaze, chipped at the base on the journey home. Bend an ear to its narrow opening and you might just catch a dim echo of Parisian market-clamour; peer in for a glimpse of Simon, younger, reaching for his wallet, hot and hungry and happy to please her with a gift. Hold it in your hands so that the palms are all in contact with the cool curve of its bowl; at a street café where they stopped for kir, Julia held it once eight years ago, just so. She lifted it and kissed it, set it down carefully, held Simon's flushed face instead, the same way, and kissed that.

If we too set it down to pass through the open double doors to the drawing room, we will find the same quiet dust here, the same hush of history pressing in. What need have you of Paris and its pretty lights? wheedles the chandelier. A crystal decanter sits upon its silver tray. Julia is scared to use it, although she remembers her aunt pouring whisky from it. Her father, a quiet man who never drank liquor except when Aunt Helen plied it upon him, would accept glass after glass because he'd rather be steaming drunk, provided he could stand and talk when necessary without slurring, than be rude and decline. In his later years, of course, he couldn't stomach it, or anything else. She remembers her mother and her aunt, after he died, drinking from the same decanter; brandy this time. She remembers her seventeen-year-old self, seeking solitude, finding solace. They looked up when she came in, they were tear-stained and laughing, and poured her a glass. And after the third one, at last, after three days of silence and a dry-eyed funeral, Julia laughed too, and cried. The taste of brandy, taken unawares, can still make her weep.

But before it was Aunt Helen's, like everything in the house, the decanter belonged to John Mackley. This is the very same decanter from which, on numberless evenings at the end of the nineteenth century, John poured port for his brother. Edward Mackley himself, who might have been knighted if he'd ever returned, held that slender neck in his strong hand. Now, you feel the weight of the thing. The wide flat bottom, the chink of the stopper as the ground glass slides out, and the satisfying heaviness of the ball in your hand. The diamonds cut into its side reflect the yellow light, everything is dazzling . . . But no, it is the sunlight. The chandelier is of course not lit. It is just past noon – the long hand of the Viennese clock on the wall has just clacked around to a quarter past twelve. The clock is old, and the beauty of its inlaid face can't be quite trusted, despite Simon's attentions. But whether his watch would tell us that it is a minute earlier, or forty-eight seconds later, it is enough to remind us that we are at the apex of a glorious midsummer day in the first decade of the twenty-first century, and it is more than a hundred years since Edward Mackley drank port in the drawing room, and more than a hundred years since he died.

The front door slams. And here in the hallway, at last, is Julia. It is dim and cool; she is suspended for a moment in the amber light from the etched-glass oval of the door. Here is Julia at last, pausing

39

at the mirror, her skin a faint shiver after the midday heat of the street. Gilt-framed, some spotting at the bottom left corner. She is still a little sun-blind and can see the room behind her only darkly; the grandfather clock at the foot of the stairs is only a tall, pale-faced brown shadow, thudding softly in the dust. She cannot meet her own eyes, unable to focus on the immediate centre of her vision; slowly her pupils grow huge, adjusting, and fix upon their own reflection. At this moment, she hangs somewhere between herself and her image, trapped by the glass.

Many hundreds of lives have been framed by this gilt. Might we yet scry something? What, after all, happens to them all, all the reflections that have passed through the mirror – might they not linger somewhere, those that have glanced or paused here? It may be that there is another young woman, another bronze-flecked gaze behind Julia's eyes, still flickering in the depths of the silver surface. The past is not to be dispensed with easily, today. Everywhere it insists itself in this house, encroaching. The chandeliers, it seems, might after all be lit.

On a fine evening in October 1897, this very glass had the good fortune to reflect the image of nineteen-year-old Emily Gardiner, who, having excused herself from the party, made a quick assessment of her appearance and found it wanting. Brown eyes far too bright like a fever

40

and a high colour in her cheeks as if she herself had just come in from the snow. It wouldn't do. She must try to calm down and refuse any further offers of punch. For Jane Whitstable was sitting in the next room and had held the same cup all evening, sipping, speaking charmingly when spoken to, even conjuring a lovely pink blush when Edward Mackley bent to kiss her hand. When a man returns from the wilderness, such is the woman he wants to find waiting. Not some red-cheeked heathen with a wild look in her eye.

But how could she not be thrilled by the Norwegian's words? As Dr Nansen spoke of his journey, of the lights, the ice, she had glanced across at Edward and felt sure that he, too, was transported; he was taut, his forearm on the mantel, his jaw. The dogs, and the sleds, and the men; the walruses and the whales, the waves, and everywhere the ice. The heave and the groan of it. And to hear the sky described so. To see the pallid flash of the lights across the night, to see the moon and then the sun circle the horizon for weeks on end. To hear the freezing sea turning, and the stars, ice white; the night deep blue-black and white. To eat plain hard biscuits out on the floe, to return to the ship for darts and beer and singing. To come home to the wife that waved from the shore, at last, after months of longing. To be the woman longed for. To lie beside a hero . . . No, this would not do at all. This carnality in the hallway; no

41

wonder her cheeks were flaming. She smoothed her stomach and her skirts, correcting the S shape so that she was, if not so swan-like as Jane Whitstable, at least something like respectable. She breathed in, watching herself in the mirror, seeing her chest rise as the nostrils pinched. Pretty as a peach Jane Whitstable might be, but her funny little nose was nothing in comparison with Emily's fine, straight, perfectly proportioned one. There. That was the finishing touch she needed and now she was ready, quite ready to resume the party with her chin (also, actually, rather good) held high.

And so she returned to the drawing room, and on that night the great romance of the Mackleys began; the story that the family has told itself for a century, that has passed down the years through a dozen retellings to reach Julia, now – the story that has been her favourite since childhood. The dashing, somewhat thin young officer whom Emily remembered, who had departed for the north when she was only fourteen and fanciful – although she might have liked him a little broader, and not quite so dark – had returned. And now the ten years between them were narrower; in the years that had passed, his chest had filled out and she had discovered poetry and come around to the possibility that a man with a brooding countenance and a flash in his almost-black eyes might, after all, be ideal. A man with a set to his jaw and a strong forearm upon the mantel.

The ship upon which Edward had sailed in 1892 – leaving Emily to her adolescence – set out to explore the known, and no more. It reached a respectable enough latitude. The summer was spent hunting, and refining the contours of other men's maps. They were far enough north to be embedded for two winters, and when the ship was released by the ice in the second spring, having survived the crush and the dull months of darkness, the captain set a course for the coast of Canada, with an enraged Edward stationed at the stern, furious to be turning back. He bade farewell to the lightening world he was leaving behind, jade and lilac in the slow dawn, and swore he would return as his own master. There was still space enough for his name to be writ large across that vast white semblance of a land, visible for ever in the snow, bright under the Arctic moon and the brilliant day alike.

When he heard Dr Nansen speak, at his brother's invitation, in the family's own drawing room, he thought: I might take that path, and sail northeast for Spitzbergen. And also, he thought: I could go further. Further than this man's Farthest North; to the northernmost point, to find it, to fix it, to feel the world turn below me. This, then, was what Emily saw burn in him, the flare of ambition outshining the fire's blaze.

Edward, for his part, had spent many months at sea without female company, and can surely be forgiven for following the wildness of his heart upon his arrival in London; but while the charms of Leicester Square's ladies were not negligible, he had, after all, his duty, and had reluctantly returned to the family home. It would be a duty sorely borne, for the women with whom he was expected to associate bored him. He was bored by their adoration for his one great adventure. He knew that the likes of Jane Whitstable would never tire of being wedded to an explorer, a hero, provided he was never so rash as to explore any further, ever again. He would for ever be known for this single futile expedition, a glory enough for the small town he'd be trapped in. And he would be respectable and sire children and his wife would sit and stitch; their girls would play the piano prettily, the boys would all be called John and Edward. There would be kippers and baked eggs and bacon for breakfast, there would be luncheons, casseroles and cutlets, and then there would be tea and muffins and buns and toast, and then there would be dinner, there would be asparagus soup then sole then quail then veal and cherry clafoutis for dessert, then cigars then port then sleep in separate beds then gout or rheumatism and then, eventually, death.

Then Emily Gardiner shook his hand, and blushed in confusion because he'd meant to kiss it, and she blushed deep crimson rather than pink and was really a terrible flirt – that is, she was terrible at flirting and didn't seem even to try. But when they spoke about the snow, her eyes danced like the light upon it. She loved him for the dangers he had passed . . . and he loved her that she did savour them. She would never hold him back from the brink, but spur him over it to greatness.

And so began the Mackley family's favourite story.

CHINA

On the table in the hallway, there are flowers in a vase. Arranged with an artlessness that says they have art enough alone – surely by Julia's hand. Bright blooms thrown together, yellow, blue, white and vibrant; imagine her, coming in from the garden, her arms full of summer, trailing hyacinth and lily scent behind her. But, you notice, they are dying. They have been snapped off and tossed in this china vase with no care for their frailty. Even as we watch, a petal shudders, seems to sigh, and slips onto the heap of those already fallen, gently and suddenly over the last hour. They are browning about the edges. Their leaves, left to stand in the water, are rotting. If we draw close enough to be daubed orange by their stamens, we will smell something foetid from the depths. There is a rusty stain where pollen has silently exploded on the linen table-cloth that John's wife, her Great-grandmother Arabella, hand-stitched. (Simon, in the city, is thinking of buying his wife flowers; but of course he is not here to witness the petal fall, and it is only a coincidence that he should think of this just as the lily is dying – he has other reasons, which will become apparent perhaps, in time.)

The last petal to fall shivered itself free in Julia's wake, for we caught her in the hallway in a momentary gilt-framed pause, and she has since moved off, breaking the gaze of the past in the mirror. In the kitchen, the spoils of her recent venture are spread before her in brown paper bags. She has kicked off her sandals and is standing in a square of light where the sun has warmed the tiles, and she works her toes into the stone for a moment. *Terracotta*, she thinks, the baked earth beneath her feet.

Terra cotta, terra firma, old maps with the infirm edges
so unlike the warm earth stone under the soles

And then a wiry softness around her ankles. Julia bends to lift Tess and press her flat cat face against her own, tells her she stinks and sets her gently down again, with which the cat is quite satisfied – she did not enjoy the hand under her belly, having gorged herself on tuna while Julia was out. Julia stands barefoot at the kitchen table, mopping olive oil with a torn chunk of bread. The tomatoes are sliced thickly, plucked from a ripe basketful on the pavement, and taste still of the sun. Italy filling her mouth and mind again, she bought three, full of that dark green vine-scent, that earthy almost bitter tang that belies the sweetness. Strawberries, too, in a punnet, she lifted them to her nose and the grocer, watching, felt his heart swell with redness. Then, next door, to the baker. It is indeed a very pretty market town, and there are still shops like these to be found on street corners, baking their own bread, selling local produce, eggs fresh from the farms, yolks of all yellows within their brown, nubbly shells.

Julia on her way back to the house, minutes ago, loaf tucked under one arm, the other swinging the bag of fruit: she's humming to herself. The hot road smells of summer, she nods to her neighbours as she passes. The grocer, filling a tray with lettuces Peter Rabbit might have plundered, soft and frilled and grassy green, watches her go. A man mowing his front lawn pauses to admire her, her pale brown back and the narrow straps of her dress, her head on one side, her hips insouciant in the sunshine, as if she's dancing home. He thinks of his wife, who died last year and was also young once; he shades his eyes from the sun. If this shopping trip is little more than another way to side-skip boredom, if Julia is momentarily elated simply to have the eyes of others upon her, this man would never guess it.

The woman who lives in the house opposite Simon and Julia's and two doors down is just locking her door behind her. She has the afternoon off, and is on her way into London, to do some shopping. She has a date this evening but is too restless and excited to wait until then; dates have been rare since the divorce, all she wants is

48

to feel she has a chance. By the time she turns, Julia has passed, crossed the road and reached the house, and slipped inside unseen. The neighbour in the dressing gown (now fully dressed) has escaped the discomfort of polite conversation with her rival.

This is the journey from which Julia returned, slamming the door to alert us; and now she is in the kitchen, kneeling on the floor. There is a splash of oil on her dress and a broken plate before her. Tess, in the corner, licks a reproachful paw.

Stand up. In a minute. I'll get up in a minute and do some work. I'll clear away the plate, I will need to clear away the plate, second thing broken in a week, they were cheap we've had them for years I must never use the good china I break everything. Aunt Helen saying silly old woman as I knelt on the rug to mop up and he gave me his hanky.

Julia's cheek rests on her left palm. With her right she holds a piece of the plate which is in five other pieces on the floor. Her eyes fix on a space somewhere between them.

Stand up

She slides her fingers down the side of her face and taps the tips against her top lip slowly.

★   ★   ★

49

Stand up and go back to the attic. Back to the animals, back to the snow, the sunrise this morning so beautiful pale blue

With sudden unexpected decision she rises, takes the dustpan from below the sink, sweeps up the pieces of the plate, throws them into the pedal bin and bends to pet Tess (who instantly forgives the alarm she caused) as she leaves the room, clasping the diary she has recovered from the garden. She trips lightly up the stairs, but pauses on the landing to admire the butterflies.

She has left a joint of lamb marinating in the kitchen, in wine and herbs and anchovy, the savoury smell of it twitching at Tess's whiskers. Tess is as agile as any self-respecting feline should be but has learned her lesson from the last time she tried to reach the top of the tall, smooth-sided fridge, and succeeded only in scrabbling at the dish there and upending a fish pie on herself. It's true she had the chance to lap a little off the floor before Julia, alerted by the crash, found her, but it had all been most undignified. So the lamb remains out of paws' reach, ready to be offered up this evening.

Julia wants to please Simon today; she knows, although neither one has said it, and despite the fact that they made love (on a Wednesday), that she annoyed him last night; that the nuisance of an evening he would rather have avoided, and hadn't expected to have to endure, will hang over

50

him all day and her too. 'Remember dinner tonight with the Watsons' – she was irritated at breakfast, imagining him saying it, when in fact it is she that should have reminded him, and didn't, whatever she chose to call them. He is right to be annoyed; she is annoyed with herself, for being so hopeless and disorganized and always proving him right. When did this lethargy set in? When did she cease to enchant him?

She remembers, with a clutch of pain and shame, her tears; the bird's black eye; when did she last cry in front of him? Not when Aunt Helen died; not when . . . there was a time when she should have gone to him and let him hold her, and could not. But it won't do to dwell on it. She must try to work hard, today; she will work hard so that he will see she is happy here as the family archivist; it was his gift, he wanted to make her happy. She must try. It will be like the days a decade ago when she told him the story, imagining it over for him as they lay safe together all through the winter, his head in her lap as they lay outstretched on the bearskin and she stroked his dark hair back, tracing with a fingertip the slightly receding hairline that only she could see. She will find something new to fascinate him. She will set about her task with renewed vigour.

So, when she lifted those strawberries to smell them, she was breathing the scent of new optimism, of hope for the evening to come – this was the hope that swung in her hips past the man in his garden, past her opposite neighbour (who is even now making her way across town, trying to make the last hours before the evening go faster).

When she tasted the tomatoes at the table, when she stroked at Tess's soft fur, when she wriggled her toes on the warm stone, she was full of the possibilities the long day proffered, wide and clear as the sky. She chopped rosemary and garlic and rubbed olive oil into the meat and watched her own strong hands with pride and imagined a version of herself and Simon sitting down to dinner and laughing together; she would think of something to say that he would laugh at and he would forgive her; there would be nothing to forgive. When the plate slipped from her hand the day threatened to darken but she wouldn't allow it, it was just a cheap plate, and tonight she would set the table in the conservatory with silver and their glasses would shine in the lamplight and the night would gleam with moths and fireflies dancing, out in the dark blue garden.

The butterflies that Julia is now admiring were not captured by Simon, although they were placed in this prominent position in his honour, for they are what brought him to her. A collection of Arctic Whites gathered in Alaska and mounted by a friend of Edward's from his first expedition, presented as a wedding gift: these are the pale ghosts now hanging in the stairwell, but they were once kept in a little-visited guest room. There are fifty of them, arranged in series, five by ten; it is one of the finest, most complete collections of this particular species of Arctic Lepidoptera, and includes – and it is this pair of tiny wings that Simon, years ago, came to see – a variety now thought to be extinct, a female, with a bluish tint. They are less than two inches in wingspan and like many northern creatures they have no need for boldness. These butterflies never know darkness; they will wait in their pupae for two years or more, shifting fuzzily, growing by increments, waiting for their day in the perpetual sun; and, once emerged, will die before it sets for winter. They are not, perhaps, spectacular. It takes a careful, patient, searching eye to see the subtlety of their whites, like an egg, like a petal, like snow. An eye like Simon's. Even when his father was chasing Ladies, Simon was content with the quiet moths and the pale green brimstones. It isn't dullness, on Simon's part. It is not a lack of imagination, but a love of the delicate.

Now, as Julia passes them on her way to the attic, she remembers Simon as he was when they met ten years ago, and feels an unexpected surge of affection which reveals, by contrast, the complacent irritation that has become her customary feeling towards him. What a strange creature he is, she'd thought then, somehow old-fashioned and adolescent at once, a man with a hobby that drives him to overcome such obvious shyness and seek out a bunch of butterflies in a stranger's house. Yes, this is the house where he found her. He wore a tie, on that first visit, he'd come from a meeting, and he held it between his fingers (which she could see, looking sidelong, were suited to delicate tasks), and he rubbed the fabric of the back of it with his thumb, a tiny movement, a kind of almost-static fidget that she caught out of the corner of her eye. She remembers his tremor beside her and the surprise she felt at the answering warmth of her skin. Taking out his glasses and pushing them on, bringing his face nearer the glass with a 'Hm' so that she, too, pushed her pointed chin forward – she had to crane upwards to follow his long finger to the particular insect that seemed to have settled on its tip.

She thinks of the ordered stack of drawers he showed her a few months later so bashfully, which have found their home now in the new shed out in the garden; the innocent pleasure of sliding out each one in turn on its smooth runners to reveal the jewels within, twenty pairs of wings to a drawer, sea-green in one, pearl in another, pale brown like her eyes he said once, in an unguarded moment (when had she last seen Simon unguarded?)

the powdered sheen, bronze into the finest line of indigo at the edges, exactly like your eyes, he said, a female Mazarine Blue, he told me, you're the only one left in England, and blushed. That word a gift

he gave me that I haven't forgotten, Mazarine,
between an antique sea and an azure sky.

Each drawer so meticulous, the subtle shifts in size
and shape and colour so carefully accounted for in
Latin. Looking at the butterflies on the landing
now, she feels inspired by the neat labels beneath
each one, still true a century later. And she thinks
that if she were to somehow emulate him, if he
were to come home to find everything in order,
that this too might somehow please him.

Let us follow as she makes her way up the stairs,
staying close to the wall to avoid the creaks that
sound softly under her feet. She is thinking of
lining the attic with glass cases and placing her
relics in them; of making a label for everything.

THE ARCHIVIST

There is a soothing continuity to Julia's life, these days; it has slowed to a comforting dawdle through the rooms of her childhood. When she sees old friends – which is rarely – they laugh fondly at her easy life, and are unsure whether to feel pleased or concerned. She seems happier than she has been in years, since her beloved Aunt Helen was first taken into care; she laughs more readily, never looks as if she might have been crying alone, enjoys herself guiltlessly again. But she is also somehow distant, somehow gauzy.

She has spent so many hours here, since she was a child, picking up whatever comes to hand and setting it down again, each handling adding to the patina, the shine on scratched glass, the lustre of a fabric now faded. Now, her wanderings have a purpose; she will eventually have to bring it all to account, and present Edward Mackley in a neat package – a catalogue, a Life, a bill of sale, she is unsure of the binding. She prefers not to dwell on it; she will know when the time comes. She prefers not to dwell on when that will be. So, she makes occasional notes in notebooks; she wraps, unwraps, rewraps; she reads letters and journals and jottings; she strays from the task to straighten cushions or make jam.

If she is daunted by her task, if she has been procrastinating, can we blame her for preferring to lounge in the sun? Can a life be composed of other men's accounts, diaries, journals, notebooks, newspapers and relics of a wrecked expedition any more than it can of – for the sake of argument – a concerto, a dead pheasant, a cat in the garden, a trace of lipstick, the taste of vine tomatoes, of aniseed, a lily? How can we hope to do more than snatch at our quarry? It cannot be netted and pinned. Even butterflies, so captured, show only one side of themselves. What of that Comma that escaped Simon's sentence of death? He would have it show its colours, certainly, but in doing so would hide the subtler underside, some would say the more lovely part.

Perhaps this underestimates Simon. It may come to pass, one summer's day like this one, this year or in ten years' time, that he will catch his Comma and find that its blues and browns and bruise purples are indeed more intriguing than the upside, and decide to buck convention (for he is not in all things conventional), and mount it downwards. It may be that he places it alone in a frame, and presents it to Julia as a gift, and she will hang it above her desk where she will, at last, have settled, and will sometimes glance up mid-sentence and pause.

But who knows if the Comma will ever return to the nettle? And what are the chances that Simon, too, will be hovering about the spot? Tess has been known to eat butterflies, has been found with a wing poking out of her shimmering grin . . . Let's not break the bounds of the day. It is exhausting enough, snatching at the past as it slides through the present, without letting the future interfere.

In the attic, Julia sits surrounded by boxes of Edward's possessions, and Emily's, which have found their way here over the years unsorted. As girls, Julia and her sister Miranda would creep up here and open them at random to pull out hats and muffs and mysterious swathes of sealskin. She remembers the big windproof anoraks they'd wear to cross the icy landscape at the top of the house together, struggling against the snow until they caught sight of each other and collapsed giggling into the icy wind. Or she would pull a fur around her and step out on her top-hatted sister's arm to an opera or a waltz.

When Aunt Helen moved out, Julia's grandfather Edward – John's son – had the animals hauled up here too. They were morbid, he mumbled, and they'd have to sell the place sometime, although no one made any move to do so. After his first shuffling visit, unable to manage the stairs even, he lost all interest in the home he was born in and had inherited from his father. Although it belonged to him he had never been its master, having lived in London since leaving to study there at seventeen, and had visited rarely in the intervening years; he seemed reluctant even to return. And now he was an old man and hadn't the energy for a sale, had money enough to see him through his last lonely years. He died quietly in his own bed in Belgravia at the age of ninety-nine, and the house here stood empty, settling into its own memories, letting them sigh down into the dust that had been so rudely disturbed by the animals' exodus to the attic. Simon, whose careful fingers are suited to such tasks, learned to restore the mounts (although they did not please him like his own winged captives), and has groomed and sleeked them back to something closer to life, patched where necessary, eyes replaced.

Now those glass eyes, some new, some old, look upon Julia for the second time today as she sits on the swept floor. In the gloomy warmth, she tastes cold sea salt on her lip.

Cold waves washing and my feet bare, my Great-great-uncle Edward somewhere out upon the water. I saw him at the prow, proud, his dark eyes looking out. Skin slapped red, I wouldn't step out of the sea, I too would one day have an adventure, the waves would lift and lull me, when the sea became rough I would batten the hatches, take in the topsail, look lively. I would grow used to the vile brown taste of rum. I would be quick and clever like Edward, I

59

would be wise and strong, I would not die in the snow.

Julia is sitting on the wooden boards of the attic's floor, tapping the tip of a fine ballpoint pen (stolen from Simon's supply) against a pad beside her. A nebulous mass of dark specks is swarming into the margin, beside where she has written

Box 004

– thinking the additional zeroes will add an air of authority to her filing, the appearance of a system –

Item 8: Rifle

– followed by an emphatic full stop

.

She sights along the rifle at the bear in the corner. Then feels suddenly guilty, and then has at least the sense to feel ridiculous. But Edward once lifted this same barrel, perhaps, in this same pose that Julia holds steadily, and hit the bear square in the eye – so the story goes, the unlikely story that explains why she is scarless. It might have been the taxidermist's skill that made her so; or she was found dead already, although she is reckoned to be only eleven, too young to have died of old age. Edward kept no records on his first expedition. The ship's log reports: 'Young Mackley returned excited from a morning's hunt, to recruit two pairs of hands to help him drag his kill back to the ship; a fine specimen, with not a mark on her, a gift for his brother he says although I dare say he might make a second killing if he takes it to auction.' Which wouldn't help Julia solve this particular mystery, even if that log was in her possession and not buried somewhere in a Kensington archive. She is, besides, happy to believe in the bullet in the eye.

Poor polar bear. Dying with a roar or posed like that. Great-grandpa John forcing the mouth wide, hand between its jaws. Holding it by the paw like a dancer.

John, white-bearded, takes the massive claw with a bow, his big doctor's hand crushably tiny in its grasp. He has to reach above his own head to ask for the waltz; the smile in his mischievous eye is captured in silver. Helen took the photograph. It hangs in the upstairs hallway.

Julia rises, her knees stiff from kneeling. In the steps between her and the bear her hobble straightens, so that by the time she reaches her partner she is quite ready to dance. Suddenly shy, she reaches to take a paw. Who will lead? The bear after all is a lady, and perhaps mindful of the conventions of her day. It might be lonely, here in the attic, with no one to admire her. Aunt Helen used to greet her whenever she came through the front door; Miranda and Julia would imitate her,

61

delighted. 'Hello, polar bear. Hello, bear cub.' It is a habit now engrained in her passage, so that every time she enters she almost says it aloud before seeing the empty corner and remembering, sadly, that the bear is gone.

'Hello, polar bear,' she whispers now in the attic.

Julia's Aunt Helen was in fact a great-aunt, her grandfather's sister, John's daughter; much younger than her brothers, she was born late to Arabella Mackley one peaceful spring morning in 1916 while shells and mortar fire tore apart Europe. She was in her fifties when Julia was born; her dark hair just turning to silver, her lively face beginning to crease. If we wish to know Julia, we must know something of this aunt, Helen Mackley, who told Edward's stories like fairy tales (of the best sort, thrilling and gruesome), who had in turn learned them from Emily, Edward's unwitting, waiting widow. To Julia, this is not so much John's house as Aunt Helen's; it was in her keeping from the end of the thirties. No one had ever questioned her right to it, since she had lived there her whole life, and her brothers made no claims upon it. With Emily she had seen it through the war, opening its doors to children from the city, sitting with them around the kitchen table, overseeing them in the schoolroom where she and her brothers had been taught, and telling stories of explorers and polar bears (the stories that Emily had told many times over, that Helen first heard from her, and told to Julia and Miranda in turn), and tucking the awestruck evacuees into beds that they thought they'd be swallowed by, so that more than one dragged their blankets to the floor by morning. The staff dwindled as the war went on. By the 1950s, Aunt Helen managed the house more or less alone, with *élan* and *aplomb* (these are words that Julia reserves especially for memories of Aunt Helen), and as the country emerged from post-war darkness she invited bright, brilliant guests to enliven the once-gloomy rooms of her Edwardian childhood, and had parties and picnics and poured wine and champagne, and posed for photographs and painted in the garden. At least twice a year she ventured alone across the Channel, travelling by train across the continent and returning with souvenirs and stories. When Julia was a child, the house was still busy with her visitors and the tales she told, brimful of the family's reminiscing, so that the departed and the long-dead jostled with the living. Aunt Helen conducted them all through the house and the garden, opening cupboards and books and secrets, each more enchanting than the last, dazzling her guests (and her great-nieces in turn) with the glamour she cast over everything.

Her strength and brightness belied her age almost to the end, until the confusion of her last years. Well into her eighties, when most of the old guests were gone, she was to be found in the garden, pruning or painting, or baking cakes in the kitchen, or inviting young men to tea. She had never married; she had taken lovers but hers, she said, was not a heart to settle. She loved children, but had none of her own. So when her nephew William brought Julia and Miranda to visit, she lavished them with attention, with Turkish delight and chocolates, and pastries for breakfast and, when they grew older, half-glasses of wine with dinner. She'd set them up with easels and let them use her paints, and didn't care a bit about the mess they made, and framed their masterpieces and proclaimed that her nieces were, without a doubt, the most talented of the many talented artists it had been her privilege to meet. Julia adored her. As a teenager she would borrow her aunt's scarves and beads and her catch-phrases, would say ironic things like 'How jaunty!' and try to raise one eyebrow. They spent summer holidays there and Christmas too, and went on doing so even after their father died. Aunt Helen worried for her nephew's widow, and besides would not have given the girls up so easily. And then four short years later, Maggie, their mother, died too, having ignored a cramp in her guts for a year that she had put down to sadness. And Miranda had just qualified and taken a job at the Royal Infirmary in Edinburgh, where she'd studied, and then she married and had her own home and children to tend to, and it was just Julia and Aunt Helen in the holidays, against the world.

There was always, for Julia, something enchanted about their nights out in the garden, or by the fire in the sitting room, preserving between them the memory of all that was lost; together in the warm, lawless places of the house, the spaces that were not all oak and grandeur but filled with secrets and softness, cushions and flowers, the smell always of lavender and roses, and upon which they cast a spell of ice so that it crept over the walls and enclosed them, glittering. The story passed from Emily to Helen and on, through a line of surrogate daughters; this is the legacy that Julia owes a debt to, both the legend of the figure in the snow, and the woman left behind who shaped the legend while she waited. In the quiet of the attic, all the rooms now empty, Julia still feels the quiver of some vibrant invisible thing about which the house throngs.

Julia's squinting eye ranges the room. She twists the telescope, which turns still with a grudging grind, until the malformed leopard's eye fills the other end with darkness; then returns it to the tasselled bag it has at some time acquired but was almost certainly never carried in, and sets it down at the end of a lengthening row of objects extracted from *Box 004*, as labelled in Julia's curled and forward-slanting hand. She returns to her desk and writes:

Item 5: Telescope. Tin. Found in camp beside grave site discovered F.J. Land 1959; believed property of Edward Mackley.

★   ★   ★

It may, in truth, have belonged to any one of the five found there; but he was the navigator, after all. And she would like to believe that through this same curve of glass he watched his wife grow distant on the shore. The lens is intact, if a little scratched, and looking through it now we might yet spy Emily Mackley trapped under the glass, waving as she watched her husband shrink, while he adjusts the focus, again and again, sharpening her outline each time it blurs until at last it will turn no further.

Edward, as his ship set sail, watched her diminish, long after she had lost him among the other tiny figures on the deck. So they dwindled from each other's lives and could only hope to be close again. The crew set about their business, glad to be under way at last. Edward lowered the telescope, and watched until the land slipped over the curve and there was only the sea, the sky, the long, long day between them, just a paleness at the far edge of the world which would in time be blinding. It was July, the nights still light. He was on his way to glory. There was a long way to go and it would only grow colder.

Their honeymoon had been spent in Norway while Edward made his preparations and recruited the last of his crew. Emily, released from stays, had learned to ski, had learned liberty. In these brief months of their marriage, she had learned what a lover is; she knew now that a wife is not a delicate bloom to be kept under glass, but a woman, with strength as well as soft skin. Arriving at Edward's side at the bottom of a slope, she slipped and skidded on her hip into his legs, laughing, and he lifted her and laughed too and her eyes were bright, her face red with the cold and her gleeful descent, and he kissed her. They walked hand in hand through the little town; they joked and played and threw snowballs, lovingly made of the softest snow, and in the evenings the trees were frosted and twinkled in torchlight and the cabin they stayed in was warm, and they ate simply, fish and black bread and a sweet brown cheese like caramel, and drank light ale, and felt whole and healthy and fell into bed almost, but not quite, exhausted.

In too few weeks, the ship was ready to sail for the north. Norwegian-built to spend months in darkness, locked in the ice and, with luck, borne up by it, to meet the spring on the other side. She was christened *Persephone*. Captain Edward Mackley stood at the prow, broke the bottle and named her, with his wife by his side.

Emily came as far as she could with him, and would have gone further, he knew; she said she would follow him to the ends of the earth, but he could allow her only as far as Vardø – which was close enough. They sailed around the coast to this northernmost point, between the islands, every fjord a gasp of awe; they stood together on deck and looked out at the mist in the mornings, the mountains and the air which Emily would never forget, would try to describe for the rest of her life, always grasping for clarity. The ship rolled in rough water; it was built for ice, with a wide shallow bottom, and Hugh Compton-Hill retched over the side for a week so that Edward wondered if the boy would stand the journey, but he couldn't be set down – his father had bought his place on the expedition with funds that Edward couldn't afford to lose. Emily was not sick once; she was, he said, his finest shipmate, and he would be sorry to lose her. She held firm and only asked for champagne when she felt queasy (a fine excuse, he said). It is hard to say if it was seasickness, or the memory of the bottle broken on the bowsprit, which explained her distaste for it in later years.

They reached the northern port late one evening and a banquet was held in their honour; they were toasted past midnight, leaving a scant handful of hours together before he was to depart at four in the morning. Masses of birds crowded the island across the bay from the small city; their cries, too alien, too early, woke them to the pale sun. She would return to England the next week, and he was assured she would be well looked after. How long it had been since they had sat at his brother's table; and how many months she would sit there without him.

Parting is the Mackley romance. Parting, waiting, and romantic loss. Edward and Emily sailed out for the north on their honeymoon; their first and only months together were a journey to the place of their leave-taking. Julia's Arctic is a dream of brilliant distance –

Everything is equidistant; everything is as far from me as he is far from me, I am heedless, I reach out from my centre towards him at the top of the world . . .

Waiting, serenely, with a pale ache. Desire over great distances: this is the romance of the story, Emily's legacy. Emily waiting, waiting, the sea growing wider and hardening to ice as she stretched out towards him, watching him grow distant.

Who is this giant, after all? A man who set out for glory and failed to find it. A man who loved his wife, but left her for something greater; had he not been handsome, he might have passed quite unnoticed. Had she not waited so faithfully, as if there could be no man on earth to replace him – this man who wasn't made for earth at all, but for a place beyond its edge. Had she not made of him a hero.

He is little known, it's true, beyond the family's circle. The memories and treasures that fill the house are, to the visitor, little more than curios for the curious, scraps for specialists. His name appears in the records of the Royal Geographical Society three times: with Godspeed and accolades upon his departure; with hope, that he will be found; with regret, when he is, years after hope is gone. His diaries remain unpublished. He might have been the century's first champion, reaching the pinnacle as the world turned under him; as it is he is only, to most, a vestige of Victoriana. Simon hadn't heard of him, until he learned that Freely's butterflies still hung in his brother's house.

Still, his dark eyes in the portrait downstairs are fixed on greatness. They see to the top of the world. There is something about him that won't relinquish, that cannot dim.

PART II

Look: here is Edward in his cabin as they sail out of Tromsø, the first Arctic city and their last port of call before Vardø and parting. The cabin is already the cosy, cramped nest of a bachelor. The shelves just visible at the top of the picture are stuffed with socks, sealskins, waterproofs; the bed is a neat nook made up with three blankets; Edward himself sits at a chair at his small desk, in a pose of easy authority, his diary open before him, smoking one of several pipes that hang on the wall. No open flames allowed below decks – except in the galley and in the captain's cabin.

On a shelf above the bed, we can make out a slim collection of John Donne's poems, slipped alongside the handful of books of reference (the ship's main library is kept in the saloon). There are several volumes of the *Dictionary of National Biography*, including Vol. 35 (MacCarwell–Maltby). It will never be known if Edward discovered, between Brigadier William Mackintosh of Borlum and Charles Macklin, the actor, the entry his playful wife tacked in, describing the life of the eminent explorer and exemplary husband Edward Mackley

– the tale she wrote for him, telling how he reached the Pole and revived England's pride and passion; his brilliant, tall sons and beautiful tawny daughters, brilliant also: the Mackleys, who shaped the new century. But if Emily knew him at all, she was surely right to guess that he would turn, from time to time, to the page that his name would one day appear on – as, indeed, it now does, not interleaved but printed and irrevocable. When the editors called upon her to check the details for the 1912 supplement, the difference between their entry and her own, which she had written with such a proud, light heart over a decade before, was a pain almost too great to bear. The volume was to account for those who had died between 1901 and 1911. It seemed by then a sure assumption. She could not pass the word 'lost' and asked John to finish the task for her.

In the photograph all this is in the future; the biographer's subject has not reached the point of departure, when the myth she'd written for him was to split from the one she had to make do with. He has not yet even entered the fog that would shroud him as he sailed from her. But when it descended, this was the cabin that Edward was to read and write and smoke his evenings away in; this was the cabin in which Emily imagined him, and this is the picture that sits on Julia's desk, the place that she too will embark from. Smoking his pipe as the fog descends: here is Edward.

FOG AND FREEZE

The earth turned under the ship, relentless, until the shore was swallowed by the horizon. Below decks, he discovered Emily's last act of love; unpacking his case of warm clothing, he found among the long-johns and the socks a photograph of her, smiling in the snow, a brief pledge of love written on the back (the ink, when it was found with his body, had almost faded). The photograph Lars Nordahl placed on his captain's breast when he buried him now sits alongside Edward's on Julia's desk. It is not formally posed, or if it was, the subject could not be persuaded to contain herself; framed by frosted pine trees, a laughing, flushed young woman (so much younger, thinks Julia, than she herself is now) in a fur-trimmed jacket and hat. This, Julia thinks, is surely Edward's Emily, as if the picture was taken from an image in his mind. This was the version of her that he was to carry with him. If, when he found it, Edward Mackley shed a tear, it is not for us to judge him, for heroes too love their wives and fear death.

He would soon address his crew. He would

commend them for their valour. He would set out the schedule of their days, the programmes of exercise, mealtimes, watches, all the necessary measures to keep minds and bodies shipshape. He knew that with adventure comes exhaustion of the spirit, that awe is eventually tinged with boredom; he had lived already through an Arctic day and he knew the longing for darkness, the ache behind the eyes which one cannot tear away from the ice even as they burn from it. And he knew that then the night comes, interminable. The captain's address would not be touched with pain, or dolour, or yearning, however; it was a rousing speech full of ambition. It is there in the ship's log.

The ship's log was brought to London by the last of the Norwegian crew. The second diary was found, as we know, along with the telescope at the last camp that Edward and his party made on the ice; the same snow-stained pages that Julia earlier abandoned, filled with frozen regret, the record of the yearning he had denied himself on board. But by then he had no crew to speak of, let alone to speak to, and could afford himself a little honesty.

As the ship headed out into the Barents Sea, the summer fog closed all around them; the Varanger Peninsula had not long vanished over the horizon before everything else vanished too. It was not the clear bright blue that Edward might have hoped for. For five days they passed blindly through it. On deck, the men's morale was as damp as their clothing; droplets clung to their beards and eyebrows, to be wiped away with a sodden glove. Water ran down their necks, it saturated their skins; soaked cuffs clung about their wrists. They were nothing but leaden smudges in the featureless air; only as they drew close could they recognize each other, put names to the shades they'd become.

Sometimes it would clear enough to reveal the three masts above them, the sails furled in the useless stillness. These pockets of misted visibility were worse, somehow, than the seamless blanket of the heavy fog. The men shuffled on wetly in the silence. Edward imagined himself on a ghost ship, cords and torn sails hanging listless on the yards, their bones full of the chill, all light gone from the world and their eyes. He began to feel that *Persephone* had tricked them, leading them into a pale grey afterlife; they had already reached the end of the world and were condemned to sail for ever in this sunless void.

It went on for days. They kept to their cabins, emerging only for the hourly night watch which dragged by for each of them in turn, with nothing to watch for. Whales, walruses, Krakens from the deep could have passed their flank by inches, and only the sudden roll in an otherwise waveless sea would have betrayed them. The dogs, battened down in their kennels on deck, rested their muzzles on their front paws and looked mournfully up at their Russian keeper with flat, saddened ears, every coarse hair tipped with dew. The Norwegian crew were stoical, but Edward's English companions did not know these seas, and had expected splendours after the beauty of the hard, cragged coast they'd set out from. Only Samuel Freely, who had sailed with Edward for the Northwest Passage seven years before (netting and pinning a host of Arctic Whites en route), knew what a northern summer was. Still, his spirits were as numb as his fingers, and he could summon for his friend little comfort. Mealtimes were dismal affairs, false jollity washed down by disappointment. They moped below decks and turned in early.

On the sixth day a bank of dark blue appeared to starboard, as if a line of ink had been drawn across the centre of a wet page; it seeped at the edges, but there it was, undeniable, darkening and hardening into contours as they watched. And as the air cleared they became sure that what they could see was land, not some trick of the water and light. Within hours, the bird-streaked coast of the islands of Nova Zembla emerged from the ocean, black and grey, crammed with the squawks and settling feathers of the summer nesting. They navigated the strait around the tip of the southern island and emerged into the open Kara Sea, stretching north, north, to a watery horizon. A blue sky arced glorious over them, almost liquid where it touched the sea and seemed to soak into it. The men stretched out on the deck in their sun goggles, lolling against each other, as if the ship had transformed into a lido. With the wind in the sails, they sped forward. How lazy, they laughed, adventure could be. To the Pole, they cried, and don't spare the dogs!

In his cabin, a month after leaving his wife on the shore, Edward woke in half-darkness and knew that dawn was close; and something else too. They were nearing ice. He could feel it. He knew where he was from the moment he woke; for the first time since they left the coast behind them, he did not expect to find her beside him. The sea shifting under him had become his own lymph-rhythm. And he knew, too, that the sea was beginning to freeze, although it was not yet August; without so much as standing up from his bed, he knew it. He could smell it, although it was scentless. Across the bridge of his nose, under his eyes, like a frozen sneeze he felt the pinch of it. Ice.

He dressed quickly, pulled on boots and gloves and coat and left his cabin. Only Janssen, the cook, was awake below decks, peaceful and floury in the galley. Edward's stomach, tight with excitement, barely registered the comfort of the baking bread; it was knotted up with that other evasive but undeniable scent, ice, ice.

He came out on deck. Lars Nordahl was on watch. Edward was wary of him – he'd been ship's mate on many a whaling vessel, recruited in Trondheim (with the bulk of the crew) for his experience and the respect he commanded, and he thought of this explorer's expedition as a well-paid whim. He was liked by the men, powerful, broad, with a mass of copper hair, and Edward had to struggle against the awe of the child within himself who had dreamed of Vikings.

'We're nearing the ice, Nordahl.'

The Norwegian, gazing north, did not turn. Edward joined him at the rail and saw it was not insolence that kept him silent; it was the same taut thrill that had gripped his own dreams.

'I felt it in my nose when I woke this morning.'

Lars turned his large head and looked down, impressed, at his captain for a moment, before turning his gaze back to the sea. In the quiet morning, this jocular, expansive man was subdued. In the pit of him, a depth of calm like the fjord he was raised beside lay placid, and his spirit was stilled by the pale-misted dawn.

'Frazil, Captain,' he said, with a nod to the water. 'And grease ice further out. Your nose told you true.'

The sea they were sailing had turned glutinous; it rolled without breaking, its dark surface covered by the rough-silk sheen that was the first sign of freezing.

'We'll reach the first floes in days.'

'It's early in the year for that, Nordahl. But I

believe you're right. It seems it will be winter soon enough.'

Mare Congelatum, it is called on ancient maps. The sea congealing.

Julia holds the edge of her desk and feels her hands clench around imagined metal, feels the chill crystallize; as a child, she stood so on a ferry to France, at the back of the ship, which, she had learned, was called the stern; and with a suitably stern, resolute expression she imagined herself an adventurer.

I would be brave and strong like Edward, I would sail through the floes, I would not die in the snow; the whip and cling of my skirt in the salt wind, the ice-white cliffs become a great frozen wall.

Emily, almost home now, sees the English coast loom out of the grey dawn, and holds fast to the handrail to steady her mind. She gathers her skirts about her as she steps onto the gangplank and imagines that the next time she sets foot on a ship, it might be to meet her husband, home from the sea. She breathes the brackish air, the last of the sea-mist freshness mixed with the pungent, gritty odour of the shrimp hauled onto the docks; she wonders if she will ever sail again. She will not.

★ ★ ★

Edward's hands grip the rail, his black eyes bright. The Pole draws closer. He is returning to the frozen sea.

NIGHTFALL

They sailed on; the sea thickened and slicked into an undulating, elastic transparency before greying and turning to rubble; true to Nordahl's word, the first of the solid fragments were soon upon them. It was bright still in the sunshine, and warm, and the holiday atmosphere prevailed, but as the evenings drew in faster the nights grew cold. They were snug below decks, swaddled in layers of insulation and heated by the galley at the centre. Out in the night air, they could feel the frost all through their gloved fingers. Edward breathed it in and took joy in every breath.

The floes grew thicker, more persistent, packing close, the smaller chunks crunched effortlessly under *Persephone*'s wide keel. The stuff of Simon's nightmare, and those of the whalers who in years before had risked these waters – chasms narrowing, closing in. But *Persephone* had reached the home she was made for and no longer rolled with the ocean; the open water had all but vanished, filled and frozen with ice. They smashed a way through or found gullies between, until they gave up on negotiating routes and allowed the ice to grip and release her at will, knowing she could stand it. At dawn and dusk, a daily cycle, it rolled and piled in extraordinary forms all about them; the men on deck saw mountains, monsters and beasts rise and topple, abstract complex geometries, gigantic crystals glinting off every surface and smashing slowly into glittering facets. And everything suffused with the sunlight that left its colours lingering, flaming brilliant gold against the cobalt sky for an hour before fading to pearlescence, the shadows hollowed out in deep lucent blue. As the dark drew in each evening, and the last of the colour gave in to the edgeless half-tones of moonlight, *Persephone* ached and groaned as the gullies narrowed about her and squeezed, squeezed, the ice insisting itself up her sides, forcing itself upon her with a giant's roar, threatening to turn her, crush her and drown her deep in the freezing underworld. And then slackened and left them in peace for another uneasy night. As the ice packed the men were quiet, contemplative, then raucous in the evenings against the silence when the din had settled and their ship had triumphed once more. No, she would not go under.

The nights grew longer until the days could hardly be said to have broken; the sun nudged at the sky for a few scant hours, hesitantly broaching the horizon before flooding the snow red again as it retreated before the quiet advance of twilight.

Early in October, in the last of these ruddy evenings, Edward gave the order to make ready: they had been held fast for days now and could neither shift nor break a path; the ice had them gripped for the winter. Ten days later, the men drank a toast to the return of the light, in 1900. The sun had set.

A collection of ink drawings between marbled boards illustrates this part of the tale; Julia lifts and turns each one delicately, with the proper reverence for old paper. The work of an unknown artist, survived by his impressions of the wilderness that engulfed him; a vision of a brave ship stranded. And a silhouette against the snow: Edward standing at the prow, a captain on watch; *Persephone* perched several feet above sea level, as if lifted from the waves and abandoned on the crag of an ice mountain.

In the strange arrest of the Arctic night, there was no wind and nothing to stir in it anyway. The ship's engine, dismantled, was silent; she had been stripped of sails, and the masts and remains of the rigging were stark, already brightly frosted against the deepening sky. She might have been there for a hundred years or more, freezing slowly into the semblance of her own white-glittering phantom. In the afternoons the ice still heaped itself against her like some ancient beast with a thorn in its side. They rose above; she forced the

85

ice under and they were borne up, at a slight list to starboard which interfered with dice games but otherwise gave no trouble. Now, in the hour before midnight, the beast had moved off once again, and Edward almost found the distant stomp and growl of it a comfort, a part of the profound peace he had recovered. He felt rather than heard the far-off boom of pressure in his chest, looking out over the strange country that had formed and set around them, boundless and muted as far as the horizon. The men below deck were resting after supper, playing cards, listening to Lars's tales of Scandinavian conquest with laughter and genial envy. Edward smiled. In England, his brother would be sitting by the fire, lighting a cigar; how strange, he thought, that they should share this ritual when there were so many miles between them, and they were in every way remote.

Filling his mouth with peppery smoke, Edward savoured the cedar-richness of tobacco on his tongue. Gazing at the red glow, he felt his whole self condensed in that ember; he was nothing but a tiny spark of light, of bright brief life, on an incommensurable plain. On those twilit nights, he felt as insubstantial as the evening he surveyed. His breathing slowed to become part of the quietude he had forgotten, and longed for without knowing it, since he was last locked in these seas. Far in the distance, the deep heart-boom.

The full moon was bright enough to see by, flooding the ice milk-blue; a ring of light circled it, and above it hung another orb, only the faintest waver betraying it: *paraselene*. Edward said the word to himself: a mock-moon. It seemed somehow congruous, in this place of phantom land and phosphorescence, which might have been another world entirely. A different sphere; nearer, perhaps, to heaven. No tumult of angels, no press of pudgy cherubim, no rush towards glory, but just that stillness, the dark sapphire immensity with its doubling moons and silver lights. They coursed above him, shivering a gossamer sheet across the apex, winding golden cords across the rosy sky, the lilac, jade, ice-blue sky . . . When he thought he had caught at a word to describe it, it changed again to elude him. If he were a god, he thought, he would spend his nights at this play, far from the flawed and petty makings of the world that turns below. He would spend his nights thus, casting silver webs across the sky.

As the smoke on his breath thinned into the mist of an ordinary exhalation in the cold, he flicked the stub of his cigar over the rail. Watching its arc burn bright, he sensed a movement on the edge of his vision, out on the ice; something alerted by the sudden glow. He turned his head slowly, and slowly took up the rifle propped by his side. His gaze found that of his prey. Two pairs of bright black eyes met across the ice. A white fox, so far north in winter but sleek, not starved, with one paw raised and frozen there; wary or impudent, he could not say. She sniffed the air and smelled him: tobacco, cured meat, Norwegian ale. The musk perhaps of his armpits, for his blood was high now despite the cold. He felt it thudding in his head (and the ice, far off, turning with a boom); he was all eyes, ears and sharpness: a hunter. He raised the gun to his shoulder, the fox still frozen to the spot. Alone on the ice there, the only living thing for miles around besides the deep, hidden fishes, and the dogs and men far from home. There had been no snow; her step was sure and almost trackless on the ice. She was ready, paw raised, to run. Edward fired.

The peace of the evening erupted into frantic shouts and barking as the men rushed on deck at the sound of the dogs' frenzy. The shot had broken their twitching slumber and they snapped and bayed, straining and pacing in a chaos of teeth and fur. Anton Andreev calmed them in the Russian they seemed to understand. His favourite, Anna the old bitch, whined towards him and he took her long head in his hands, letting her lick his face; yesterday she had bitten one of the whelps to death, but Anton couldn't help but forgive her.

They searched for Edward, calling for him over the dogs' cacophony on deck and below, until Freely, knowing his friend better, pointed to a dark figure on the ice. Edward had climbed down from the deck and reached his kill, and was kneeling to inspect her. A clean shot to the heart. He lifted her like a babe in arms and made his way back to the ship, with no triumphant trophy-bearing.

'I'm sorry I woke the dogs, Anton. My brother would never allow me to let a beauty like this pass us by.'

There is no white fox in the collection at John's home, of course. She sank, presumably, with the ship.

Edward caught at least one other. He describes it in the diary he took with him to his death: 'A fox on the ice today. Shot it with one precious round. She was weak with hunger, as we are. A pity to watch her last breaths. Call it an act of mercy. Our vegetarian is now a happy carnivore, picking at the carcass and sucking at the bones like a child on his thumb. We skinned the meat and divided it as fairly as we could, and ate her raw. Foolish to waste fuel on fresh meat. We are become as savage as the dogs, which tore at each other out of boredom.'

In fact, the days of boredom were long past; the dogs had wolfed their dead companions down, skin and all, one by one as they fell or were shot for the only meat Edward could afford to spare them, until there was nothing left but two corpses. He is reluctant to go into detail and does not, or cannot bring himself to record if the men too ate their own pack, who had dragged them, panting, for so many miles towards their goal. But he writes that their keeper Andreev is starving and 'yet cannot take what meat there is'. Julia, who is not squeamish, hates to think of them feasting on the fox in grim silence, but cannot stop her mind worrying at the scene:

hands trembling hungry and slick with innards, painfully portioning it out, dry mouth flooded suddenly with the smell of blood. Fresh red, a shock against the snow, cramming meat into mouths and stomachs cramping . . .

One day, near the end, this is his only entry:

> In past days we would talk always about the meals we'd eat when we got back to our countries. Lars listing lutefisk, sild, salting and pickling an endless litany of fish – and the sea all about us empty, it seems. Stoic Anton longing for his beetroot soup. Hugh's childish sweet tooth, aching for Eton mess. Beef stew; whitebait, poor Freely's favourite. I believe now it sickens us to think it. We have forgotten the sensation of hunger. Now, when we talk, which is rarely, we talk of dying. None of us can take comfort in a God, it transpires. I wish just one of us could bring that solace and save the rest.

These are the pages that Julia couldn't bear to read this morning, now safely closed and waiting on the desk to be revisited. She has set out with him from the beginning, and this time will not fail him; in time, she will come to this part, and give death its due. But there were months of dull civility before barbarity set in.

GIFTS AND A THIMBLE

Julia is bent forward, chin resting on the desk, peering into a thick, greenish glass jar. The jar has a label that reads – in the elegant copperplate of a man with time to take care over his handwriting – *Porifera, Crustacea, 18 August 1893, Beaufort Sea, 72° 21′ N, 125° 64′ W*. A sodden sponge floats sadly in the murk; if we peer a little closer, just as Julia is, we will also see a collection of very tiny, pale eight-legged things, some specks of silt; the alcohol only faintly discoloured urine-yellow; and, beyond, Julia's yellowed eye pulled wide by the curve of the glass then retreating. She sighs; she struggles to find the contents interesting and it is true, they are rather dull.

Indeed, even Edward, the label's author, would agree; and yet it was from the depths of this inauspicious specimen that his illustrious, if brief, career was born. Drifting off the coast of Canada as a green young officer, it was his task to dredge and examine silt samples from the sea. Having little else to occupy himself with, he did his duty and wrote out label after careful label in his cabin (Julia, imagining him thus, lends him Simon's

91

stoop). Once, on an impulse prompted by boredom, he took a sip of the preserving liquid, and his curiosity was rewarded by a violent attack of vomiting. Edward was not a scientist by nature any more than he was by training.

On his second expedition, he personally undertook no such experiments. The monitoring of flora and fauna, scant as it was, fell to Dr Wilkinson, who had little else to attend to as the small crew remained in remarkably good health for as long as they remained on ship. An acquaintance of John's, a fellow collector keen to see his trophies in living motion, he had volunteered with the Geographical Society's backing. He was not a seafaring man and could not grow accustomed to calling young Mackley, who as a swaggering lad had poked fun at the postures their mounts were made to adopt, his captain; he called him by his first name as he always had done. There was no lack of respect meant and no offence taken. Edward accepted him as his brother's friend, and an elder, with a right to familiarity.

I complained to our doctor of a mild headache this morning and the poor man could hardly contain himself as he brought out the medicine chest and dispensed two pills, which did their job admirably. I thanked him profoundly, but he seemed almost disappointed to have lost his only patient, upon hearing of my return to rude

92

health over lunch. He has gone back, I suppose, to his specimens. I shall express my deepest interest in his latest catch when we meet at the card table this evening,

writes Edward in the ship's log – the one that he left with the ship, in which he entertains himself with such observations of his companions and their lives on board through the long months of winter and summer.

He is even-handed and cautious, of course. When Hugh Compton-Hill, the diplomat's son, refuses the taint of meat and insists on a greater share of the precious vegetable matter they have brought, and will otherwise eat only porridge, bread and chocolate, Edward seems to indulge him. 'It's true the boy's eyes are bright and his health and energy excellent,' he notes. He cannot betray doubt or distaste. It is his duty to preserve them all – not only to bring them home, but for history. These months must make good reading, for they precede his victory, the victory of *Persephone* over the top of the world, and his diary will be the account of it – the camaraderie, the good cheer, the courage.

Julia turns the pages carefully, making occasional notes to herself, points of cross-reference and queries to verify later. The months pass with little incident, until she catches at a sound from those pages and hears, as if she were there, the chink of glasses and a toast to the Queen. A favourite

scene so often conjured that she feels the eager-
ness of approaching festivity as if she were once
again listening to Aunt Helen tell it; as if it were
a childhood December, pine-scented and fairy-lit
and thrilling.

Christmas 1899: a holiday. They were far from land
now and long since locked into the sea. The crew
were relieved of their duties, such as they were.
Christmas Eve's after-dinner entertainment was
provided by the making of garlands, and they
decked the saloon with scraps and oddments of
paper, tin foil and bright cloth. Edward smiled to
see them, the frown of concentration creasing
Nordahl's wide forehead and the paper snowflakes
falling from Freely's clever fingers.

Edward woke in the morning feeling, absurdly,
a frisson that had last seized him when he was a
boy of six or seven, waking early in the dark and
feeling the hush of the house charged with expec-
tation, a full bladder bursting with excitement.
Knowing that below him in the drawing room
lights were twinkling and presents waiting, and
seeming to smell already the spices on the air (and
indeed, although this didn't touch young Edward, the
cook and parlour maid had been up for hours).

A break at last in the monotony, which seemed
to have stretched so much longer because there
was so much longer to go; and a gift, not beneath
a glittering tree, true, but immediately below his
bunk and just as brightly wrapped. Something of

Emily to make her memory new, which he had resisted opening all those months.

For the crew she had given a dartboard to hang in the saloon, with an inlaid message around its rim: TO THE *PERSEPHONE* – A TARGET TO PRACTISE ON! How wonderfully simple, that bright red bull's-eye, unwinking at the centre of the perfect circles. Edward, the marksman, would hit it again and again in the year to come until it seemed to taunt him with its ease, while their true target lay so many miles to the north and they seemed to draw only inches closer by the month. Tock – the dart hit home again – We're not yet even on an outside ring, he would think – tock – we've barely hit the cork – tock – embedded here as if in the wood of the wall like one of Compton-Hill's poor efforts. He would sigh and pluck the darts out, returning to the line; three bull's-eyes again, for all the good it would do him.

But as a Christmas morning's entertainment it was a resounding success, and the captain's wife was roundly toasted – especially as she had also provided a generous batch of cigarettes to add zest to their wagers. The winners, leaving the field to the gasping hopeful, made frequent retreats to the galley to smoke (much to Janssen's affable annoyance as he basted and chopped). So the hours before dinner were spent, after a breakfast of marmalade, fresh bread, Gruyère, and the first of the day's treats: a Christmas cake from their cook, with the luxury of marzipan, iced like the landscape in miniature, sculpted with a knife ('*Zaztrugi!*' cried Andreev. 'Like the wind-blown snow!') and planted in the centre with a Union Jack.

'How long have you had this up your sleeve, Einar?' asked Freely, for the cake was moist and dense and the fruit had soaked for weeks; Janssen, who hummed happily through his days and spoke little, peered up inside his huge tunic to the cavern of his armpit and shrugged.

In such good humour the day passed quickly. Dinner was a grand affair: smoked oysters, soused mackerel, a reindeer roast with peas, buttered potatoes and redcurrant sauce (not a scrap of raw fox meat anywhere in sight). The tender meat was, to Edward's palate, finer than any venison he had tasted at his brother's table; he thought of the club they attended in London and smiled a victory over pale insipid gravy as the rich maroon coated his tongue. And then – chink! – to the Queen, to *Persephone*, and to Emily Mackley's tobacco and all their wives and children.

Janssen had a word in his captain's ear then, and Edward announced that they'd stewed in their own juices long enough; it was a fine, clear night, the moon required their presence and all must step outside. What could be more invigorating than a walk in the snow at Christmas? He quieted their protests – 'Patience, boys, you shall have your pudding.'

They staggered on deck with much griping, and

clambered down onto the new-fallen snow, where their grumbles were slowly appeased by the beauty of the night. Every granule on the ground had its glimmer, and the sky was almost as close-packed with the powder of starlight. White on black like the shine in Edward's eyes, as he strove to see wide and far, to see everything, longing to bring this perfection back to Emily; if he could only close a glass orb around it and carry the universe home to her.

And then Janssen appeared with his pièce de résistance – he couldn't have lit it in the saloon, but out on the ice, the green-purple flame of the plum pudding was a beacon of cheer, an indomitable flame in the darkness. He bore it out to them, red-faced and beaming, and set it down among them as it guttered out. Overhead, the same green-violet fire flashed suddenly over the vast sky, a spirit burning incandescent. They looked one to the other then, in the hush of the milky moonlight, and shook hands in silence as they passed Nordahl's flask between them.

Later they played sports on the ice, racing each other and clutching at full bellies, laughing like children let off school and delirious with snow. Janssen, spinning and spinning with his gaze skyward to the stars, fell giggling at Nordahl's feet. Having worked so hard to bring comfort to all, in that place so far from any of their homes, no one could begrudge him a nip of the pudding brandy.

And at one o'clock, after an evening's indolence

and yet more gorging on candied fruit, nuts and macaroons, after one last smoke, they retired. And then, at last, Edward drew from beneath his bed that other, smaller parcel meant for him alone, which he had saved all day, which he had for months savoured the thought of.

A pocket watch, fine-filigreed, engraved *To Edward – For our hours apart, and so that he may find his path and come back to – His Emily*. He wound and set it and held it to his cheek, a cool disc against his skin, the ticking through his jawbone like her distant heart. He smiled as he thought of the pucker of her brow, following the trace of his diagrams as he explained how longitude is reckoned by the hour and the angle of the sun. Attentive, intelligent Emily, the brightness of her eye emblazoned always on his mind.

Just as he thought of her then, just as Julia imagines her now, so she might still be sitting in the dining room, if we descend to seek her there. See: fires are blazing in every hearth in the house, a beacon of welcome. All the curtains drawn against the frosty night.

Emily's face burns; she thinks she will surely stifle; a dark flush colours her cheeks as it did the night she met Edward; she is sleepy with heat and wine and longs to run out to the garden and press her face into the frozen grass and imagine it is snow. When at last she is free to retire, she will open the window and turn down her sheet, and climb into the cold cotton with a sigh. She will take up the little bound notebook he gave her, which she unwrapped this morning in the dark, and read over again by a candle the poem scribed in his fine hand on the first page. The lines she has known, since she was a girl, by heart . . .

> *Thy firmness makes my circle just,*
> *And makes me end, where I begun*

They are no dull sublunary lovers, who have spent months in the light of a constant sun. He has filled the words with meaning for her; this is his gift.

But now, at the table, she is far from the lonely bed she longs for and the little comfort she can draw. Her hair is caught up in the loops and curls that are forever reluctant to stay in place. Her shoulders, skimmed by the cut of her dress, are slender but strong. She shows her teeth when she smiles and laughs and cannot manage to simper; her hands are long but not tapering and must be kept in check, as they tend to gesture. She rests them interlocked on her legs and feels the hardness still in her thighs from skiing, under her skirts. Her eyes are bronze-brown and bold.

She is not quite of her time. She looks, in fact, a little like Julia.

Julia sat in that same chair – or so it would be pleasing to imagine, the seating plans were not preserved – just over a century later, last

Christmas. In the drawing room, in the bay window, there was a fine Scots pine just like perhaps the one that little Edward once imagined twinkling as he thrilled in the darkness. The house was full of the smell of it, and of spices and port, of orange and clove, of sage and roasting, of the warm nostalgia that has been worked into the wood for so many years – the festive glow which Julia had relit, resplendent. She had sweated and fretted over the goose in the kitchen, but now it was brought forth, complete with potatoes roasted in its fat, sprouts of course, redcurrant and bread sauces, a rich brown gravy and, most proudly of all, the chestnut stuffing (the liver dutifully identified and recovered by Simon from the plastic bag of innards). Her sister sat to one side of her, Simon to the other, and Aunt Helen wasn't there but it was all in her honour, and Julia would do the day justice. She was wearing a dark red dress – yes, cut to show the angles of her slim sharp shoulders – her hair caught up in a failing bun, her colour a little high with heat and happiness, and Simon watched enraptured again as her hands looped and curled her words, her laughter flowing free with the wine, at last at leisure.

This is the only occasion on which Simon and Julia have used the dining room, although it amuses her sometimes to imagine them sitting at either end of the long table, politely smiling at each other, too distant to converse. They eat in the kitchen, or on laps in the sitting room, or on a night like tonight – if all goes to plan – in the conservatory with the doors wide to the garden. But in the days when families were formal, and the damask was darker, the shine of the pattern more crisp, Emily took her seat at table thrice daily with her brother-in-law and his wife. There she sat, always the same seat, opposite Arabella, feeling like an unwanted relative's orphan or a maiden aunt. John would attempt a light political sally, into a debate that a woman might have formed a view upon, not wishing to appal or confuse her; Emily, uncertain of her bounds, would respond politely. Then Arabella would yawn in a manner she thought discreet, and all would consider the matter resolved, as far as that table was concerned. It was a missed opportunity, for Emily's mind was quick and John's was surprisingly open. Arabella, for her part, had long since given up on broaching any subject of interest to herself, seeing that the endlessly fascinating activities of their acquaintances, and their intrigues and hat trims, were of apparently no consequence to her rather peculiar sister-in-law. Besides, these were not appropriate topics for the dinner table; she had no wish to irritate her husband, and anyway Arabella liked to dedicate her attention to the task in hand, especially if it came with a cream sauce. And so Emily's first months at her brother-in-law's table passed without interest or incident.

Come Christmas time John, knowing that Mr

Gardiner, Emily's father, would be alone for the festive season, invited him to stay at the house with them too; and now here they sit, it is Christmas Day, and a select band of the town's luminaries have been invited to share the goose. Arabella, with the tact she considers foremost among her talents, has placed Mr Gardiner beside Mrs Dempsey, a widow of her acquaintance who has kept her good humour despite her loss, and a nice womanly figure besides. Daniel Gardiner, a kind and quiet man who, for his part, will never quite recover from his wife's departure, replies to her teasing in awkward monosyllables; he tries to respond to John's generous attempts at conversation, but is a little hard of hearing and finds the words are lost in crossing the table, swallowed up in the nudging, pealing laughter of his neighbour. Well, he thinks to himself at the peak of one particular crescendo, perhaps tonight I might consider the Lord to have blessed me with deafness. And as he smiles his mild smile, he catches his daughter's eye across the table. Emily is seated too far away for them to speak, between a clergyman and a lawyer, he surmises; she smiles back, helpless, and he knows that all her vivacity, as lovely as it is, can only be for show. Still, how lovely she is tonight. With her mother's pale gold skin that he liked so much better than the fashion for blue-veined pallor.

She does her best to be gay. She wears the pink shawl Arabella gave her, with no apparent attention to Emily's taste and colouring. She nods and agrees and avoids engaging the clergyman in any conversation that might be thought incendiary (such as why she should believe). She sings along to the carols although they are too high for her and her voice feels strangled; she imagines Edward singing Norse songs with his crew, his loud, easy laugh.

The plates are removed and she has barely time to sit back and ease her stomach with a sip of wine before the pudding is brought in – as if, she thought, another flame was needed here. By now she feels her own head might ignite (and wouldn't *that* give them something to talk about). Portions are served, her protests ignored; Arabella likes to insist that she needs fattening and Emily will have to swallow her distaste along with yet another spoonful. A great, weighty, steaming slab is placed before her, slathered with brandy butter, and she dutifully digs her spoon in. And hits metal. And knows that whatever it is will pain her and tries desperately to cut around it in the hope she might remove it discreetly, whatever it is; Let it be the coin, she thinks, she could keep it hidden under her tongue perhaps, she would even manage a simper if it meant she didn't have to speak. But the coin has just been discovered – by her father, which pains her more greatly. 'Ah, good fortune is yours, Daniel,' says John, smiling at Emily and back to him as if to say he had his wealth already in the daughter he'd been given, hoping it would be enough for the company to let it pass. But they are already congratulating him on the riches that shall be his – this man who lives with just the charwoman to tend him, who can't afford to keep his own daughter, who is relying on a younger man's benevolence to house him for Christmas and never has guests at his own table, and Emily can't bear to see him smile and nod and flush so and she holds it aloft, whatever it is, announcing, 'The Gardiners are in luck tonight, Father!'; she holds it aloft and it fits, neatly, the end of her finger. The thimble.

Did Arabella's eyes gleam a little then, or was it only candlelight and brandy?

'Oh, but that was meant for me!' cries Mrs Dempsey. 'The thimble, for a happy, single life – I live it, each day, as you can all see for yourselves! Had you not taken so large a piece, my dear, it would have come to me!' she says, using Mr Gardiner's arm as a surrogate for the nudge meant for Emily. And Daniel Gardiner, despite his growing bruise, warms a little to her then for her kindness.

'I had thought the thimble was for the spinster,' observes the lawyer on her left, quite failing to register the awkwardness forcing the others' jollity.

'Well, that may be, Mr Worthy, but might they not equate?' says John, and could kick himself because what comfort, really, could that be?

'In either case,' says Emily, 'I should think my husband will have something to say about it when he comes home to find I am quite content alone.'

And from somewhere she conjures a carefree laugh, waggles her thimbled finger, and with a pretty moue and a pert little shrug slips a mouthful of pudding between her lips. How her father admires her for it; only he and Arabella, still watching, see the shine in her eye and the corners of her mouth twitch for a moment, as she reaches for her glass to wash the heavy lump down.

Everyone in the house had had their turn on Stir-up Sunday; any little maid might have dropped it in the bowl, not thinking of the hurt it would cause Emily should her spoon strike it. But it does seem that Arabella, who always enjoys the dessert course, is this Christmas particularly relishing her pudding.

Later in the evening, as they bid good-night, John presses Emily's hand and says quietly, 'This, I think, was the token meant for you, sister.' In her room, she opens her fingers and sees that a tiny silver anchor has left its impression, squeezed against her palm. Safe harbour.

UNSENT LETTERS

Emily wears a silver charm on a chain about her neck; Julia's hand goes to it unconsciously, to touch where it now rests between her own collarbones. But the *Persephone*, still held fast, had no need of an anchor. The earth turned, inexorable, beneath the still point.

Edward and his crew could do nothing but wait for it to turn, through its one, long day. The sun rose again; they celebrated like pagans, with meat and wine and feasting, and staged a play in the saloon. Freely's free adaptation of *The Winter's Tale*, to mark the passing of the season, with much made of an exit pursued by a great white bear (Janssen, stumbling over the verse, was content to roar). They tended to the rigging, set up wood and metal workshops on the deck, performed the exercises Edward prescribed to keep them fit and occupied, and began, as the summer drew on, to make preparations for the following spring. So the days passed, and the evenings too, which grew slowly to resemble the days; they went to their beds in bright sunshine, knowing the darkness below decks to be false, and lay awake like children on a long school holiday, sensing the daylight they couldn't see. The nacreous dome of the polar day encased them like an oyster shell. They took to late nights, lingering in the saloon. Life became one long, timeless afternoon. There were always more stories, and when reminiscence failed, there was another hand to be played, the same songs to sing, the jokes at Compton-Hill's expense which never seemed to pall (and which the boy, to his credit, took with patient condescension).

If living in such proximity was ever an irritant, then Edward does not betray it, although his diary is filled with solitudes – and he had, after all, his private berth to retreat to, while the crew slept four to a cabin. He was often to be found out on the ice alone. Miles from the ship, he would imagine himself free as he sped over the ice on snowshoes, or pulled by the dogs that at last, after months of practice, did his bidding. At the end of every day, after the turning back that he must always wrench his mind around to (it would be so easy to go on, and on, the ice so flat, less than five hundred miles now), he would lie on his bed and feel the pull in his thighs still, and let his body speed in his dreams through the night. The ship edged north, slipped back, drifted west. The light, everywhere, reflected off the surface and suffused what should have been shadowed. As the summer drew on and the ice broke up, they began to see the tell-tale dark cast of water against the flat sky, and could sail at a stretch across occasional polynya, the wide lakes an inky shock in the expanse of pastel white. Travel on foot across the ice became impossible; even a short distance from the ship could prove fatal if the current parted the floes, stranding the hapless walker on a tiny drifting island.

Come late August, twilight and the ice closed in again upon them. *Persephone* groaned, but would not crumple. By crunching, painful degrees, they edged onward. Every other day, the measure was taken, with compass, quadrant and watch. Edward marked their route on the map, a scribble of increments which crossed and recrossed. He was frustrated, but not concerned; he had seen the same tangled knot of progress, drift and backslide in other men's accounts, and he did not doubt he would reach the Pole. It seemed to him that since he was a child in the nursery he had been toddling on uncertain legs towards it, waiting to grow strong. He could not remember a time when this desire did not consume him. Had he joined the navy only for this reason? It seemed so to him now. Others had set out for the north in the service of ambition, to advance up the ranks; for him, the career itself was a means to the end of this sole purpose. He would reach it; he must.

But what of Emily? Was there room in his heart for her? She was always in his thoughts, at his side. Her passion met his own, spurred it on; she kindled to his ambition and her flame kept his burning through every long night. Every night, when he lay down to dream and let his mind loose on the ice, he was striving towards her, where she waited at the Pole. In the ship's log, he never uses her name. He wrote no long laments at her absence; it haunts every line, as if she is just at his back as he sits at his desk, a hand upon his shoulder as if it were their drawing room, not some cubby-hole on the border of the civilized, the known and charted world.

All through the pages of 1900, all the long year, he makes his promise to her: 'I shall surely reach it; it is within grasp.'

If a man repeats his conviction daily, how could his belief be doubted? How, indeed, could it fail to come true?

And the year was passing for Emily, too, with no promise of adventure. She did her best to take pleasure in the daily round of visiting and strolling in the garden and gracious welcomes. She was cheerful and bright and helpful, doing what she could to assist Arabella in the running of the house, taking on her share of invitations to tea. Her laugh was attractive, she had gained confidence, maturity, composure. She was at all times exceedingly composed. Her heart, thoroughly laced in, was breaking.

She was alarmed to find that ladies were expected to be ever more wasp-waisted. There was a great pinch between the centuries; tottering about with chests thrust forward and backsides held high, the women of England were an absurd and uncomfortable flock, and Emily had no choice but to join their feathered ranks. No more could she loll in her liberty bodice; whalebone (culled at such cost from the seas her husband sailed on) gripped her tight. Her only escape took the form of a tennis dress, donned for an occasional lady-like game when Arabella could be persuaded; her opponent puffed and fanned and grew quickly bored, as did Emily of her meek returns. She longed for the cold, for the speed and freedom of the snow. She wished to be nothing but the laughing heap she had been at her husband's feet. Instead, she patted the ball, back and forth. Her body did not fit the age. Her shoulders were too square, her legs too strong, her back too straight. It did not want to curve, and when she unlaced herself at last and lay down at night she felt the hollow at its base, where once he had kissed her, aching against the bed. The too-soft, empty bed.

At the little writing desk in what was once Emily's bedroom, the hundred letters penned and blotted there leave no trace. Its walnut shine betrays nothing of the sadness that was spilled over it in neat lines of ink. Its drawers are still lined with the papers she placed in them, the vestige of rose-scent long since overwhelmed by beeswax, polish and the acrid tang of camphor. But the desk is still there, as solid as it was when she took her place before it every day, at first, biting the skin inside her bottom lip and gripping its edge to keep steady and writing letter after letter that she couldn't send.

They were left in their drawer for fifty years or more, tied with black ribbon, and carefully replaced when at last they were found. Julia has taken them from the room they were written in and brought them up to the attic, seeking the Emily that lived in Edward's absence, listening out for her voice, which is quieter than his; she is addressing only her husband, whereas he must address the whole world. Julia remembers sitting with her mother and sister on the side of Emily's bed (which Julia slept in as her aunt's guest) and slipping the bow, the dusty satin still shining where it had been knotted; she loosens now the knot her mother retied all those years ago, and which she has slipped and fastened so many times since. The half-learned words loop an indigo line across her mind, writing themselves over as she reads them. The rhythm of the ink is constant and strong, never smeared with tears, resistant to despair. 'You will be pleased to learn that Arabella is teaching me to crochet. It is slow progress, I fear; I am forever unravelling. By the time you return I may just have completed a tiny blanket, with which you may cover one knee'; 'Your brother I find has excellent taste and my big monkey hands, as you once so dearly described them, have been put to task stretching octaves at the piano nightly'; 'It is spring, and the cherry trees are showing off, all pink and blowsy about the town; the little apple tree at the bottom of the garden blossoms white and quietly, and as I sit beneath it they fall about me, like snow, my sweet, like snow . . .'; 'Today we rode out to the country and I thought how green, how lovely, and wondered, do you miss the smell of earth, of leaves and grass, darling? As I sorely miss the sharp scent of mist and salt water . . .'; 'I have been wicked and not written for a week, for my thoughts, like my days, are quite empty. It has been gloomy and dull this month past and the summer is over; and you will be trapped again in the darkness. Under the same moon, but I cannot see it – there is only some will o' the wisp, haunting the clouds.'

'I have been so long without you now. What colour are your eyes? They are almost black, of course; I remember. I pray that they look upon this earth still; that they look upon its summit, even; and then recall that you and I are heathens with no one to pray to, and must content myself with hoping.'

'All the leaves are fallen now, with no word of you, and so I know I must wait another winter – as you warned me I might, so I cannot call you cruel'; 'What hope blooms in me with the coming of this spring! I shall see you again, surely, in a matter of weeks, you cannot be far now'; 'We have been taking tea out in the garden, these last warm days, as you and I used to – it seems an age ago, another time. Everywhere life at its fullest, yet you are absent still from my side and the green world is grey to me until you return.'

'Where does this letter find you? Will you come home safe to me? May I hold you to your promise, Edward? As I have been true to mine. I am waiting.'

Julia reads each one, and wonders if they could bear a different sort of scrutiny, a harsher light; if they would withstand the transition to print, if a woman's courage and hope can be called history. Taking up the stack, shuffling them carefully to align the edges, the bundle she reties seems a very frail weight. She remembers the three of them sat on the bed together, knowing what Emily could not – that her hope, by the time of these last letters, was already misplaced.

Squashed up together on the soft mattress, Mum in the middle, making a dip that the two of us leaned into. Outside the open window, always sunshine, a willow shuffling, the breeze pale green, the old song – willow, weep for me . . . the scent of clean linen, of lavender, my mother weeping, mother singing willow weep for me . . .

Maggie, her mother, hovers at the edges of her memory and haunts the rooms too, absorbed into the past. There was lavender growing in the garden once, and it flourished all over the house for a time; Maggie brought it in by the bunch, stuffing it in bottles and bowls. Julia clipped a sprig to lay on the coffin and imagined she could smell it burning when she saw the smoke rise from the crematorium as they drove away. When they moved in last year she wrenched it out of the soil, while it was still winter, before it had time to flower (Simon came home to find her muddied and panting in the dark, unable to explain herself, and laughed at her, fond and nervous). And now with a similar wrench of will she banishes the scent from her mind.

The contents of *Box 004* are lying upon the floor. She reads over her inventory, glances over the morning's notes. She has tried to bring it to account. She has tried to redeem the day, to give it meaning, to stay true to her purpose. The work of the last hours is arrayed in a neat line, and accounted for. She has reckoned dates, materials, origins, costings where she knows enough to esti-mate; she thought she would feel neat and clean, like Simon's labels, but it leaves her feeling faded, dirtied, like the cardboard box lying on its side emptied of promise, become ordinary. These boxes of treasure that she rummaged as a child now just a succession of artefacts that she cannot place a value on. What use is it all, after all; what purpose in disturbing the dust? These relics and facts and guesses cannot come near to the sum of the man she is seeking. They are not the man that strides through her dreams, and they are nothing like the Edward that Emily remembered; he is more than the sketch of a silhouette, and will not be constrained in her mind by that outline.

Is there no other way to approach him? She must not give in yet again to *ennui* – a word she prefers to less glamorous, more worrying alternatives (why can she barely keep her eyes open through an afternoon? Surely not because she can't think of anything worth staying awake for. Not that). She stands and takes up the second diary. She knows the story so well that she cannot remember the last time she read it first-hand.

A CIGARETTE

A square of unhurried sunlight stretches and slides over the floor, as if seeking something. There is a silver filigreed pocket watch, looted from Edward's grave, now waiting to be accounted for among the miscellany on the floor in the attic; but as it is irreparably broken and will not be wound, it cannot tell what hours have passed. If, however, we were to extricate the small brass ship's clock which is currently muffled by a velvet wrapper in *Box 002*, it would reveal that the time is now a quarter past three. In fact it is closer to half past; it is still winding down from the last time it was brought to light a few days ago, and each second it counts off is just a little longer than the last; and why, after all these years, should it be in a rush to catch up?

Outstretched, Julia's limbs are arranged in a manner appropriate to the chaise longue they're draped upon. One hand trails upon the floor, palm up, in the manner of an opium addict. She is enjoying the *chaise*, italicized exotically in her mind. Since she was a teenager she has draped herself upon it, just so, reading one of her aunt's books of poetry, feeling tragic, Romantic. The soporific warmth of the attic in the hot ceaseless summers of the south of England, of her girl-hood. She is enjoying the memory of her body as it was then, the way her new breasts ached and the fine hair on her legs, and hours and weeks stretching out upon her, her life somewhere off in the hazy distance that she'd set out for sometime. She is enjoying the quiet and the sound of her own breath. And most of all, her head back and resting on a rose-pink pillow, her eyes half open and watching her own hand and its long fingers and the thin plume of smoke curling bril-liant through the dust in the light from the window, most of all Julia is enjoying her cigarette, her guiltiest and most delicious pleasure. She has cut down dutifully, from twenty, to ten, to five, to this one, unnecessary and perfect. Sometimes in the morning with coffee. Sometimes with a glass of wine at night. Sometimes she smokes when she's angry or nervous and the pleasure is spoiled and she is disappointed in herself and in the ciga-rette, annoyed that she has squandered it. But the best cigarettes are those like the one that we've found her smoking now, for no reason at all.

By the river we sat, my sister and I, and we smoked. I liked the narrowing of her eyes when she inhaled. I liked the way she pulled her hand back and held it out defiant and the pause before she breathed out.

Watching the flash on the water, the bright empty air and the yellow dust on the dry paving and the disapproval of the people passing. We pretended not to care what our parents would say as we frantically chewed mints and sprayed ourselves with perfume in the chemist. I chose the one my aunt wore, in a white china bottle. Old-fashioned floral. We must have smelled like smart old ladies, those ladies that go to matinées together, with high heels and set hair and two-piece suits: comfits and freesias and the faintest waft of fag smoke.

Julia laughs at herself gently in the attic, all these years later, twisting her neck to extinguish the stub. Her body could not be moved now from the cushions, is becoming one with the furniture; *chair* she italicizes, in French it means flesh, *ma chair, ma chérie*; she smiles again, sleepy.

The pages dig into her belly; a line of pressure, of solidity, through her middle. On either side, above and below, she is slowly, heavily vanishing, like a sheet of bible paper weighted only by a fold. The words are barely visible in the brightness, through her eyelashes; like Edward

Item 11: Snow goggles, leather, rubber and tinted glass

sunblind. Light diffusing through dust. She lets the diary fall against her chest, so that her entire body is no more than that square of paperweight, a weight made of paper to hold her down; she is

118

acutely aware of her fingertips and the book warm from lying in the patch of sun from the window that has at last found her.

Brightness, blue, blue and white, silent still; skin against the snow. Sky deep above me, ice deep beneath and ocean deeper. The sun has risen, rose and gold. I am elated, I am waiting . . .

The hot, woody dust-smell of the attic grows thicker as the afternoon draws on, the heat of the house rising and gathering here and the sun beating on the roof unabated. She tries to let the blank sky blot and fill her mind, letting time grow as dense as the air about her, until she can see him as she knows he was, setting out and holding on to hope as he sailed into the unknown; holding on to the hope of the Pole, an idea to be mastered, a mast to steady the world by.

When I was a girl we cut holes in the world. Opening a way into an unused air, cold and clean and sharp as snow. Putting our faces close to the gap so we could smell it, taste the pale blue bite of it, careful not to slip through.
   I shall walk into that other air and strand myself, after all.

Far in the dreaming blue distance a figure, she thinks, approaches; too far off to see yet if it is man, bear, apparition even. There is the steel-white

119

of the snow, the deep and bright impossible sky, and emerging between them a figure: yes, a man. She can make out sealskin, furred fringes. His pace is purposeful, he is still strong despite the cold. Tall, bold, strident; more than simple history. A Hyperborean, a heavenly being, beyond the world of men; he has passed through the storms and emerged into brilliant, sunlit, infinite myth. She sets out to meet him.

He is next to her now, they have covered the distance so quickly. 'Good God, woman,' he says, 'you've not a scrap on you, what the devil are you doing?' But he is laughing as he says it, and she looks down at herself and, seeing that she is naked, she laughs too. 'I'm waiting, I was waiting for you,' she says. And he opens his coat and folds her inside with him to keep her warm, but she is warm already and in his coat it is cold, his skin against hers is cold, and he takes her hands between his to warm them but his fingers are black all through, and she looks up at his face and his nose is black too, and it spreads and his black lips pull back from his teeth and his eyes turn to milk as the lids contract and she feels his body spasm and shudder, cold against her, and this is how, more than a hundred years ago, Emily woke beside her husband for the last time, for this is her dream, recurring always.

'Please, don't go,' she says. She can hear his breathing, as steady as his spirit. He lies on his back. He jerks again in his sleep; this is what woke her (already the horror is fading to unease). He is righting his balance on deck, she knows it. She too has felt her legs remember, the sea roll under her, as if their bed were cast adrift, not safely landed in this snug room. It is the first night in two weeks that they have slept on solid ground. It is the last they will spend together; tomorrow, they sail on different ships, bound for different seas.

The fire has burned out to embers and there is only the faintest orange light on his lovely face. This is not a word she uses out loud, she would be laughed at. But here, in this quiet glow, tracing with a fingertip the line of his brow, she sees only loveliness in the gloss of his closed lids. Too fine and strong to be merely handsome. Furniture and dowager aunts are handsome.

The fire has burned out but the room is still warm, the heavy drapes at the windows shielding them from cold and brightness alike. So that it might almost be night-time, real, English night-time. Many miles from them, their homeland sleeps in darkness; in a couple of hours it will begin to recede. It is June, the spring has come to fullness. Dawn has crept in earlier each day, peeling the night back a little more each time with a sly thief's fingers; and now those mornings have come, which seem to come so suddenly, when one wakes to a pale and fragrant air, the curtains thrown wide, and one must no longer dress in the dark. She remembers now that sunlight from another life, her bedroom, lilac, rose, palest peppermint green, virginal. How she would wake as fresh as the dew, untouched by the night. How she would think of the day's engagements and think, Perhaps today is the day that He will come for me. Some tall and foreign stranger with dancing eyes. And later, when He had a name, she would think, Perhaps today Edward will come, a different thrill, not romantically abstract but physical and real and not to be spoken, not to be thought of until safely stayed by whalebone.

She turns now and curls against him, wishing they could stay in their den for ever, warm beneath the furs like savages. 'Please don't go,' she says, and then sees that his eyes are open and smiling. 'I'm not going anywhere. I'm quite content where I am,' he says, reaching for her. But it is three o'clock already. 'For only an hour more,' she says helplessly, unable to stop herself, suppliant for some last kind words to add to her store for the months and years ahead. He sighs, and strokes at her temple with the tips of his fingers. 'I can't leave you for ever. I shall have to come back for my heart.' It will have to be enough.

'I will reach it, Emily. I will reach it,' he promises; he has murmured it to her every night like words that lovers use, and they are what she loves him for. Under their blankets in the dark below deck, with no windows.

'I will reach it, and I will come back to you'; he whispers it every night when she is far from him, in ship's cabin and cold tent, as he did when she was near.

'I will wait. I will know when you have reached it, if you think of me,' she answers. She pledges this in return, the night before he leaves her and every night since, in a strange Norse cot grown suddenly chill, in the narrow bunk she longs to share as she sails for England, and in the too-soft too-wide single bed she sleeps in alone for so many years in a place that wasn't meant to be her home.

'I think of you always. You will know.'

And night after night she waits for him there; lying there waiting at the still point, the world turns under her and still he does not come.

Bare skin against the snow. Bathed in the clean air, scentless. I am waiting.

PART III

Q uietly, now.

In the dimming attic, Julia's breath comes slowly, the constant sigh of the house filling and falling from her chest. A hush has settled with the dust, the animals ranged patient about her. And below, the remnants and traces of lives are stilled; the echoes that people the rooms make barely a whisper; the years and the heat weigh upon them. Caution and grace, now; do not stir them.

The sitting room: at the corner of the ground floor, sheltered from eyes from all sides, facing into the garden. The alembic into which the quiet distils. It was once, many years ago, amplified by the double-time tick of a fussy French carriage clock which remains on the mantel, but is now for ever halted. When the otherwise speechless seconds were counted by its insistent wittering, this was the morning room – the room in which the ladies' mornings dissolved seamlessly into afternoons, punctuated only by lunches and tea and the pricking of needles; the silence of this room, now at peace, was once stretched thin across every half-second the clock counted.

Helen, as a child, would sit and sketch between her mother and her aunt, until she thought the scrape of her own pencil and the ticking and ticking and the faint ponk of needles puncturing taut linen and the hiss of silks drawn through it might make her scream; instead, she sat and sketched. When Arabella died, Helen and Emily stripped out the stuffiness and lace, the spindly fretwork and wicker that had clung precariously to its edges since the end of the last century. They did not rewind the clock, so that it is always noon or midnight here; even Simon, after his one attempt to wind it, agrees that each of its prissy tickings is a singularly miserable sound. They painted the walls and ceiling a daring maroon and hung them with dozens of photographs and paintings; they installed a gramophone, which sits now in gracious retirement, having given up its place to uglier, more functional devices. They tossed tapestries and cushions over every soft surface, and covered the floor with a bearskin, upon which, years later, Simon would lay out his own most treasured memory.

Imagine now a night in October, ten years ago. It is warm, yes, but suppose it is the heat of the fire, lit in the grate to ward off the night; with the heavy drapes drawn we can believe in darkness. The fur of the rug is long and surprisingly silky, a bear-hug of a rug if laid upon. It tempts

128

the palms of the hands and the soles of the feet, the cheek, the bare belly, all the parts of the body that most love softness. It is a rug to scrunch into. Julia, in the attic three floors up, won't know we're here; imagine her laid out here, her eyes golden in the light from the fire, her warm limbs soft against the fur, barely breathing, but close enough to damp his skin. So she lay beside Simon when first they lay together.

And again, hush: listen for the whisper, lingering here still, of a secret she hasn't told him: she imagined, that first time, that she was Emily. Since she was a little girl, hiding in a hot, damp pocket of duvet in the bed Emily had slept in, in the sleepless half-light of bedtime, she had imagined over and over the romantic farewell. The promise of return, the yearn of the years and the miles which would soon stretch out between them, which made the hours so precious, before she even understood what such hours might be filled with. Still when she thinks of love, she thinks of longing. It was not a conscious fantasy but a habit of mind, then, to imagine that the man whose quick fingers slipped her dress off and tangled in her hair was her Arctic hero (tall, dark, lean, like Simon), that it was her great-great-aunt's wedding night and that the fire they stretched before was burning a hundred years ago . . .

Soon we will sail for cold places and make our den together through the long nights; soon we will sail and

129

too soon we will part and I must take as much of him as I can before then, I must take him in and hold him here for as long as he will stay. Because soon he will sail on alone and I will wait for his return and he will not come back to me . . .

When Julia thinks of what a husband means, the impossibility of giving herself up daily, she thinks of her sick father fading and her mother clutching after him, fading with him, so that her teenage years were spent on tiptoes, not wishing to break into the hush that surrounded them.

For Emily, waiting for her Edward, there was no slow souring, no flagging indulgence; and no need to witness any gruesome, petty, griping illness and death. There is only a hero, vanishing; his wife a figure on the shore.

So he is emerging from the snowstorm that obscures him: Simon's rival, frozen in his prime. The man that Julia has helplessly loved, like all the women of her family, since she and her sister first stood on either side of their aunt in the drawing room before the portrait of the two of them, Emily and Edward, and heard the story. His hand rests on her shoulder; he is at once fond and fierce. The iris she holds in her lap, for faith, wisdom and valour, is velvet-purple against her white silk skirts. On a table by her elbow lies a compass, to signify her constancy, which will keep his course true. His love will burn as bright as his ambition.

Julia, it would seem, is not planning to move far this afternoon, and can perhaps be safely left alone to her wanderings in the snow for the time being. What of her husband, Edward's avatar and rival? It may be that Simon is no hero, is unworthy of a hero's niece and her devotion. But it is not entirely Simon's fault. There are other kinds of love story. Simon, too, wants to be loved, and loves, as much as he can. Simon's love story is not epic in scale, but he has no desire for anything grander. He would like to be admired, he would like to be needed, he would like to be noticed. It is not always simple to live with the flicker he fell in love with; he has for ten years now flown relentlessly into her flame.

TO THE CITY

Here he sits, in his spacious, uncluttered office in the city. How different from the house he left this morning; no surprising corners or unexpected stairways in this building, just a succession of fluid identical spaces, full of air, and nowhere to hide. No obstacles to thought and nowhere for memories to nestle. And yet Simon, today, is unusually beset by them, as if he has helplessly trailed the house's aura with him.

Simon is devoting only the smallest possible part of his mind to the plans spread before him. These complex diagrams and calculations, with their very precise angles and firm graphite marks, are Simon's greatest professional pleasure. Following his always accurate lines, structures emerge that are sound, balanced, in three dimensions in the real world, and for Simon, his part in the symmetry of things is a reward greater than any other. On most days, then, we would find him quite absorbed, each day growing a little more curved in the back as he bends close to the fine paper, relishing the pencils he has always used for these first drafts. But today he is out of sorts.

What then, while his wife roamed the rooms of the house until she came to rest in the snow, has Simon been doing? Julia's morning smile and his breakfast eggs have so far, sadly, been the only pleasures of his day.

So, to circle back:

He arrived at work rather later than he'd hoped to; there was an accident on the road. Within half a mile of his turning onto the short stretch of dual carriageway that takes him to the station, the traffic stopped inexplicably. He waited. He took off his jacket. He was still hot. The windows were down but the air, like the cars, was at a standstill. One by one people switched off their engines, leaving their music playing so that he was assaulted from all sides by anodyne presenters, and hits from the Sixties, and, for pity's sake, Neil Sedaka. And the man next to him was listening to a classical station broadcasting one of Simon's favourite Bach concertos, but it was a poor recording and the radio was staticky, the bass chords lost, the ivory high notes thin as plastic, so that he wanted to get out of his car and get into the car of the man next to him and turn it off so that the extremely eloquent and pithy lecture on the value of actually listening to what you listen to that he was currently rehearsing could be very clearly heard and perhaps even understood. But, thought Simon with a sigh, trying to relax his angry grip on the wheel, what hope was there of understanding? I hope your crappy radio makes your battery flat, you ignorant arsehole, he thought. He restrained himself from saying it out loud. Julia was correct, Simon almost never swears, even when he's alone, except in his head. His head, in this stationary traffic, threatened to implode with all the words he wasn't saying out loud.

There were sirens. They waited. Simon drummed his middle finger on the wheel and checked his watch every twenty seconds or so, knowing he'd missed his train, wondering if he'd miss the next. Listening to the sirens, waiting, Simon was thinking that this was Julia's fault. He knew this was quite irrational, which served only to add to his irritation. It was her fault he was tired, and that he was going to be late. He'd been tired when he came home from work yesterday and the last thing he had needed was an impromptu dinner party with the sodding Watsons, with their nice wines that yes, he was sure he'd better not have even just one little glass of, with their poussins ('Just pick it up, we don't mind!') and the fuss over the bottle of wonderful Pouilly-Fuissé and their lovely suburban home just a short hour's backwoods drive away, with her big breasts in his face and his big belly laugh and the endless Bordeaux . . . all of this was too much, unforewarned, at the end of a long, stressful day and a horrible hot journey home. When he had stepped through the door to find Julia emerging from the cellar with a bottle, and saying '*There you are*' with a blithe kiss on the cheek, his heart sank even before he knew why it might be that she had expected him earlier.

'Do you want to change?' she asked. She was wearing a short puffy skirt she knew he disliked. She should have known, at least.

'What for?'

'For dinner. We're supposed to be there by eight.'

When he walked in the door it was 6.52.

'Supposed to be where?'

Simon knows, deep in the appointments diary of his soul, that he wasn't told of wherever it is. He doesn't forget appointments. He makes a point of writing them down even though he knows he won't forget them. Now, he pointedly takes his diary from the inside pocket of the suit jacket (which has crumpled on his way home). The evening, as he knew, is filled with nothing but blue feint lines.

'We're going to James and Michelle's,' she says, uncertain now.

'Are we. When did "we" arrange this?' He feels a nasty satisfaction in seeing the precision of his punctuation hit home. She was in a good mood but it's fading now.

'Last week.'

'Dinner with the Watsons.'

'With Michelle, and James, yes'; as if he might somehow have forgotten their first names.

'Julia . . .' he sighs. 'I wish you . . . you could have told me before now. I'm tired. I've been in meetings all day and I have to be at work early tomorrow. When did you . . . why didn't you tell me?'

'I did,' she insists, but Julia's inefficiency has been proved too many times for her to attempt indignation for long. 'I'm sure I did. She called last week. I remember, you were upstairs in the study so I called up to you and I assumed you'd heard.'

'You assumed. You shouted up the stairs and took my total lack of response or acknowledgement as a tacit acceptance of the invitation.'

Julia smiles sheepishly, even giggles a little. It may be a nervous giggle; she knows she's in the wrong. It is certainly, regardless, a very annoying giggle under the circumstances. Simon walks past her, ignoring the hand she puts to his arm as he passes. He makes his measured way up the stairs, not stamping.

'Simon? Are you . . . what are you doing?'

'I'm going to change.' He stops on the stairs but doesn't look down at her. 'I believe I was meant to get changed.'

'I just thought you'd like to. You don't have to, if you don't want.'

'Hm. I've been wearing the same shirt since I got up at seven this morning. I'm hot and uncomfortable and yes, I'd probably like to change, for dinner. With the Watsons. Thank you for suggesting it.' He stamps the last six stairs and blames her, too, for the hot peevish flush he feels as he reaches the bedroom.

He descends again a quick wash and a fresh shirt later, sharp-creased through the sleeves and collar (James will be all rolled-sleeved linen lightness and starchy Simon will despise and envy him for it). Julia is gone. He finds her in the sitting room, and is astounded to see her painting her toenails. He hates painted toenails, and they are running late.

'Oh, that was quick. Nearly done,' she says.

'Shall we go, then? I assume I'm driving?'

'Oh, I don't mind really. What do you think? I just need to wait two minutes and I can put my sandals on. If you're driving I can just carry them to the car, actually . . .'

'I've arrived at this assumption on the basis of the prior assumption that you haven't, in the twelve hours since I last saw you, learned to drive and obtained a licence. And if we're expected at eight, we're already late, so yes, my dear, I think you will have to set out barefoot.'

Julia winces. Simon's terms of endearment are infrequent and almost never affectionate.

'Sorry. I thought you might want to take a cab, is what I meant.'

'Have you booked one?'

A very small voice now: 'No.'

'Then I'm driving. I don't want to drink anyway. It's fine. If we leave now we'll be there by quarter past.'

Julia checks the silver watch he gave her, six years ago, as a gift. Before then she said she'd never had much use for one and he sometimes wonders if she's worked out how to read it yet.

'I should call them. They said seven-thirty for eight, actually – no one ever means that though, do they?'

'So when you said an hour, you meant half an hour. For God's sake, Julia . . .'

'Well, I didn't know you'd be back late.'

Simon, instead of shouting, So now it's my fucking fault that you can't even tell the time, calmly takes his car keys from the table by the door and marches out into the evening, which is as unpleasantly hot as the day has been and shows no sign of relenting; the growing darkness has only condensed it. He waits by the car and tries to subdue the infuriation which increases with every passing second of her non-emergence. It would serve her right if he did, he thinks (without allowing himself to imagine the thing he might do, without allowing himself to contemplate the possible consequences of a misplaced kiss); but he knows it wouldn't. Still it remains to be seen if he will do it anyway.

Suddenly the traffic started moving again, the gasp and roar of engines all around jolting Simon back to the morning. A mile and a half on, two cars and a van had been hauled to the side of the road. A man that Simon took to be the van's driver was talking to a policewoman. He was sweating and his head was cut; Simon couldn't tell if he was crying.

One of the cars was badly dented, the other crushed from back to middle, the front almost comically intact, half of an accordion, and there was blood all over the windscreen, and then there were people putting up screens but Simon had already seen enough to imagine the mess of hair matted into the glass. He thought again of the pheasant. He remembered driving too fast. He imagined Julia's head, instead, hitting the same spot from inside, making the same noise, not bang or crunch, and spending the rest of his life shadowed by the guilt of it, and of not having forgiven her. He asked himself why he was imagining such a thing. He felt sick. He kept imagining it over and over until he reached the station, egg yolk gluey at the back of his throat. As he locked the car he could hear his train announced; as he ran up the metal stairs, terrified of slipping but determined not to miss it, he heard the train pull in; he slipped through the doors at the last possible closing beep and had to stand all the way to Waterloo, shaky and damp until he gathered himself, and reached the office late, flushed and already crumpled.

The lift was crowded and it stank of commuting. Simon was worried that he, too, must smell by now. He slipped a furtive hand into his armpit, lifted it to stroke his cheek (still smooth) and discreetly sniffed the palm. Soap. Good. But he'd worn a blue shirt and there was sweat down his back soaking through. Joanne was sitting at her desk with her mug already; she gave a little guilty start when he came in, and quickly closed a window on her screen. He hesitated before asking her to make more coffee for him. He didn't want to patronize her; it wasn't her job to serve drinks. Was it? It wasn't her job to check private email or read gossip sites either. She was his personal assistant. He could ask her to go out and buy him a fresh shirt if he wanted.

'Would you mind making me a coffee if you can spare the time, Joanne,' he'd said, before closing his door with an unnecessary bang.

By this time, evidently, Simon was irritable in the extreme. Don't judge him too harshly: he was sticky, hot, he'd been the victim of musical travesty, he'd driven past death, he was plagued by visions of skulls sliced against glass and metal, he'd almost been crushed by the door of the train, he'd been sarcastic to a woman he actually liked and respected and sat down to his desk already feeling small for it. An evening appointment was casting its long shadow already on the day; a decision he didn't want to think about making, a mistake he didn't want to make worse, that possibility he can't allow himself to contemplate. He'd lost forty-five precious minutes with his pencils and his plans, and all he really wanted was to bring a little balance to the world.

By half past eleven he was feeling a little better, and had almost recovered from the morning. The sound of a head hitting the windscreen had not thudded into his thoughts for an hour now. He had succeeded in resolving the problems that the proposals before him were proposing, and was pleased with the progress of another project, taking its early miniature form out in the open-plan office. It would nod to neo-classicism while evading pomposity or pastiche. His part in the design cleverly resolved the question of the windows. But this brief satisfactory respite lasted only for the hour before lunchtime.

An oak-panelled old-fashioned city steakhouse: while Julia scents strawberries, swings her winsome hips, slices tomatoes, breaks plates, Simon, meanwhile, sits before the remnants of his tasteless sirloin, feeling jaded. An empty sauce-smeared plate before him, empty years stretching ahead (his thoughts become maudlin when he is overfed and bored – don't mind too much his pessimism). Feeling hot and bloated in a loud restaurant, the staleness of the morning's sweat lingering under new dampness. Everywhere the bray of businessmen at leisure. He is thinking of a kiss he can't take back and a phone call; and he is also remembering Julia's skin against the fur before the fire. He is thinking of buying her flowers (just as the lily shivers off its last petals).

When he considers the matter more carefully, he is not sure that there is a practical way for him to do so. Because he always buys from the same stall close to the office, but the evening meeting that he is not allowing himself to think about (and about which he is constantly not thinking) is arranged for a pub near the station, so he would have to either return for the flowers – which would make him even later than he will be already, which is possibly suspiciously late – or take them with him, which is as unthinkable as the meeting itself. To arrive with flowers and to say, 'These are not for you'; no, he could not be so callous. Would that be more or less cruel than to say, 'I love my wife'? This is also something Simon may prove incapable of saying. How terrible, that such a statement should find a context in which it could be cruel. That he could have made such a context possible.

Anyway he knows that flowers won't solve anything.

Opposite him, his client is contemplatively picking scraps of meat from his teeth. Simon cannot understand why some people don't chew sufficiently in the first place. The client is new and needs to be impressed, but not important enough to spend too much on. They shared a bottle of mid-range wine and ordered distinctly average steaks – that is, the steaks they ordered were distinctly average, they didn't order them to be so. Simon drank one small glass and watched his client wash down his meat with the rest of the bottle, and is considering if he can bear to offer whisky. Protocol would demand it; but even a minute longer with this man might be more than he can stomach (the rich sauce sloshes). Midway through watching the second glass go down, it became apparent that his client was going to tell him about his mistress, was going to use the word 'mistress' (a word Simon doesn't care for, especially today), and would be expecting Simon to make the correct faces and noises, which Simon duly did. His client spoke almost continuously, and also ate without pause, so that inevitably his mouth was required to fulfil both functions simultaneously. Simon watched, fascinated and appalled, his client's cheek bulge out as he stored the chunk he was eating there for a moment to speak, before allowing the purple-grey bolus to slide into slimy view before swallowing. By listening only to inflections, he found it was possible to pick up the correct face and noise cues without having to hear the details of the affair, which allowed him also to block out at least the audible aspect of the processes of salivation and mastication.

He relents, offers a digestif. It is inevitably accepted. They stand to move to the bar; Simon likes to stand beside potential clients – especially squat, self-important, slightly balding ones. He is feeling particularly tall today (Simon is tall in relation to most people, although it's true he is especially tall in relation to Julia who, remember, is quite small, and has a place for her head on his chest which has been there for years, since

143

they first held each other, a few weeks after they met).

The client is saying something which Simon anticipates will be followed with a laugh, and prepares himself to join in. Crash, bang. The flensed carcass of a whale is called a *crang*, he thinks, and wonders when his mind grew so incongruous.

A KISS

And now here we find him, hunched over his plans as ever, but strangely inattentive. Simon is tired. His eyes ache. He should have them tested, he knows: he has worn the same glasses for years. He is having a long day and it is only early afternoon. His own writing, neat with a slight back-slant and a subtle serif, is somewhat too small for him to read; he finds himself squinting, sighs when he makes out the word 'buttress'. A clunk of a word for a clumsy feature; this is what the client demands. The proposal document is open on his screen, and he'd like to finish it before the end of today, if only so that tomorrow he won't have to contemplate turrets or tudor façades. He is nothing but a slave, he thinks, to the vulgarity of others.

Another cup of coffee which he needs but feels he shouldn't drink sits before him. Joanne brought it to him, having noticed the darkness under his eyes, although she knows he has a rule about caffeine after lunchtime. He focuses his attention on the screen. His desk phone, and his mobile, obtrude upon the edge of his awareness, and his eyes flick to one and then the other at intervals, as if nervous of a pounce. He is thinking of two women: Julia and her amber eyes, her hair the colour of nutmeg, and the smell of spice on her breath; and another, with blonde curls and a big, generous, bitter mouth. Bright laughter, red and full, brightness brushing his skin . . . But he does not love the showy moths. He likes the muted ones, tawny, bronze and brown, the intricacy of their patterning, how they shine under scrutiny. So why this persistent brightness, as if from the corner of his eye?

He thinks of his father, who liked large, brilliant Blues, as big as birds; and he thinks of his mother, miserable in South Africa before he was born, depressed by this relentlessly vivid country. Wanting the grey-brown scrub-field mud, the grey-blue sky, the grey buildings of her memories of England, insisting they return to raise their boy there. And he thinks of them together, of his childhood, his father lost in Shropshire craving colour and his mother hating butterflies. And he wonders, did he whisper to her ever, or kiss the top of her head? Did he leave her any comfort before dying? He wonders if his mother is at least content now, without him, without the burden of pretending, when she has never been up to the task of happiness. She no longer wears turquoise on her eyelids.

He remembers a meadow, he remembers her smiling and batting at the wings all around her, sitting on a picnic blanket, and remembers running after his father, running back to her with his net streaming behind and a jar with a big burly purplish thing hurling itself at the glass, his first catch, holding it out before him as he ran and then stopping, confused, at the edge of the blanket, because she was crying. It was hayfever, she said; no, she wasn't sad.

Simon's mouth becomes full of a phantom pork pie, heavy, greasy, dry, the yellowish jelly. A mouthful of queasy disappointment that he can't choke down. His stomach gurgles and he swills his mouth with coffee.

And you, Simon? asked James last night (and well he might). Are you happy?

Last night, after dinner: Julia and Michelle are in the kitchen, Simon and James in the living room. James lolls on the sofa; Simon has taken the edge of an armchair, one knee optimistically advanced and askance, ready to leave. He is thinking of the drive ahead and his early start. Listening to Julia laughing in the next room, he is beginning to feel depressingly sober, and, having spent much of the evening listening to the others talk, he feels that some conversational gambit is now required of him.

'Hm,' he announces, the little pedantic cough, born of awkwardness, that makes him seem more middle-aged than he is. 'Hm. Did you know, I read recently, did you know that there's no single definition of the Arctic's southern limit?'

'I'm sorry?'

'I came across this book of Julia's, the other day. There's the treeline, the latitude where the sun doesn't rise or set on the solstices, the reach of the ice. Some of them are perfect circles, others are all over the shop.'

There is a pause. James looks expectant.

'No fixed centre, and no single edge,' he adds, a finger pointing and orbiting the point, to clarify.

Simon's mind circles and circles the Arctic's unsatisfactory edges; this is the spiral that will later trap him through his sleepless hour. An Arctic map, he explains, is a map of concepts. A red line, scribing an uneven round, denotes the icecap's furthest reach, as at a particular date. There is another line beyond which no trees grow. And then again, circumscribing the ice and crossing through eight countries, a line at a latitude of 66° 33' 39" (assuming the map is moderately recent, for this line too shifts with time). Stand upon this line or north of it and the sun, on at least one day in the year, does not rise, and at its other solstice does not set: the so-called Arctic Circle.

'Is that right?' says James.

Simon laughs, shakes his head, becomes young again. He hunches forward, pinches the bridge of his nose although he has taken off his glasses.

'You're looking at me like I've gone mad.'

James, too, laughs; he has known Simon long enough. 'It's not that I'm not interested. It all sounds fascinating.'

'Julia's been sorting the archive,' explains Simon. 'All the uncle explorer's stuff. In the house.'

'Ah, of course. How is the house?'

'Last week we were invited to contribute pasta salad to a street party. It's very . . . It's very pasta salad. Associations. A real grocer. Butcher, baker, et cetera. The house and the town and the market. It's charming.'

'Charming, you say. No doubt.'

Simon waves the hint of his own cynicism away. 'It's great, really. It's very peaceful and calm and there are no sirens at night. Julia seems happy.'

'Seems?'

'As far as I can tell.'

'Have you considered asking?'

No, Simon has not considered asking. He does not want to think of her saying that no, she isn't sad, he believes she would say yes, she's happy, and is not sure he'd believe her, and would prefer not to have to question why. James is frank with drinking, but Simon hasn't touched a drop.

'She's got a cat; she always wanted one. We have a garden.'

'And you?'

'It's good to have space. The house is ridiculous, of course. Crammed full of dados and cornicing and coving and corners – lots of corners. Lots of little poky spaces and big grand inefficient ones.'

'You love it.'

Simon smiles, shrugs. 'I can't help it.'

It's true. Simon, who likes his lines clean, his palette neutral, his angles sharp, has come to find comfort in the senseless arrangements of the house, so different from the hard cities he helps to build.

But would Simon say he is happy? Well, again, he would not consider asking himself this question; he would prefer not to. He certainly seems, to himself, to be. He has his extraordinary house and his own shed and a job he often enjoys and his butterflies, and the moths at night in the garden, and his wife.

And yet – we may as well pry, now, having asked the question – yesterday, Simon answered his office phone to a strange number, and a remembered kiss rose to his mouth like bile when he heard the voice on the line. Simon had almost persuaded himself, until he regrettably answered that call, to forget a stray business card, mistakenly handed over in a moment of confusion; it had been efficiently filed away in the corner of his mind that he prefers not to visit. All sorts of things are in there: the time he accidentally killed their canary in an experiment with the oven. The time he accidentally broke the wing of a Fritillary that his father had been pursuing for hours and given him to mount. The time he accidentally lost his virginity to a girl who didn't deserve it. The time he has spent in silence, not saying what he should say to his wife, not knowing what to say.

The time he hasn't spent with the children he doesn't have . . . This shameful little crevice is where Simon has stored a single kiss, the one unfaithful act he has ever committed. Is this, we might ask, the behaviour of a happy man? And what, precisely, was the nature of that errant kiss?

Two weeks ago, the woman who lives over the road cornered him in the corner shop, thrusting out a large and well-manicured, red-nailed hand to be shaken. She was wearing a suit with a silk blouse, high-heeled shoes that had rubbed her foot red at the base of the big toe but in which she walked as if they didn't hurt her, and a strong musky perfume. She had just moved in, she explained; they'd been there less than a year themselves, he said. A fellow interloper. She laughed, showing off neat white teeth and a quiver of pink tongue, and he was pleased by this moment of complicity, by her private smile for him. They should all get together, he said. The 'all' was deliberate, so she wouldn't get the wrong impression. And why would she? Why for that matter should he worry that she might? It was surely not disappointment that made her mouth twitch; he had probably imagined it. He was only hoping to make friends with the neighbours, thinking of Julia alone all day. He even thought he might make a joke about being chatted up by a *Telegraph* reader. Except in the end he forgot to mention it to Julia at all. He thought that she wouldn't like this Sandra – she would find her overbearing, and the choice of newspaper was a bad sign – and this may be why he didn't say anything about it. Those nails, that lipstick – Simon allowed himself conveniently to forget that it is he who disapproves of red, as Julia has learned long since. But then when the phone rang one Saturday a couple of weeks ago, and Julia was out shopping, he heard himself inviting Sandra over and saying, 'I don't bite,' rather unconvincingly. Unconvincing, because this is not the kind of phrase that comes naturally to Simon, and he wasn't sure why he was using it; not because he might bite after all. That comes later.

Two and a half hours later, in fact, and it turns out to be her that bites; they are in the conservatory, perched together on the wicker sofa, and she is vibrant in a poppy-printed summer dress, her blonde hair bouncing, she has laughed loudly at a passing joke he has made and pushed his thigh gently as if she is a little scandalized; she does not take her hand away and he feels himself caught now in those long red talons. He notices that one nail is chipped and a little bitten, and feels a reddening surge of something like repugnance or lust and in its ebb something like pity or tenderness; then he feels the other set of nails press into the flesh under his chin to turn his face to hers and he knows she's overpowered him, and finds that it is easy, allowing himself to be powerless. And suddenly she is nipping at his neck without restraint; and, in fairness, he is not attempting to restrain her. Julia returns from her trip into town just as a manicured hand is making its determined way down his shirtfront, tormenting that ticklish torso so that he is already starting to squirm away from her when the door slams – you have to slam the door to make sure it closes, remember, and thank goodness, for Simon's sake. He jumps back and the brazen neighbour makes a quick recovery, her heart beating so hard he can see the silk of her dress twitch; she laughs and gives him a wide-eyed 'Naughty me' look, finger-tips to her mouth. She stands and asks for his business card, which, bewildered, he gives her; she leaves through the garden gate. Simon is flustered. He rubs at his neck, hearing Julia calling for him. 'Ah, here you are,' she says, and plumps down beside him on the sofa. She doesn't notice the sticky smell of perfume that he is sure is all over his hands; or if she does, he thinks guiltily, it would never occur to her to question it. She shows him her new leather notebooks happily. Now she has all that she needs to really set to work. All she was lacking was the proper stationery, she laughs.

'Is your neck okay? It looks awfully red.'

'Hm. Just been out in the sun too long, I suppose.'

She looks at him quizzically – he is not one to linger in the garden – then shrugs, with a little shake of her head and a frown, tells him he should be more careful, and makes them some tea.

★　★　★

153

Simon loves his wife. He might well suffer in comparison with the portrait that hangs in the drawing room; certainly he does not feel heroic. True, he too is dark, cheeks hollow, tall; if he could be persuaded to grow a moustache – and Julia has tried on occasion, only half joking – he might just look the part. Strength and fidelity, surety, courage. Would she wait for him so long, if he were to set out so bravely? He would not want her to, perhaps; perhaps the world is no longer so romantic. But he loves his wife and he would like to make her happy; he is forever striving to cross that incommensurable distance, to meet her. He has no desire to betray her. He suspects he will always fail her.

In his worse moments, Simon wonders if he would have Julia at all had he not been there when she needed him, when they first met; and now all these years later he would simply like to feel that he can sometimes meet that need, knowing that he has already failed her once, at least once, constantly ... He recalls her tears last night, and all of her tears, so infrequent he thinks he can remember every one; and those she would not weep, when he wished that she would come to him and weep. His love for her, the frail and lovely edifice that is the wife he loves, is built as much from the knowledge of the sadness she keeps hidden as it is from the shimmering he first longed to capture; the memory of her head against his chest when she was suffering is painful of course, but it also brings him pleasure, to remember being needed.

BUTTERFLIES AND BEARSKINS

It was Simon that suggested they make the house their own, two months after Aunt Helen died. She had by then been living in a 'home' for seven years – not once did she fail to voice those inverted commas when referring to it as such, although she didn't resent it. It agonized Julia to think of her there, but she knew she couldn't give her the care she needed; and Aunt Helen had been furious at the very suggestion that she should spend the first years of her marriage looking after an old woman. In her clean, sunny, bland little room, she turned the pages of Edward's diary peaceably, laughing out loud sometimes or sharing some particularly gruesome detail with nurses, doctors, fellow inmates, the empty room. She had meant to find a publisher for it, to make sense of the last fading pages and present his tale to the world, restored and whole; but she somehow ran out of time. She knew the story by heart, which was just as well as she could no longer hold one sentence in her head for long enough to connect it to the next. When Julia visited, they would exchange tales of the ice as if

155

the memories were their own. Simon remembers now the vivid recollections that they span together as he took a seat at the edge of the room, listening, remote from them as if watching through a window while they played in the snow. She died on a high-summer's day not unlike this one, last year; Julia and the nurse on duty found her in her chair by the window, napping, it seemed, in the peace of the bright afternoon, her skin warmed on the surface by the sun but her blood quite cool.

Come October, autumn was giving way to a drizzling winter and dark afternoons. The will was settled, the grieving ostensibly over, the house empty for too long and full of the family's things, waiting to be cleared.

Simon came home a little later than usual one day to find Julia in the bath. She looked up and slightly past him and smiled, when he came into the tiny bathroom – she had left the door open. He hesitated over his intrusion, then knelt beside her, not quite sure of her or himself or desire, but when his hand bent to cup the water over her skin, he found it was cold; not just tepid, but freezing as a northern sea.

'How long have you been sitting here?' he asked, very casually, feeling it was important to betray no alarm or haul her out and wrap her in something warm or hold her, although these things, too, he felt were important things he should do.

'Not long. I don't know. What time is it? Half an hour, I think.'

Simon checked his watch. He had come in the door at 7.43; he remembered glancing at his watch. He reckoned perhaps six or seven minutes had passed. Nevertheless, he checked again and could not help but indulge for a moment the pleasure of his correct estimate.

'It's almost eight' – 7.49 – 'Julia . . . the water . . .' How to address this? 'Isn't the water a bit cold? Are you sure you've only been here half an hour?'

Simon imagined her leaving work early again, without telling her colleagues (and how long could they continue to indulge her? How long is one allowed to grieve?). She would have arrived at home, run a bath, left a pile of clothes on the floor and climbed in, hours contracting as the water cooled and Julia blank as the surface of the water. But he put this vision from his mind because it was surely the behaviour of a mad person, or a person who is too unhappy to be reached.

'Oh, yes. I know.' She knew. Relief rinsed over him until he realized that this was not, in itself, an explanation.

'There was no hot water left. So I just ran it cold.'

'I see. Then you got in. It really is. Cold.' Some silent minutes passed. In the flat above, a washing machine thumped through its spin cycle. When Simon thinks of the Balham flat now, of the years they spent there, he remembers the muffled constant banging of other domestic lives all around them, and he remembers also the bathroom

157

window, the muck-streaked runnels of rain lit orange in the streetlight. All their life together compressed into a black square of ugly frosted glass, curtainless, letting the night in. A car horn blared in the street; somebody shouted, an engine snarled a threat. He perched on the side of the bath, staring into nothing.

It's easy to be drawn to Julia and her beauty, her lightness, her vagueness. Just hearing her cat's-tread upon the stair, we follow. But sitting on the side of his wife's cold bath, Simon wondered if that elusive quiver he'd fallen for might elude him always. There is, after all, reality to contend with, as well as romance. Simon sometimes grows weary with unworldliness. He cannot always be the one to bear the world's burdens alone.

Suddenly she shivered violently and crouched forward with a chilly splash that shocked Simon out of his daze, his sleeve soaked. She pulled her knees up like a child and hugged them and seeing the bones of her spine all down her narrow back he was touched almost unbearably; she had thinned to transparency, in the last months; all the gold was gone from her skin, she was as pale as blue-shadowed ice. He would have liked to cry for her the tears that were dripping silently from her chin into the water. Then at last he lifted her, taking her elbow and raising her, guiding her, numb and pliable, from the bath, folding her in a towel and in his arms and letting her sob sound-less on his shoulder.

Later, they sat with cups of tea in the sitting room, Julia wrapped in a blanket and occasionally convulsing from the cold left in the corners of her. And he remembered the year they met, the weekends at the old house. He remembered their first Christmas together there, with Aunt Helen and Julia's sister and her husband and their first baby, feeling embarrassed and pleased to be part of their warmth. At Aunt Helen's table, he had thought guiltily for a moment of his parents, spending Christmas alone together for the first time since he was born (he didn't know it then, but it was also the last – the next March, a vessel burst in his father's hard heart). He imagined them sitting opposite each other over a turkey far too big for the two of them, dried out in the oven by his mother's caution. Then he thought, No, they won't be opposite each other because they will sit where they always sit, my father will not relinquish the head of the table and will leave my place empty in recrimination and my mother will have to sit across from my absence and will not allow herself to consider what might have caused it. And instead of allowing his parents' bitterness to twist into him across the distance, he looked to the head of the table where Aunt Helen had taken her place, brandishing carving fork and knife over a glistening goose and laughing. At that time she could laugh at her own oddness, she'd say something entirely out of place and then put her hand to her lips with a surprised giggle, as if someone else had used her mouth to say it.

He did his best to relax. He wore his paper hat, and forgot after a while the hot itch of it.

Sitting in a flat in Balham on a wet, dull night almost a decade later, he imagined a family of his own in that house. He thought of the bear rug in front of the open fire, of laying Julia down upon it again, as he had years before. How much warmer, wider, easier life would be, away from London, away from the dirt and the shouts in the street. How much happier she might be, in the house where the first days of their love affair – as tentative, gentle and delicate as any Victorian courtship – were played out. In the house where he first lay beside her . . .

Circling and circling, his mind returns to it. Among the clutter that catches at his thoughts in hints and snatches, Julia lies resplendent on the bearskin like a vivid half-forgotten dream. Is it possible to know her? Even what is past is not constant. Countless versions of her coalesce, flicker, disperse. She is lost moments and habits too familiar to recall and a turn of the head one Tuesday afternoon; memories will fold and flutter and resettle themselves; no, a lover cannot be set and pinned. Still he pursues her always; still he does love her, he tells himself, whoever she is. There is more than one kind of love story.

Simon and Julia met because of the butterflies, on a warm spring day, ten years ago. In the very same room in which Dr Nansen lectured and Emily, seeing ambition blaze, set her sights on Edward; in that same room around a hundred years later, Simon gallantly gave up his handkerchief, and with it his heart, which Julia returned in a damp crumpled ball. He washed the handkerchief when he got home, but his heart never quite recovered.

Julia, too, a damp crumpled ball, and summoning a helpless smile; her head on his chest, which was later; the bearskin . . . We will come to all this in time. For now: they met because of the butterflies. He came to see the collection. When Aunt Helen was alive, the house functioned as a sort of ad hoc museum, much of its contents untouched since Emily Mackley returned alone from her honeymoon at the turn of the century to wait sixty years to die. Her husband was everywhere; his brother John had adorned the safe, solid walls of his home with the spoils of vicarious adventure. Aunt Helen somehow, through the mysterious channels of communication that formed the fine silver network of her world, let it be known that visitors were welcome. In her heyday, the house had been open to all comers – friends, artists, admirers, lovers, serious historians, dilettantes and dabblers. Simon was one of the last. He had come to see . . . When the door opened, he found himself helplessly pinned by pale brown eyes and a smile that went off to one side as if distracted. He made no move; behind her in the dim hallway, a polar bear was ready to pounce. It had not yet retreated to the top of the house.

Julia introduced herself and invited him in, happy enough with the explanation that he was Simon and had come to see the butterflies. Browsing a specialist journal that he subscribed to, he had caught sight of a poor and greyed photographic reproduction of a mounted series which, nevertheless, his curiosity snagged upon; there, in the far north, these creatures thrived in the bright, cold summer. He noticed the photo credit – 'Gift of Lieutenant S. Freely, Mackley Family private collection' and the name of a town not so far from London. He had heard of neither the benefactor nor the Mackleys, but when called for a consultation a few months later – the streets of this town are all subsiding grandeur – he remembered the name of the place, sought out the Mackley address and took the opportunity to pay a visit. A few months later and he might have forgotten; so coincidence shapes us (or fate if you prefer, but Simon, a rationalist, does not). He had written two weeks before to ask if he might see just this one of their treasures, and received a prompt response from a Miss Helen Mackley – it happened that her niece would be visiting that day and they would both be pleased to see him and show him whatever took his interest.

Was there, even then, some presentiment on Aunt Helen's part, which lit the spark in her matchmaker's eye? Fanciful, perhaps, the imagined

162

flash just a reflection in the light of what came after; but a man who would go out of his way to see a host of white butterflies, and who still took the time to write letters by hand – such a man might well be deemed worth a try.

Whatever the case may be, Simon, who had asked to see this single artefact, found when the door was answered by a gilded young woman in a faded summer dress that he somehow could not bring himself to cut short what was evidently the customary tour. He trailed behind her, this Julia, the youngest of the Mackleys, trying not to bump into things as she showed him the snowshoes and the skis on the wall, the diary, the portraits, the china, the decanter, the photographs, and back to the hallway for everyone's favourites, the big and little polar bears. 'These are everyone's favourites,' she said, giving no hint of her own preference one way or the other, and Simon, twenty-five and fumbling, heard himself say surprisingly, 'Are they yours?' At that moment Aunt Helen clipped into the room wielding secateurs with a flurry of pleasure and remonstration: Julia should have told her their guest had arrived, she had just been out in the garden, she had just been . . . the roses . . . would he like some tea? Wouldn't Julia make some tea for them? Hesitant, her niece obliged, and returned five minutes later to find Simon in the drawing room politely bewildered as Aunt Helen, miming snow-blindness, modelled a pair of goggles from 1893. Embarrassed, Julia laughed, and then Aunt Helen did too and poor Simon blushed all up his neck.

'Oh, what a silly old woman. What I must look like to you, Jonathan, like a lunatic.'

'It's Simon, Aunt Helen.'

'What's that?'

'Simon. Our guest. Jonathan is still in America.' She turned to Simon. 'My cousin. She gets names mixed up.'

'Don't we all?' said Simon kindly.

'One of those families where there's only two names for boys going round. It's hardly surprising really.'

While dark, gaunt Simon, as we have noted, could well be mistaken for a Mackley, in fact it would be hard to confuse him with Julia's cousin, who inherited the less fortunate looks of their Great-grandmother Arabella. As it happens, at this moment Jonathan is mopping his wide brow, as flushed as the red hair above it, in a business meeting not very far from Simon in the city; thinking of the garden in the sun, he remembers he must buy cigars . . . but he will arrive later in the day, soon enough.

On that afternoon ten years ago, Aunt Helen had removed the goggles and was pouring tea into a cup; and then there was a quiet thud and she was staring at the cup on the floor and the tea spilled out over the carpet, and for a while she kept pouring into the growing stain. Julia took the pot from her gently, not feeling the burn on her hands. Everything seemed to be happening very sedately, without panic or exclamation, thought Simon, feeling strangely detached until he found himself leaping up and offering to fetch a towel.

'Oh, please don't worry.'

'What a silly old woman,' said Aunt Helen again, but she sounded unsure this time, there was a quaver in her voice and when she looked up, she looked lost. She focused on Julia. 'It just slipped out of my hand, Maggie.'

'I know, it's okay. That's why they made these carpets dark. Think of the wine that's been spilled in here, Aunt Helen. Why don't you take your tea to the sitting room and have a listen to the radio? Come on, I'll bring it through . . .'

Simon, blending desperately into the furniture, wondered what room this was if not the sitting room; the house he was raised in had just one small lounge, and he envied for a moment the wealth of parlours and drawing and living and morning rooms that he knew a house such as this was stuffed with. He noticed that he had adopted an indulgent smile that he was hating his face for, not knowing what to do with it or any other part of himself. Julia led her aunt out and the twenty elastic bands that were holding his limbs together simultaneously snapped. Poor Simon. He only wanted to look at the butterflies and here he was, immersed in the terrible embarrassment of a stranger's ageing, and also falling in love, which was not something he was accustomed to or would have encouraged in others. Edward, at his wife's side, looked on fiercely from above the fireplace at the limp figure pressing his head back into the hard sofa.

Julia came back in. She looked shaken. He sat up quickly, and stood.

'I'm sorry, perhaps this was a bad time. I hope I haven't troubled you . . . Thank you for showing me around. I think I should go, I do hope your aunt is all right.'

'Oh, but you haven't seen the butterflies.'

'Another time, maybe . . .'

'You came all this way and they're so beautiful. Please, do come and see them,' said Julia, extremely brittle, the ease with which she'd ushered him around the house now vanished. 'Really, they're just so lovely, you must . . . have some tea anyway . . . oh, there's none left. I'll make more, it won't take a moment, I'll just go and . . . I'll just clean this up and then . . .'

Julia, on her knees now with a hopelessly inadequate paper tissue, was dabbing at the carpet with her back to him. He stood, useless, his arms hanging awkward at his sides like those of his lanky boyhood, which he thought he had long since mastered. Then she stopped, with a slump of her shoulders and a dip of her head; then, alarmingly, she blew her nose loudly on the tea-soaked tissue. And at last Simon sprang into action. He had a handkerchief in his pocket, how stupid not to have thought of it! He bent behind and beside her, put a hand on her shoulder and pressed it gently into her palm with the other. The handkerchief had a blue stripe around its edge and had been ironed, neatly, into quarters. Julia shook it out, scrumpled it up and pressed it to her damp nose before looking up at him – and her brave smile was so charming that he almost didn't mind the soggy ball she handed back.

'God, what an idiot,' she said. 'I'm sorry. I don't suppose this is quite what you were expecting from this afternoon.'

Simon smiled back.

'Do you think I could see the butterflies?'

So Simon found himself standing in a tiny room which clings to the end of a corridor on the second floor; it was once Emily's maid's bedroom, and the blue floral print that papers the walls peels at the corners. A faint smell of damp rises from the sheets, so long unslept in, still neatly turned on a single bed that occupies most of the floor. It is chilly here, now, despite the heat of the afternoon; rooms grow forlorn and fade like printed cornflowers when there are no bodies to warm them, and the memory of the butterflies is barely a flutter now, having been remade elsewhere. Julia has entered only once in the ten years since she came here with Simon, and that was to lift them from the wall. There is only a sad browned rectangle left behind, framing a field of brighter blue blossom. But all those years ago, when Simon came to see them, they hung there still and he thought they were wasted in that lonely little room. He was also very much aware of the bed, taking up so much space that the backs of their knees almost pressed against it and they were forced to shuffle together into what little gap there was between it and the dressing table, precariously close to touching. He gazed for a long time at the bluish tint he had come for but his mind, truth be told, was elsewhere, as if those serried ranks had flittered free to batter about his ribcage. His left side tingled to Julia's nearness as he pointed to that particular specimen he'd come for, and she stretched her face upwards to follow his finger, which longed then to trace the hollows of her long throat and instead kept foolishly pointing.

As he stood by the front door ten minutes later, stammering thanks, he didn't think once of that precious blue tint on the wing; he thought only of the woman before him that he wouldn't meet again, tawny and gold. And then Aunt Helen emerged from the sitting room (which, it transpired, was down the hall on the left) and rescued him; quite recovered from her earlier confusion, she seemed twenty years younger again, eyes clear and lipstick refreshed, and informed him that since she had behaved so badly today, he would be coming to tea next Sunday so that she could make up for it; and she looked at Julia with an eyebrow raised as if daring her to back out of it.

Julia turned to him with an awkward flap, insisting it wasn't necessary, that he must be busy, but Aunt Helen was stubborn and she gave in; with a smile she said, 'Of course we'd love to have you round. My aunt makes very good carrot cake. Will you?'

And Simon, urbane, amazed at himself, said, 'Well, if there's cake,' and they waved him off at the door and he held her smile cupped in his palm all through the week until Sunday.

In hopeful, nervous increments, each succeeding visit brought new intimacies to add to his hoard; she kissed him goodbye on the cheek, squeezed his hand, kissed him closer to his mouth, held his gaze a moment longer each time, kissed him on closed lips and said she tasted aniseed, the bronze in her eyes warming. They met always at weekends, always at the house, a sanctuary. Since they did not meet in the city, he did not have to see her dimmed; he did not know until later how she faltered there.

One week they went for a walk in the park, with Aunt Helen again as chaperone. They stopped to look out over the pond; it was late April, it had been a fine, wispish day, and now the sun was lowering, softening into the sky as it sank. It was no flashy summer sunset: a pale yellow, silvered over and reflected in the water which was silvery too under the surface. And as the sun began to vanish behind the buildings, it warmed to gold, and left behind it a last elegant wash of brightness, salmon, apricot, peach, into pale blue and darkening to indigo above them.

'The light fades so slowly, you don't notice it going, do you?' said Aunt Helen, lucid as the evening, with a rueful smile. She linked an arm through each of theirs and they walked home. She was a tall woman, but stooped now, and the bone of her wasting forearm pressed heavier on Simon's as they walked; by the time they were home she had begun to glaze and wander. She couldn't remember where the plates were and stood in the middle of the kitchen as if helpless or lost until Julia showed her and she said, 'Yes, that's right, in here, dear' in a voice like a quivery old woman's, not her own. It was sad and, for Julia, frightening, to see her neck craned forward awkwardly, her uncertain hands held out slightly and shaking before her, unsure what she'd meant to do with them. She would move sometimes with a sudden start, as if she'd just remembered something she'd forgotten, or the way that cats do, startled by some unseen ghost. Over tea she called him only Jonathan or Edward until Julia gave up correcting her. As the evening drew in, Julia made the thick hot chocolate she liked to take before sleeping and saw her to bed.

'Going to bed at eight like an old lady. Oh, Maggie, don't ever get old, it's desperate. Dull. I am tired, though, it's true enough. Goodnight.' Simon hadn't meant to stay so late and, embarrassed, would have left then, and might have shuffled awkwardly out of Julia's ambit for ever. But when she descended to find him waiting in the hallway, she came to him dry-eyed, wordless, and it was then, when they were alone for the first time together, that Julia's head first found its place on Simon's chest. They did not kiss; she came to him and leaned her head against him, her arms hanging by her sides, leaving a cautious space between their bodies so that there was only this heaviness against his breastbone and no other contact between them, and he wanted to gather her in but only let his mouth rest on her hair.

There was a period of stillness, in which everything slowed to the ponderous tempo of the old grandfather clock, time and his heart alike; after this long unreckoned pause, without raising her head she said:

'Maggie was my mother, in case you were wondering. She didn't get old, as it happens. At least there is that, I suppose, that little mercy.' And she drew back from him with a smile to reassure him. There: this is the Julia that Simon thought he could reach out for and rescue; he fell in love first with light and laughing, shoeless Julia, who met him in the doorway, but there is also this – strength, sadness, restraint.

She was the only one left, she explained: her parents were gone, her sister Miranda was in

Edinburgh. She was at the house most weekends. The constant flow of visitors had fallen off in recent years, and she worried that Aunt Helen would be lonely (and, although she wouldn't admit it, she was lonely too; she didn't belong to the city). Simon would never suggest that it was in any way unusual for her to spend every weekend with her elderly aunt. They were quite content to potter their days away, she said, lying in the garden, smoking, talking, drinking wine in the evenings. And when Aunt Helen started calling Julia Maggie, sometimes, and when she came into a room looking for something she was holding in her hand, or when she stopped in the middle of a sentence and Julia said, 'And . . .' and she said, 'What's that, my sweet?' and Julia said, 'You were saying . . .' and Aunt Helen said, 'Was I?', it seemed almost mischievous, almost in character, and easy enough to ignore. Until that day when Simon first came to the house, and Julia came in to find Aunt Helen in the snow goggles, it had been quite possible to pretend there was nothing the matter at all. Julia explained all of this in her quiet, even voice, not crying, and looking at his breastbone; and then met his eye with a sudden bronze brightness and asked:

'Would you like to stay for dinner?'

Simon appeared in Julia's life, then, just in time, with a place to lay her head.

Midnight found them in the old morning room, the hour stilled by the unwound clock so that the night might last as long as they needed. Sated by Simon's henceforth favourite meal of slow-roasted lamb, snug and a little drunk, they sank into the sofa for a last glass. The sofa is low and pillowy and all too easy to reach the floor from. Simon, whose tastes have been trained to run to the minimal, found himself in a deepening ruby-rich haze that felt dangerously bohemian. But when Julia slid onto the white rug, turned back and took his hand, he allowed himself to slip down beside her . . .

And so again, full circle. It was this that he hoped to recapture when he thought of them living there; after too long watching her pall in the city, after the latter years of loss unbroached, of unremarked emptiness and silence, after the last months of sadness too ice-deep and cold for him to fathom, he hoped to warm her there, to lay her down again upon the fur and see her skin again flush golden, see her again as she had flickered then in the firelight, her eyes widening just before she closed them. In a chilly flat in London where the damp seeped through every crack and the mucky clouds smirched out the stars every dirty wet October night, he remembered that other October ten years gone and hoped, as we all at times long hopelessly, to rekindle the past.

After weeks of rain, they set out on a miraculous Saturday of cold clear November sunshine that

Simon, who does not believe in tidings, still took gladly. They left as the sun was setting and arrived in the evening with a car full of suitcases. Julia had been quiet all day and spent the first part of the journey looking out as London passed away from her. As the roads narrowed and the bare trees began to arc over the road, she grew more animated. She talked about Aunt Helen, and about Miranda, how they must have Miranda to stay for Christmas again, how she would cook a goose, she had never cooked goose but Aunt Helen always said it was easy, she would make the same chestnut stuffing. She grew sad at that; it wouldn't be the same. She didn't have the recipe. She'd spent all those hours by her bedside and not once had she thought to ask. She'd have to look online and how could Google possibly bring her aunt back?

'It had liver in it, from the goose,' said Simon helpfully.

'How will I find the liver? What does it look like?' she wailed.

'It'll be in the little bag with the rest of the bits. I'll help you. It's the largest organ in the body. I'm sure we won't miss it.'

'Is it really?'

'So I'm told.'

'By who? How can they be trusted?'

'I don't know. It's an expression.'

Simon hates driving and was trying not to snap at her. She switched on the radio and rejected the contemporary and the classical and settled on something easy, easy listening, and sang along to an old jazz song that Simon, after ten years together, was surprised she knew.

The song ended and they sat through the next two in silence.

'And definitely sage,' said Julia, suddenly loud in the darkness.

'Yes. And onions. Or shallots.'

'Which?'

Simon bit back 'Does it matter?' and offered instead definitely shallots, for the sweetness, which seemed to convince her.

She sang along to 'Piece of My Heart', Dusty's version. Simon was relieved; he can't bear Janis Joplin. He cannot bear to hear a note screeched, even if it is in tune. Simon, who doesn't like to sing, has perfect pitch. Julia does not, but she has a low mellow voice that he finds he can forgive, mostly.

'You know you got it, if it makes you feel good,' she sang to him, with a playful little nod.

If only, if only I could have just a little piece, he thought. Do I have even the smallest chamber to curl up in?

Two miles more of quiet driving. Then a sad, flat crow at the side of the road; Simon opened his mouth, remembered that he'd mentioned the law about pheasants an hour ago (passing a smear of pigeon), and was interrupted anyway by Julia:

'Shall we pick it up for dinner? We weren't the ones that hit it, after all.'

175

'It's just pheasants.'

'Oh,' she smiled. 'Silly me.'

In the pause that followed, he could feel her deciding whether or not to push it. Some invisible betrayal of irritation warned her not to.

'It would be nice, though, wouldn't it, to have Miranda down?'

'Of course.'

'Molly must be getting big. It's been three months since we saw her.'

They had last seen Miranda and her three children at Aunt Helen's funeral. Which meant that Julia had calculated from that date; it was unlike her to remember a lapse of time so precisely.

'It's amazing she finds the time to look after them all,' said Simon, for something to say.

'She's a great mum. He's a good dad, too, for all his faults.'

'Of course they are.'

Matthew's faults, in Julia's terms, include a lack of imagination, and having poor taste in shirts and footwear (shiny pointy business shoes, awful sandals in summer). In Simon's view Matthew is just dull, a television sports spectator. Julia's sister presumably has her reasons for loving him.

'They're great kids.'

In the car, Julia and Simon fell again into silence. She no longer sang.

There are many words that have gone unsaid in those ten years, to fill the silences that widen between them. There are all kinds of things they don't say. They think about hospitals. He thinks of rushing to her and finding her thin and bloodless, knowing that flowers wouldn't have helped anyway but wishing he'd brought just one useless rose, at least, wishing he wasn't so empty-handed, so helpless. These are the spaces between them that they may not, or may yet, cross. Unsaid words and empty hospital vases. And this is the feeling that troubles him still, which he cannot articulate, as he sits in the office not thinking about it; Simon's troubled and stifled thoughts all circle about this lack, always gaping at the back of his mind, the space between them that he cannot reach across, the impossible white distance beyond which she lies heedless.

By the time they reached the house, Julia was once again bright. Since he'd first thought of it, of bringing her back here, Simon had imagined himself catching her up to carry her over the threshold they met across all those years before; he had thought the gesture would be fitting. He would carry her through the hallway and lay her down on the fur where they first lay together. Now, as he pulled up outside, he realized the impracticality of his plan and felt foolish to have rehearsed it so carefully; the night before, he had carried her in and laid her down, carried her in, fur against skin, looping relentless against sleep. Now here they were and he had barely killed the engine and she was out of the car, keys in her hand because of course the keys were hers, the house is hers, and she waited for him at the door but he could see no way to do it, now, to lift her, and it would be dark and cold within, with no fire in the grate. With the key in the lock already she turned back radiant and he followed her in. And every time he enters this house, he feels that he follows her in, as she was then, for ever an echo of the first day he met her, the first moment he saw her, for ever framed in the doorway, inviting him in.

They spent their days unpacking, shifting furniture, pictures, china, silver, to find spaces for the surviving remnants of their own meagre home. He gave up helping, seeing how anxious it made her if a particular teaspoon or box of broken beads was moved out of place, and not knowing what was precious to her or why. The master suite had not been used for years; they couldn't get the heating working for the first week and slept under a mound of chilly blankets, with heavy stone hot-water bottles wrapped in wool socks that made Julia nostalgic for her childhood holidays there and stubbed Simon's long toes. He couldn't sleep for the weighty tick of the grandfather clock in the hall below, although it was he that had reset and wound it. The old bed creaked, and Simon and Julia, who had always lived with neighbours above, beside and below through only a wall or floor's thickness, could not get used to allowing it to do so, but did not speak of abandoning the old frame. They made love tentatively, holding back vigour, not wishing to wake the ghosts.

He came home one night, a few weeks after they arrived, and spied her shadow in the corner by the lamp in the drawing room, watching for him through a barely parted gap in the curtain. The door opened just as he raised his key to the lock; she swept him in from the cold and kissed him – 'Aniseed! I'd know your kiss in a million,' she said – and took him by the hand and led him up the stairs half-backwards, without needing to see or even count to know the steps, her other hand slipping up the oak banister with the surety of those who had smoothed it for her. She was flushed and sheened with excitement, anticipation flecking her eyes golden, leading him up the stairs well before bedtime, and he was stirred by her and just as he was thinking it was unlike her to be so bold she stopped halfway up on the landing, with a 'Ta-da!' – she had moved the butterflies. The picture that had hung there – he couldn't recall it – had left its outline on the wallpaper, framing the smaller frame.

She wanted to please him, and she did; it was a gesture to the memory of their own romance, and he wanted to pick her up, so small and slight after all that he can lift her easily, to pick her up and carry her down to the bearskin, but did not.

FLAG

Poor Simon, stretched out thin and torpid with the endless afternoon, chilled by air conditioning, clammy with caffeine-sweat, eyes aching from the glare of the screen; when he looks up the vast spotless sky filling his window offers no relief, the river dazzling like glass (or snow or ice). No, he absolutely will not think of it. He will not think of cold baths or bearskins or tissues, or red lips; he will not think of coming home to a glass of wine and the warmth of his wife and family, a sleepy well-behaved boy waiting up to say goodnight to him – this last in particular he pushes away, merciless, only to find himself confronted with the cold bath again. No. The clock in the corner of the screen, synced with the meridian – no foolish margins for error – shows 16.23. His mobile phone, aligned with the edge of the desk, agrees, but Simon has not glanced at it for over half an hour now.

He pushes up his glasses and turns to his drafts. Yes, he is a long parabola of precision, from his dark eye through the hunch of his shoulder to the tidy, quick fingers that trace over the page. He sharpens his attention to a point, letting all fall with the curling slivers of wood that he carves away from the graphite. Fresh pencil shavings: this is one of his favourite smells, along with mint leaves, cedar wood, aniseed and honeysuckle, which blooms abundant in the garden, drawing dusty moths to its scent when dusk falls. But he is not thinking about the moths in the garden or honeysuckle. No, he will not think of her, in that house where dust drifts like snow in the corners until she's as frosted over as every other relic, a living memory of the first time he lay with her; this endless reaching for her, every time since, as she retreats from him and he watches her across the distance and waits for her to dissipate . . .

And here, however we try to tease it out, his mind pulls to a stubborn halt. Because every act of love echoes every other in retrospect; and last night was no different from any other time, and although he loves her and desires her still there is always, as he enters, this halt; and it is this, in the end, that he won't allow himself to think about for fear of what it means. Every time, her limbs freeze for a second like a panicked animal, every time; and then she lets herself surrender, but she surrenders only her body and retreats from him – as he seeks the depth of her she retreats from him, further than he can reach. She doesn't care if they leave the light on, but she always closes her eyes. Yes, as she acquiesces, she dissipates. He cannot grasp her; even as her fingers clutch his arms, his back, her heels grip about his thighs, even as she holds him so fast it sometimes bruises and he watches amazed as her head tilts back, in that moment she is lost to him, she dissolves into the air –

Skin against snow, spread out across the sky . . .

And when it's over and she opens her eyes, the pupils widen with pleasure but for a moment, he's sure, they are pinpricks, as if flooded with brightness, so that she must adjust to the dim world she returns to from wherever she's been, lost in the snow.

He loves his wife and does not wish to betray her, especially with a woman for whom he tells himself he feels no desire at all. And yet that same woman called yesterday and, if he were honest with himself, which he isn't, he felt the scald of red-hued lust; and ignored it but still agreed to meet, since (he told himself) it was the decent thing to do, to say it to her face; and the evening is near enough now to be inevitable, and he is tired and wishes he had not slept badly. He will not think of that single, wet, illicit kiss, or of unspoken irritation and guilt, or of any of the things he lost sleep not thinking of. He is pressed upon from all sides; he is still trapped in that Arctic he dreamed of, jagged, bitter, hard, crushed by the frozen sea.

He stares out of the window that stretches all

across the wall to his left, over the city, as impressive a view as one might hope to find, and brilliant in the sun today. Today it is especially fine. The leaves are filled with green light; Westminster is pale and golden against a sky so massively deep blue and clear that it almost hurts to look up. But Simon isn't looking at the sky or the trees or the towers, he is looking at the river, and he is seeing a cold grey sea, and between its banks, just drifting past the plane trees of Victoria Gardens, an iceberg is jutting out absurdly into the summer day, vast, overwhelming, vertiginous.

He pinches the bridge of his nose under his glasses. When he opens his eyes again there is nothing but the dirty old Thames, glittering brightly. A dream of an icy sea . . . but Simon doesn't dream. He's not a person that ever dreams.

He takes a sip of lukewarm coffee and measures to the point. He checks from another angle. He marks the cross. He knows beyond doubt that the place is the right one.

For a moment he thinks of a flag in the snow.

(The flag that Julia's Great-great-uncle Edward failed to plant was also buried with him, six hundred miles from the North Pole. Emily, a woman singularly lacking in the skills the age expected of her, had nevertheless taken silks, needle and thread and assiduously stitched the pieces, blotting her pricked fingers on the red cross of England, trying to avoid the white and the blue.)

183

Simon hauls himself back, one last time, from the brink of distraction. He will not be diverted by dreams or flags or family myths, or anything else that is insubstantial, or kisses and their consequences for that matter. Yes, the point he has marked is the right one.

What Julia would call finicky (with a kind of affection), Simon would call just and true. Since the painstaking years of his childhood, Simon has loved balance. A well-engineered structure has its own grace, without which mere ornament is a shallow flattery. Elegance is born of unseen depth and strength, like a cathedral, full of light (like an iceberg glittering in sunshine . . .). Even as he takes pleasure in the sureties of his profession, a phrase skates across the surface of his thoughts: Foundations cannot be laid in snow. Simon barely even shapes the words, but as we've caught them passing, they are worth catching at. What solid thing, after all, did Edward Mackley ever lay upon the surface of the world? Where is the edifice that attests to his greatness? There is none, there is none, there is only his body, still frozen where they found it and buried it again, more than fifty years after he died.

PART IV

North:

(   )

Blank, white, vast and silent but for the slish of the summer ice. It is not the heave and roar of the darker months, but a constant drip, the rush of a hundred rivulets. A slick sheen over everything as if coated in glass. There are no shadows here, beneath the Arctic sun. There is no sense of depth, only massive solid forms without contour and, between, the black sea. The sky is almost white. Don't look up, or let your gaze rest anywhere for too long. The sun is in everything; try to keep your eyes half closed, the brightness will blind you.

Beyond this shore is nothing but the uninterrupted ocean; and, somewhere at its centre, the Pole. We can go no further north on land, although if it were spring we could travel on foot across the ice. Six hundred miles merely, the length of the British Isles, to an invisible point in the whiteness; we won't know it when we get there. We will take bearings

187

and will have to believe that we have aimed true and hit the target. You wish to set out? Six hundred miles of this treacherous, tearing white, cracked with black. Row across the open water – it is freezing and unthinkably deep, there are mountains below us – hope the kayak has not been too damaged from months of dragging it over the winter ice. Hope there are no walruses waiting to roar out of the depth. Stand on the floes and they might split beneath you, or drag you back to behind where you began. It will shift and yawn and grin into gullies before us; it will betray us. Time, suspended by the constant sun, will begin to spiral. It would be folly to attempt it. It is too late in the year.

Beneath our feet, the holes where Edward Mackley's eyes were stare out of his leathered skull, which still half resembled him when it was last dug up; they stare for ever across this hopeless distance, his last vista. He came closer than this. He turned back to find land. This is where he came to rest, just as the sun was setting, hoping to wait out the winter. This is where he was buried, before he saw the sun again. The tin cross there marks the spot: the fourth one, on the right. Below, he lies in a makeshift coffin, which was once the kayak he hoped to sail to safety in. They couldn't tell what he died of by the time they found him, his skin blackened but intact, his insides melted to slush. Starvation, exhaustion, guilt. Frustration and failure.

He could not have known he would end here when he set out all those months before, as Emily waved him off from the shore. He had thought to be better, greater.

PAPERS

The ship's log remains open on the desk at the page where Julia left off reading, the point at which, halfway down the page, a more scratching and less eloquent hand has taken up the pen. On the last day of February 1901, the captain of the *Persephone* recorded his last entry. As he prepared to depart the next morning, he expressed his confidence, both in his own venture and in the ship's eventual return; they would rendezvous at Franz Josef Land and either attempt to sail south or, if need be, weather another winter in the ice; he was certain that the polar current would eventually bear them out to the Atlantic. He entrusted the ship, the ship's log and the lives of the crew to the last remaining Englishman on board, an officer in the Royal Navy, Raymond Parkes (a melancholy man who had kept to himself for much of the voyage, and is barely mentioned by Edward before this; in the depths of another long winter, he hanged himself in his cabin and was left on board in the coffin they'd meant to bring him home in). On the eve of his select team's departure, Edward made a last speech to his crew. He thanked them for their vigour, their good cheer, their expertise; and he assured them again he would not turn back. He told his party that it would be no shame if they wished to, that they could do so at any time, but if he had to push on alone he would.

On 1 March, Edward and his five men set out for the North Pole. He had waited two long winters and a summer for the moment; he had waited, he thought, his whole life. They had spent months preparing kayaks, sleds, provisions. He had borrowed much from Nansen, bucking British convention by using dogs, studying carefully so that he might take the same wise precautions, calculating weights and capacities, but for one detail which he knew would be his making or undoing: he would not turn back. Six men set out, intrepid, for the Pole. None returned or were heard from again.

In the autumn of the following year, four Norwegian sailors, the survivors of a desperate band who had left the *Persephone* still frozen and failing three months before, were found by a Russian whaling vessel, frostbitten, exhausted and barely alive on the shores of Spitzbergen. They had lost toes, fingers, companions, almost all hope. The ship, abandoned with the hanged corpse of her surrogate captain in the hold, was never found.

They were warmed and changed, bathed and fed. They ate soft white bread for the first time in two years; they smoked real tobacco, they drank ale like nectar. There was a new monarch on the throne of their captain's country, they were told; they raised a glass to King Edward, and another and another to their captain, who had not returned. In the hard months of their toil, their struggle through snow and cracking ice and salt-sludge seas, they had told each other tales of a Union Jack, planted at the Pole beside their own flag by the brave English officer. And now they learned that he had not triumphed, that nothing was known of him since the day he left the ship more than a year before them. So they raised a glass to his country, to his king, and to Edward Mackley, with tears in their smarting eyes. There was a picture in *The Times*, on the third page; a carefully pressed though yellowed copy remains among the family's papers, the same presumably that was laid by an unwitting butler in its usual place on John's desk, when the ink was fresh as the morning's bread.

'Four Norwegians have been found on Spitzbergen,' John Mackley tells his brother's wife, standing in the doorway of the morning room. 'They left the *Persephone* in the spring.'

Emily, drawn and tear-stained, looks up from her reading.

★   ★   ★

192

No. That cannot be it; she cannot have wept since the day he departed, she cannot have cried all that time, while Edward fought and lost against the snow. Julia knows that she too was noble and strong. There is scant record to call upon of those years as they passed quietly in the house he'd left behind, and it is hard to imagine how his wife might have lived in his absence; but a woman cannot live on longing alone. She must have called upon the forbearance that her husband had trusted she held in reserve; she must somehow have found a way through her days.

Emily simply looks up, then, from her reading.
'And Edward?'
'Was not with them. Emily—' John steps into the room, closing the door behind him. In one hand he holds the newspaper; he puts out the other as he approaches, as if to console her, but finds he does not know how to do so and lets it fall on the back of a chair as if that was what he had meant.
'Edward left the ship in March last year, as he'd always intended. To walk to the Pole.'
'And did not return?'
'And did not return.'
Emily is silent, looking past him into a distance he can't measure.

Everything is equidistant, all is far from me as he is far from me and I will stretch out over the distance, until he returns, I am peaceful and will not weep, I am waiting

'I am very sorry.'

The sound of her own voice recalls her. 'Do they bring news, the Norwegians? Do they know anything of him at all?'

'They waited at the meeting point; Edward didn't arrive. They were under instruction to sail before the winter set in. They drifted too far north, the ship was trapped in the ice again and couldn't break free in the spring. Their supplies were running low, the man Edward left in charge has . . . was ill. He died.' John is scanning the story over as he speaks, glad of the paper barrier of simple reported fact. 'They had to abandon ship. A party of twelve set out to seek help. They thought the ship would soon break up.'

'Of twelve?'

'Eight died.'

'God help them,' said Emily, who did not believe in God. And then, perhaps, went back to her book . . .

There is no known surviving record, in fact, of Emily's immediate response, which was of a greater significance than Julia could guess at – but all in good time. What Julia knows, what has been passed down, is this: in the course of the month that followed the announcement in *The Times*, NORWEGIAN PARTY FOUND AT SPITZBERGEN, Emily tied up the last three years of letters with black satin ribbon and stowed them in her bureau; she made what calls she must upon her neighbours; she laid away skirts and furs; she ordered a great stack of books – natural history, poetry, French novels, Gibbon, Walter Scott – and then went to bed, for the better part of a year. Julia finds it possible, almost, to imagine this period as a perpetual dozy morning, laid out on the cool white sheet, tracing the wedding-cake patterns of the ceiling rose, as she herself dreamed hours away in that room as a girl; time had passed so easily then, unnoticed, or so it seems to her now, when the days take so long to fill, although the years slip by so quickly. So she envisions Emily's blank limbo of not-waiting, not-mourning.

However it was that the time passed, it is known that one morning in 1903, not long after midsummer's day (four years since she had bidden him farewell), Emily woke – perhaps to the sound of her new nephew's cry in the night nursery above her, or to the dream that plagued her of her lover decaying, or perhaps just to the birds at the window; whatever it was that woke her, she got up and dressed and appeared at the breakfast table smelling faintly of the mothballs her clothes had been kept in. She said yes, she would take an egg, and some toast. She said yes, she felt a great deal better, thank you. She said no, she had not given up hope. She could wait. She waited. She put away finery and would wear only sober dark blue and

195

dove-grey (but never, for the rest of her life, black). She did not open that drawer again and her letters remained unread until Helen tugged at it after she died; it unstuck and released the last of the rose scent, so carefully captured there for more than fifty years and sour with sadness.

What had happened to Edward? England asked the same question, for a year or two. Then began to forget; then in 1909 an American claimed the Pole, and any last vestige of interest in a British attempt waned; and the century went on to fight its wars and revolutions without him. And then, in 1959, his body was found, unsought for decades. And with it the diary he kept, open to the first page now and spread on Julia's knee, as she sets out with him:

> I looked out upon this morning, this first of the month of March (1901), under one of the first risen suns of the year, and of the new century; never have I seen the ice so lovely, so bare. The blue shadows long in the shallowest ridges, the sky pallid. So short a stretch it seems until we attain our goal; and just a stretch longer until we are home, my dear, and you can tell me what has passed in my absence, and we shall between us plan what the next hundred years may bring.

This is the first entry, written on their first night on the ice, snug in the tent after supper. They drank champagne and raised a toast to the Pole and the last of luxury. This diary, found buried in its aluminium canister with his body, is quite different from the official ship's log that he left for Parkes to maintain, which was brought faithfully to England by *Persephone*'s survivors. This diary is a testament to his best self; he writes as a safeguard against the loss of the man he was, husband and hero; it is the voice that Julia hears when she listens for him. When they were children, Aunt Helen read to the girls from both the ship's log and the diary; a judicious editor, she honed out an adventure, sparing them the days of nothing but weather reports, bearings, dredging and sounding, and retaining just enough gruesome detail to make the tale exciting. So Julia, who has been told this story for as long as she can remember, embellished by the years curled up in bed or by the fireside, cannot comprehend Emily's many years of not knowing, or what it meant to know after so long waiting. For her, Edward has always been complete, his words so familiar that she hardly needs to read them; she has known him always as a hero to the last. But Helen had read the diary before, many, many times over, to Emily, whose eyes by then were milked over with cataracts, and who had for so many years not known the man he was in his last days. Nothing was left out of that telling, there were to be no improvisations or edits. She was urged on through suffering by a wife who had waited too long to bear any more omissions; it was all she could do now to flesh out the shade who had always walked beside her.

He knew that, if he returned, he could rework a public version which obscured any trace of the too-sentimental (or, later, of despair); otherwise, it would be found by some other, or never found at all, and he would be past caring. And if it was found, then he wished his Emily to know he loved her; this slim, leather-bound book is one long address to the wife who was waiting, and her hundreds of letters may be weighed in the balance against it. He could not have known that it would come into the care of his brother's great-granddaughter, that eyes like Emily's would one day scan the pages, on a glorious summer afternoon such as those he dreamed of through the Arctic night. His life in her hands – strong, long hands like Emily's. She must do it justice now; no omissions; but what of the gaps? Has she the right to imagine?

The diary's partner, the book he left his wife as a gift, remains curiously empty but for the poem he wrote in it, and on the next page a single entry in her hand, undated, incomplete as if interrupted: 'Edward, what will you think of me? I cannot go on without' . . . Aunt Helen gave the book to Julia on her sixteenth birthday; how she longed to know the end of the sentence, and how she longed to make the remaining pages her own. But every page she scribbled on would be squandered, every line would lessen the blank perfection of its possibility. She has it still, unfilled.

TENT

Julia casts herself out into the white expanse that would swallow his story for more than half a century. There are pages in the diary that are water-stained, the ink leached pale; places near the end where there is only the barest trace of graphite; but as she turns it slowly, we can still make out the words, although parts are indistinct. And for us there is always the liberty of what may be conjecture, even if Julia, supine on the chaise, struggling against her own legends, does her best to reject it.

Edward set out, then, into the unknown. Doubtless, dauntless, sure-footed upon the snow that would bury him.

At first, they travelled in half-darkness for much of the morning, marching on in the pale twilight and stopping when the barely risen sun had fully set; by the end of the month, it was almost light when they woke. Taking turns to ride upon the sleds, the men gave in to the breathtaking rush of beauty, speeding towards triumph on their dog-drawn chariots, exhilarated in the violet flush of the long dawn. On plains of sheer ice, the pack was fast and tireless, and on snowshoes the men too easily covered the distance. At such a pace, it seemed they would reach their goal in moments; they were higher upon the world than any man now, far beyond all that was ordinary, like gods in a land of immaculate light and splendour.

For the first weeks, they made good progress. They were fortunate: the weather stayed clear, the ice for the most part passable. The sleds crossed easily over narrow gullies when they came to them. They covered nine or ten miles on a good day, trudging on over uneven patches, hauling the sleds where the dogs could not pull them, speaking little to keep their breath in the thin air. Careful not to exert themselves too much, for despite the ever-encroaching sun it was bitterly cold, and sweat freezes at such temperatures; but always moving enough to keep warm. They rested twice only in ten hours of marching, for only five minutes' pause each time, stamping up and down and clutching chocolate in awkward mittens to stave off the cold. The ache of every limb, of thighs and arms and across their shoulders when at last they bedded down, made their relished sleep as deep and heavy as that of exhausted children.

The tent they carried was made of silk, light-weight and strong, round, and large enough to accommodate a stove at the centre, and the six of them in three double sleeping bags – the advantage of shared body heat having long since overcome any English regard for privacy. Freely and Edward were old bedfellows; Hugh Compton-Hill, the diplomat's son, was paired at first with Nordahl but found the mild Dr Wilkinson more tolerant of a squirming, muttering sleeper – truth be told, the good doctor was reminded of his wife, and after months alone in a narrow bunk which had seemed to him luxuriously wide was oddly comforted to have his nights again disturbed. And so Nordahl and Andreev, both large but stolid men, squeezed into the last bag and lay flat on their backs together like kings on a marble tomb, as if cast from the monument they deserved but would not, alas, receive. This was Edward's team of brave men – and the boy he was compelled to bring with him.

Each evening, as the sun spread across the horizon, the day's march was called to a halt and the tent assembled, the white silk like the snow bathed crimson. They made it fast, secured the sleds while Andreev tended the dogs, and on a clear night could be snug inside within forty minutes. They climbed into their bags and waited for their clothes to thaw – stiff with ice, they cracked and squeaked as they flexed their limbs and it took an hour or more to warm themselves. When they could move again, they set about preparing supper; the simple, repetitive bill of canned and reheated fare seemed manfully spartan after *Persephone*'s lavish spreads. At night they slept in their wet clothes, drying the sodden wool lining of their boots with their own body heat, laid like compresses on the chest, so tired they barely felt discomfort.

The days were varied only by the changing consistencies of light and snow, the lowering or thinning clouds, the thickness of the air and the depth underfoot. Edward's diary is a series of measures assiduously taken, the reckoning of rations and of the horizon, the scale of the ice forms that towered about them more vast than any they had seen aboard ship or had imagined, 'great monuments and temples such as gods might toss up effortless, in their own honour'. Through it all, pride and love and the promise of triumph and return. And beginning every entry, that essential measure: how far north. Almost every day is otherwise much the same, but for that figure creeping up daily through the 80s, recorded first and foremost without fail. The priority is never forgotten, so that more exceptional events are recorded as an afterthought – on 28 March, for example: '85° 52′ N. We must surely reach soon the 86th parallel; we are fast covering the distance', and also: 'Last night we were attacked by a huge bear. None were hurt but for one of the dogs; today we have been feasting.'

The story of the bear proved a favourite with the girls. Julia's father would prowl about the tent, growling, and the sisters would clutch at each other laughing, terrified, needing to pee. Early versions omitted the details of the murder, but one summer, by the campfire, Aunt Helen decided they were old enough to hear it, and knew when she saw their narrow faces aghast with grisly satisfaction that her judgement, as ever, was true.

Edward and his men sweated and steamed in the damp heat of their own bodies in the tent, and cracked coarse jokes of which no record remains (not an appropriate legacy, thought Edward, to leave to his wife or the world). One night, Anton Andreev halted them with a raised hand. The gesture in itself was so unlike him, who rarely joined their banter with more than a bobbing, smiling laugh, that all were hushed.

'Listen. It is Anna.'

They listened. There was no wind, no sound, only stifled breathing; no leaves beyond the window, no familiar house-creak, no night-bird's cry. Only the endless, patient quiet of the Arctic. They grew nervous; the tent, after all, a warm little glowing circle of solidarity, was very small, very thin, very lonely. They sat rigid, spines straight with attention, for minutes like hours of silence, until Compton-Hill slumped and laughed.

'What did she say, old boy? You'll have to translate, you know: we don't speak Russian – or wolfhound, for that matter.'

'Listen,' Andreev said again. His features seemed carved by the orange light of the stove, his eyes shining below his dark brow. And then

204

they heard it: a whine, very faint, but distinct. And another.

'They're dreaming of rabbits, Anton,' said Edward, to calm his men, feeling their fear creep over his scalp.

'No. They are not sleeping.'

Edward held the Russian's gaze. 'No,' said Edward. As carefully as he could in the cramped space, he slid himself out of the sleeping bag, staying Freely as he did so but motioning Andreev to step out with him. And then, crashing through the silence, the barking started; a furious frightened din, alarmingly close to them. In the tent, the men froze. Edward and Andreev's eyes met and they began to move with quiet speed, pulling on boots and loading rifles. They heard the clamour subdued to a growl as they unlaced the tent. As their eyes adjusted to the dim light afforded by the new moon's sliver, they saw the clear line of savagery, from the straining leashes through the slavering pack, long snouts all low-snarling at the point where a dark trail across the snow ended. A bare twenty yards off, the poor carcass of one of their number was still pinned by a pair of massive claws. As the men emerged, the bear raised its bloodied muzzle for a moment before deciding there was time enough and returning, placid, to his feast. They were close enough to hear the soft grunts, the rip of gristle. Close enough for a good clean shot.

Bear meat is a delicacy relished by all who

venture far enough to taste it. Andreev mourned for the dead hound, Yerik, an old friend; but it may be that revenge lent his supper that night an especially sweet savour.

In early April a light snow began to fall; the air closed in upon them and thickened to a pale bright grey as dense as the snow beneath their feet, so that they could not see the meeting point between ground and sky or even a hand outstretched. Shadow and contour vanished. They were forced to send scouts ahead without the sleds, to find a path; any step might have run against a wall or plunged them into an unseen gully. They marched on, back and forth across the same ground to gather the whole party in increments, disorientated and frustratingly slower by the day, carrying the weight of the water frozen into their clothing so that they dragged the landscape with them at every step. Tiny fine crystals clung to their clothes, their eyebrows, rimed their nostrils. From the front, they were frosted white, driving into it; their backs remained dun-coloured, so that they might have been pop-up cut-outs from an ice plain made of cardboard. Every hour the flakes grew fatter.

Flurries and blinking conspired to blur their vision impossibly; their heads were so swaddled they could barely hear; so when Dr Wilkinson, bringing up the rear, plunged his foot deep into a hidden crack filled with slush, they were thirty yards on by the time they heard him calling. A faint and lonely human sound in the blizzard. They ran back, at the sinking helpless pace of a dream, hauled him out; he was quite all right, he said, just couldn't get a purchase to pull himself up; his trouser froze solid so quickly that his leg wasn't even touched by the cold. But Edward at last had to take the sign; it was too risky to press on. They made camp, picking at frozen knots with numb hands, wrestling with the sleds and the tent for two hours against the wind, then crawled inside and prepared to wait it out.

They spent two nights in a strange, muffled proximity, the snow insulating the tent so that sunlight and sound were dampened. Every couple of hours they would check, in turn, the weather, and report back to their companions of the void. Groundless, depthless, airless, white. They could not take a bearing without sun or stars, compounding their frustration; they might be anywhere, or nowhere in the world. The dogs, in a makeshift shelter outside, curled about one another and slept all day and night; and the men, too, felt a curious instinct towards hibernation, their blood and breathing slow in the dim-filtered light.

On the second day, Edward startled himself and the others awake with a shout. The silence pressed in again immediately, so that the sound replayed itself over in their minds, absorbed into the half-memory of the clouded sleep that had been broken by this violent rousing. He had dreamed, he wrote, 'some horrid, frenzied madman's act, which I cannot set down here for fear of being condemned as such. We must start again soon. We are losing time. The snow will swallow us.' A troubled sleeper since childhood, he was haunted now by the blood-spattered silk of his nightmare all through the cloistered day. When darkness fell he lay with wide eyes beside Freely, waiting for the dawn, which brought him an hour's fitful respite.

And when he woke to this third day he saw that they were spared. A new light pushed its way through the walls of the tent. Edward opened his eyes to the bright silk and thought, perversely, of the town fair's marquee, as if he might step out onto well-kept parkland, a neat green lawn peopled by long-skirted ladies twirling their parasols, aghast at his bearded and oil-black visage. He laughed at the vision and woke the men again, who worried for a moment that this might be some further sign of a loosening mind before seeing for themselves the sun's return, Edward already unlacing the flap. The tent was half covered by snowdrift, become part of the brilliant new landscape that had fallen all about them and gleamed now like a white Eden in the world's first light, under a blessed blue sky.

Julia looks out through the skylight at a blue so deep and clear that clouds seem impossible, the height of the summer day soaring above her, and feels her mind expanding into it, her body filled with his joy.

208

ICE

Just as it is almost impossible, on a day such as this one, to imagine the need of a woollen sweater or a blazing fire, so after many months in the north and the weeks of walking in the cutting wind, Edward could not now imagine heat. The thought of himself sipping an iced drink in his brother's garden, in a light lounge suit, seemed an exotic fantasy which could not belong to his own experience. The thought of skin exposed to air was an absurdity. He couldn't quite imagine his hands without gloves on. He was beginning to find it harder to imagine holding Emily's in his own, her long fingers laced in his.

Hugh Compton-Hill complained of a frozen chin; it was too numb to speak properly, he said. Nordahl suggested he might keep silent, then, and concentrate his energy on growing hair to cover it. His own beard, which had been enviable at the outset, was now a thick, dark red thatch which he plaited in two to amuse them, a true Viking. Emily would not at first have known Edward; his always neatly sculpted sideburns and moustache had run amok, extending into a beard that followed the

209

point of his chin like an unkempt Mephisto; 'You would think me quite piratical, and call me your buccaneer,' he tells her. Sixty years later, when she heard this, it would raise a wet chuckle as she pictured him: he looked more than ever like the poet he was not.

The snow, blown by low cross-winds, was scalloped and smoothed and ruffled like icing in striations of shadowed blue. *Sastrugi*: the Russian taught him the word. Shaped with a knife. It was how he imagined a desert to look, it was like a massive desert rose; he had seen them in the British Museum. He had never been to a hot country (and could not now imagine heat). It is beautiful, he thought, as they stood in despair looking out at the sculpted surface. Like an ocean in arrest. Crests and flats, the light trapped in hollows, elsewhere deep blue shadows pooling, or a roseate rainbow in a translucent arc of ice; in places the snow curved over itself, a wave in the moment before breaking, creating a cave that he longed to curl into. Such a landscape is beautiful indeed, and treacherous and almost impossible to cross. They laboured over the uneven surface for hours, plunging feet into drifts that seemed solid, dragging the sleds over toughened ridges that they couldn't slice through, upending into hollows and hauling back out. When it was possible to use the sleds as a bridge over a narrow crevasse, the dogs had to be driven across one by one, in sullen succession; one afternoon the whole pack halted without reason and refused to go on. Under the whip, they would shamble forward a few steps before sitting again, stubborn; it took an hour to cajole them into moving of their own accord. Boris, dour and dragging a hind leg at the back, was singled out for the dogs' dinner that evening. The pack was diminishing; they grew leaner and the hunger whined in their eyes. It had always been part of Edward's plan to pare off their number as the sled-loads grew lighter, and their only sustenance now was their own companions. When one weakened and fell and could not be stirred, it was almost a relief to poor Andreev to be spared the choosing of another for slaughter. He had taken it upon himself to slit their throats, although Edward would not ask him to serve the still-furred meat to the others.

They had been marching for weeks now, sometimes against the drift and current, so that a day's labour barely brought them inches towards their goal; but they were drawing slowly, slowly closer. Time was collapsing; Edward remained hopeful and recorded daily their bearing, every twenty-four hours carefully tracked in the absence of nightfall; they were closing upon the target set by Nansen, which he was determined to far surpass. It would not be enough to merely draw a little closer – there could be no triumph in a more successful failure. April slipped away; he had hoped to have come further by the month's end, knowing the ice would be at its worst in May.

They had brought provisions ample for a hundred days; he began to limit their rations, knowing they would already struggle to make it to safety with what they had, nevertheless not doubting that they would. No one mentioned turning back – or at least, if they mentioned it to Edward he did not record it, to spare them the shame. They would push on, determined even as the plain began to fracture, leads opening all around them.

The ice grew ever more fragmented, the channels widening so that they were forced to scout ahead to find a way around, taking hours to cross a twenty-yard stretch. It was not yet broken enough to allow them to sail, and Edward was reluctant to stop and lose the time it would take to secure the kayaks before he had to. Their legs burned with each step, far beyond aching. All too soon, they were becoming too weak to bear this frustration.

In the endless daylight, days became the same. Ritual kept them alive; it kept them trudging when they longed to stop, and compelled them to rest when near-delirium would have pushed them on. The tent was pitched according to the well-practised routine; they crawled in, warmed themselves, and prepared one of two or three possible meals, always the same amount, divided between them gram by gram, spoon by spoon, square by square (although the chocolate had dwindled, from three squares to just one). Although they sickened, they swallowed down their ration; although they starved, they did not give in to feasting. They rose as dry and warm as possible, and assembled their layers about their bodies, trying not to look at their own blistered, bloodied feet as they wound them in still-damp wadding and forced them into stiffened boots, and furled the tent and stowed the sleds with their heavy load, and trudged on again, far enough to get far enough, halting on the point of exhaustion.

Ritual meets bodily needs; but the mind and the spirit, too, survive by it. When there is no land below, just the false, cruel floes that shift underfoot and drag the traveller back to where they came from, so that nothing is sure; and when, too, the division of days is lost in the relentless light, so that the world itself seems to have forgone the cycles that once seemed so sure, a man needs this.

As they rested, they imagined the rituals of home, the lighting of cigars, the starched buttoning of evening dress, the dinners, course by course, the seductions. Lars spoke of the many women he loved – 'It's true,' he declared, 'I love them all' – and described each in detail; Freely swore that when he got back to London he would propose to the girl who had once, in Greenwich, fed him whitebait with her fingers, the finest meal he'd ever eaten; Edward recalled a certain unladylike crimson blush. They roared at Compton-Hill's invented conquests, and Andreev laughed along quietly. Even Dr Wilkinson spoke fondly of his wife, who would be comfortably star-shaped across their double bed without her narrow husband to take up his strip of space at the edge. And these imaginings, too, were a ritual, to remind themselves they were not animals – a ritual indulged in as they whiled away the sunlit evening hours picking lice from their furs like monkeys.

Here, weeks truncate into the space of a few pages, reduced to a stretch of wearisome struggle and aching that Edward could not attempt to convey, and which we, perhaps, like Julia, cannot comprehend; it is no common thing to push pain beyond the point of tedium. He wrote barely a sentence each day, struggling to take readings and record them in the glare of the crisp, fine snow. When there is nothing but tiny crystals of ice on open ice for miles, each one a brilliant pinprick, the effect is dazzling. The sun was relentless; they crossed the plain with half-closed eyes and hoped there were no surprises. The clouded sky refracted the light, so it suffused the whole flat world around them, shadowless and too bright to bear. The snow goggles served only to slice a narrow, searing strip of white fire across the brain. Edward could have wept to see Freely's eyes, too pale and wide to stand it, two angry red sores that he could barely open, trying pitifully to look up at the doctor as he swabbed hopelessly at the inflamed skin with cocaine solution.

Edward was becoming a somnambulist, his

swollen eyes closing before he noticed, so that he could pace for miles in a peach-flooded glow of numb agony. When one of them stumbled, it was more often a slip into sleep than a trip. The body falling to the bed it expected, and waking when its knees hit the snow. Their rations long since reduced to the minimum, he no longer felt hungry but found himself, in this dreaming daze, reciting menus. Asparagus soup, then sole then quail then veal then cherry clafoutis for dessert. How delicious a cigarette would be. How rich and deep to let a sip of port linger on his tongue. How he longed for intoxication, something other than this half-delirium of roasted joints and great glistening fruit platters laid out before him on the clean cloth of snow.

One morning, close to dawn, Edward heard birdsong. Could it be that they were nearing land? Had he taken a wrong turn, or was there here some undiscovered island? He could not see them – he could not see – but he could hear them, all around. Not the harsh, distant cries of seabirds in flight, even, but songbirds; it was as if he were lying beside Emily again, in his brother's house, her forehead clear and dreamless, her dark brass hair on the pillow, unleashed from the complex arrangements of the day as only he was permitted to see her. The sweet, mossy smell of a spring morning on the breeze through the window and the birds in chorus in the garden, the coming of the lark which soon would surely wake her, and her pale brown eyes meet his . . .

He lay back and listened, trying not to laugh out loud in elation. In his white blindness they were all about him, as if to bear him up on a thousand tiny wings and carry him back to an English garden. The trills and chitters and thweeps of a joyous choir, finer than any angels could be.

Freely grunted as he turned beside him. Edward jolted, and then recognized the sound of his restless bedfellow, shifting in the silence. He cracked his eyes a fraction. Yes, it was silent. He had been sure he was awake, that it was the birds that had woken him, but told himself it was a dream, he had been sleeping after all; he would not give in to delusion. However it was that his mind had tricked him, there were no birds here to sing. Not even the horrid squawk of seabirds on the wing.

In that realm of improbability, the birdsong that woke Edward might conceivably have been the same that stirred Emily from her slumbers, perched in the whispering branches of the willow and trilling through the open window, reaching him across the sea, across the ice, to announce his wife's waking. The same feathered flock whose yolk-line persists in the chorus that still gathers about the house to greet the dawn, competing with Simon to be the first to rise, their bright refrain penetrating the pillow that is commonly to be found, at this time, clamped over Julia's head.

In that realm where all probability might, however unlikely or brief, be made manifest, where the wide ice desert grows false mountains that men mark on maps to mislead those that follow, where suns and spheres burgeon and throw out great bright lances to spear the sky, where banquets spring from the endless barren plain, Edward's insidious nightmares crept always beside him, vivid against the white wasteland of his nights.

Hours bleached into days and weeks, relieved by snatches of poor, troubled sleep. In one restless and exhausted slumber, a creak sneaked its way out of the ice into his dream: an ice cube squeaking between his teeth; he was taking a drink before dinner with his brother. Their father was there, the wheeze of his whisky breath, a stern smile; the tonic was bitter, or was it the gin? Edward was a young man again and had not tasted either before . . . the ice squeaked between his teeth. Then it was cutting his gums and he could not chew through it or spit it out, it was broken glass in his mouth and it was cutting his teeth out, he was choking on blood and cold glass and his own teeth and his head was filled with the most terrible crunching and cracking, so that the plunge into freezing water that woke him was a momentary relief.

But the awful cacophony that had cracked through his skull was echoing still all around him, and if he was awake then this was a worse nightmare, he was trapped in a soaking, freezing heavy shroud and the sound of the ice breaking was resounding all around him and something was struggling and kicking against him, and above, a bright white silk canopy descending like a parachute but it was water, not air, they were falling through, there was nothing solid for miles below them and they could not breathe even if there were safe ground to stand on, no, they could not breathe in water, and the tent deflated and slipped away like a jellyfish collapsing . . . A pair of red-pale eyes met his, huge and wide; it was Freely who kicked and struggled, fighting to fly free of this wet-furred cocoon; his eyes were terrified, his hand was grasping at Edward's shoulder and shaking it, slowly. Freely was moving with a strange exaggerated slowness, his head gawping from side to side and streaming big bubbles from his open mouth, soundless. Somehow in the tangle of the bag they found each other's feet and with a great shove were jettisoned out.

Speed and lightness and no more pain, buoyed by the sea; what a joy it was to float free. Everything was falling away around him. The water so clear. There was nothing living here to see but it was so clear, he could see sunlight above them, everything vivid with a green-blue liquid clarity. It was peaceful, the water was very different from beneath the surface, from above it was dark glass, but from beneath it was so luminous, vast caverns of deep green, a vaulted ceiling of ice and light. He hadn't thought to find this cathedral here. Beams of pale gold spilling through the splintered roof above; passing his hand through it, he could see every dirty detail, every cracked knuckle and oily whorl, and hoped this cascade of light could yet clean him. He could see his compass, floating too far off to be reached. His last squares of precious chocolate, foil-wrapped, sinking to the seabed like doubloons. Two pennies from his pocket – what had he hoped to purchase? Let it all go. It was hardly even cold. It was cold enough to be perfectly clear. How foolish to struggle. There was the watch that she gave him, trailing its chain like some fantastic silver fish. The watch she gave him to navigate home by, engraved with her name – his Emily.

He reached out and grasped it as it sank past his eyes. He had promised to reach the Pole. He had promised to return.

A stream of brilliance guided him to the surface; he swam up through the thousand tiny bubbles of light that his friend left in his wake, elated now, so close to the air, enraptured by brightness.

Then he felt huge hands under his armpits hauling him onto the ice with a rush of sound, crashing out of the muted underwater thrum into splashing and shouting; with a roar he was fighting to cough and to vomit at once, water pouring from every part of him, a sluice out of nostrils, ears, sleeves, and coughing, coughing the sea out of his stomach and lungs on his hands and knees and then, his weak arms giving way, sinking to rest his face on his splayed hands as the dogs did in despair.

Beside him Freely stretched on his back, moaning, painful salty retches racking his body.

The others had been further off, working on the kayaks. Unable to persist any longer by foot and sled alone, compelled to enter the water, the party had taken the first opportunity to pause on a rare stretch of seeming solidity, and had rested there for three days while they made the vessels secure, taking the work in shifts. It was a mercy, then, that the rest of the team were spared the plunge and their supplies were for the most part safe. They carried a second, smaller tent, in case the party had ever needed to divide, and so still at least had shelter, without which they would quickly perish; but they had lost the better compass, a precious day's worth of provisions, one of their two rifles and a valuable case of rounds, and, disastrously, the Primus stove. They would have to improvise to heat water, and without the efficiency the stove afforded could no longer waste fuel on cooked meat.

Edward, propped in the lee of a hummock, the best shelter they could find, looked on shivering while the others worked to erect the new tent. He was grasping something in his hand; he opened it to see. He still had her watch. He traced over all the fine filigree of it; it was as if he could feel the delicacy of its patterning through his filthy glove, through the numb calluses that were his fingertips. He would have it repaired at the first port he reached, and never tell her it had stopped. He had made a promise to find his way back to her. He had promised to reach the Pole and come back to her.

Was it then, swaddled in furs and helpless as a baby, that he felt the first bitterness of doubt? Of worse than doubt, even; of failure?

Freely sat slumped against Edward, spent by his effort to reach the surface, unable to stay upright on his own. After an hour, Edward felt a twitch against him, heard what he thought was a tiny sob; but shifting so that he could see his friend's face, careful not to let him flop forward into the snow, he saw that it was laughter that shook Freely's wasted frame. A smile that opened alarming red cracks in his chapped lips, horrible against the black and the crusted white of dead skin, and a hacking chuckle, half a shiver, that ripped at his exhausted ribcage.

'I'm glad to see you in good spirits, Samuel,' said Edward with an effort.

'I was thinking' – Freely could barely speak for gasping – 'I was thinking of the lass at the Trafalgar Tavern. H . . . Hat . . . Ha, haha, do you remember? With the red ringlets? At the Trafalgar? Ha . . . Hattie?'

'Was that her name, Sam? Hattie? I remember the girl.'

'Hat-at-at at the Tavern . . . come sit on my knee . . . I'll be your sailor come back from the seeea . . .'

At this, Freely collapsed in an agony of cackles, leaning against Edward with a hand to his chest.

221

'Oh God, God, Edward, I think my lungs will burst . . . do you think young Hattie would care to sit on my lap now, Edward? All skin and bone and my hands all black?'

'She'd sit there gladly and feed you whitebait with her fingers, Sam. As would any woman.' Edward forced a laugh that rent his racked throat to tatters. 'Yours will be the most desirable lap in England when we return.'

And seeing that Wilkinson was beckoning them, he got to his knees and with a great heave dragged his old friend to his feet and staggered towards the small tent, managing four steps supporting both of them before tottering forward and feeling Nordahl lift the weight from about his shoulders.

Once inside the tent, they couldn't get warm for hours. They stripped their wet clothes, lit a precious fire and huddled together in every spare set of woollen underwear they could find, in Wilkinson and Compton-Hill's bag. The boy, curiously eager and bright-eyed, had set to work with the doctor on making a new one out of furs and sealskin. Edward lay beside his friend and watched his blue lips chatter. He held him tightly, felt his body jerk against him, the cold in his joints now, in his kidneys; he seemed to only grow colder the longer they lay there. Edward imagined icy caverns for lungs, every breath frosting them over, like the empty saloon of an abandoned ship. They swam in and out of sleep, rocking on troubled seas, falling again and again through the ice and waking with violent starts before almost immediately drifting back under. In the restless stretches of that long, bright night, Edward watched as Freely's eyelids flickered as if under the weight of the dark purple greasepaint that seemed to coat them, and his heart, too, beat like some desperate creature trapped between the palms, banging against Edward's own chest where he clasped him close. At last, seeing his friend drift off, Edward slept, exhausted, for no more than an hour, he thought; he woke to the same hard light and wondered blankly how much time had passed and remembered his broken watch as he came to, and found that he held a corpse in his arms.

Edward's diary was preserved in its aluminium case at his breast; but his fingers and his heart were too numb to make much account of his grief that day. A note, merely, of what was lost: the tent, the equipment, one man. Two days later they were ready to set out again. He writes:

> The kayaks are secure. We have killed the last of the dogs, we cannot risk capsizing and they are of little use alive to us now; we have taken two aboard but hope we will not have need of them. Freely is gone, the ice grows ever more intractable, and it would be madness to push on. With fractured eyes and sodden instruments I take our bearing

223

to be 86° 31'; if I am right then we have outstripped Nansen. We stand farther north now than any man has, and that shall be my achievement, the seventeen fractions of a degree my friend died for. Today we turn south to seek land. On this, the 30th June, 1901, Edward Mackley turns back.

How noble he sounds in defeat. The disappointment so honestly borne. Here is the turning point in the tragedy, the moment of capitulation which signals the coming fall; Julia, turning back with them, feels her heart sink as it always has with a heavy relish. Edward turns back but he will never find his home, where his wife waits expectant now, thinking she will see him before the year is out. But now, in the half-daze of the afternoon heat, in the house where Emily waited, Julia hears a whisper, what he could not bear to write: 'Emily, I did not reach it.'

But I was waiting, I was waiting for you there at the still point, outstretched . . .

He did not reach it, or come back to her. He could not even be sure how far he had gone, and even if his reading were true then, when they dug up his dead body at last, it no longer mattered, it had long been surpassed; and as she listened to his tale on her deathbed, this was the truth she learned after so long waiting: Edward Mackley turns back.

SEALS AND SAILING

When the weather was clear they pushed on for hours at a stretch against unknown currents and choppy waters; aching in their arms and shoulders, the rhythm was all that they knew, ceaseless. Despite the pain they paddled on, even when aided by their makeshift sails, to stay warm in the icy, damp wind. They spoke little, took turns to lead, Edward, Compton-Hill and Wilkinson in one kayak, Andreev and Nordahl in the other with the bulk of the provisions and two dead dogs. They rested on any floe large enough to offer sanctuary, sometimes pitching camp on a rough circle of no more than twenty feet across, which might at any moment split beneath them; but they must sleep. They did not speak of Freely's fate.

Once, they woke to find the current had carried them many miles back upon their own path, dragged to the east and, which was worse, to the north they had turned their backs on, as if the Pole's magnet was taunting them now. Although there was no landmark, no land, to be certain how far, their readings showed that the last two days' efforts

225

at least had been wasted. Nordahl threw his oar so hard against the floe that it stuck fast; for a long minute there was no sound but the ragged trapped rush of his breathing. Edward stepped forward, gripped the post, and with surprising strength yanked it from the ice and handed it wordlessly to the shaking Norwegian.

'I am sorry, Captain. That was foolish.'

'To your place, Lars. We must row.'

With every stroke he could feel their anger, lending them at least new vigour against a powerful wind from the south, which drove the ice across the surface with alarming speed so that the closer floes crashed together and they had to weave a perilous route to avoid being crushed between them. The great chunks of it were like clouds scudding over a blue sky. But the sky itself was cloudless, filled with a heavy pale fog, obscuring the sun and spreading a painful wash of light.

As they drew slowly south, they came to realize that they were no longer alone in the water. Long dark forms could be seen moving with enviable grace and speed beneath them; from time to time, a sleek seal's head broke the surface. Edward took a shot at a fat female basking on a floe, and they lived off her much-needed blubber and flesh for four days, a welcome and delicious reprieve after two weeks of insipid bouillon and ship's biscuits. (Edward's diary makes a careful account of their depleted rations; again, the dogs' bodies are omitted from the account.) Their clothes and exposed skin were saturated lead-grey, their hands inside the gloves on the oars slippery with the seal oil that provided vital fuel for a fire to cook the animal's own meat in. 'I could not touch you now, Emily, and leave your gold skin smeared with filth. How I long to; but even if you were by some miracle beside me, I could not.'

Emily, who dreamed nightly of her husband's face frostbitten black, pulling back from his bones and rotting, would have gladly taken his poor, chapped, oil-slick, living hands upon her. She had no reason to despair yet. The date of his expected return grew closer, and her days were filled with speculation about the married life she had been waiting for, which would so soon begin. What would she wear to meet him? What words would he have to greet her? Where would they live, how would she fit their home, who would they receive there, what would their sons become? Would he lay his hands on her rounded belly and tell his child tales of the sea as it swam in her salt-water womb? He would lay his hands upon her . . . She lay down each night and longed for this, and almost felt his touch as sleep came – and such was the meagre portion of bliss meted out to her, this moment when her hands became his as she tipped between waking and sleep, before the dream came to turn them black. And in the mornings, the different bliss of very brief oblivion, of waking to the fragrant morning and knowing nothing before the day encroached, bringing the awareness of his absence; and the next thing she remembered was the imminence of his return, which was all she had to fill the empty space beside her and the hours to come before bedtime.

With a clear sky above them, they gazed out over a stretch of rippling water one morning, or afternoon, or it might have been the dead of night – resting for a spell while the sun was warm and the wind carried them gently forward. Edward felt a strange calm upon him, and thought of the round pond in the park at home, of his little boat sailing beside John's, one impossibly distant and tranquil evening when they were boys, watching the two white sails bright in the soft yellow light of September . . .

'It cannot be far now, Captain,' called Nordahl. 'We will soon sight land.'

Edward heard something shift and snuffle on the floor of the kayak behind him.

'Is that true?' asked a piteous voice. The diplomat's son had been growing quieter since they'd set out on the water, humming to himself with vacant eyes, and Edward regretted the bullying he'd met at their hands almost as much as he regretted bringing the boy along at all.

'If our readings are true, we should be nearing Franz Josef Land, Hugh. I expect to come in sight of Prince Rudolf Island any day now.'

In fact, Edward had expected to land at Cape Fligely, on the island's north shore, some days since. This had always been his intended route, to proceed from there by land and sea through the islands to Jackson's camp at Cape Flora, where they would be collected – although he had expected the outward journey to be faster and, of course, successful. But even when he turned back, even in his misery he hadn't despaired of finding the way. Now he knew that their battered equipment or his own calculations must be doubted, that their bearings were wrong; he could not know when the fault occurred (and he could not allow himself to think now, when their survival depended on withstanding despair, of the implications – that their northernmost reading might well be a nonsense, an unknown which could never be confirmed or recovered). He could only hope that the reckoning he'd made to adjust their course would not put them so far out that they bypassed the archipelago altogether. He knew that they could not endure the expanse of open sea they would then have to cross to reach Spitzbergen. There was a limit to the number of lazy, bloated seals likely to drift across their path for the taking. And he had heard, last night, the monstrous blowing of a walrus bursting through the surface not far off; if he could shoot one they would be lucky, but if threatened they were unlikely to survive an attack. These were dangerous waters. He could betray no desperation, confiding only to his diary, and to Emily, the hope that they would come to land west of the British Channel, which split Franz Josef Land through the middle, if they did not sight the northern group soon. 'Forgive me, there is no more I can do,' he confesses, 'but lie to them, and pray alone to the current and the winds.'

'I will keep a look-out, Captain,' whispered Hugh.

'I cannot deny that his eyes, looking out, were huge and wide,' writes Edward; 'but they would just as soon close again.'

The boy seemed to manage barely an hour of paddling when they set out each day before his head began to nod and he settled back, a beatific peace fixed on his tender face. Edward could not bring himself to rouse him; his weak strokes barely stirred the water anyway, and his always slight frame had grown so sparse in the last weeks that they could as well have carried a broken sparrow in the well of the small craft. He pecked at the crumbs he was portioned; when Nordahl growled that the rest were hungry if he wasn't, and would take what he couldn't manage, Edward shared his frustration but said only, 'Eat, Hugh.' And Hugh chewed dutifully with a wan smile before curling up like an exhausted child. Yet he was always the first to wake, and would be restored by the time they set out again, his youth shining like some new Apollo beneath the grime that matted his blond curls black.

★ ★ ★

Another week passed with still no sight of land; the precarious nights on the floes were taking their toll, and each man, exhausted by anxiety, wondered privately how long they could go on. Edward pushed forward, having no option, dark blood tunnelling his vision to a tiny spyhole focused on the prow of the craft and any obstacle it might encounter. He did not know how many hours they had rowed for, how long it was since they had rested. Very far away, a man's voice said his name.

'Edward.' It was insistent, almost certainly real, a man calling him by his first name. Deeper and older than Samuel's fine tenor; Samuel, he reminded himself, was dead. The friend he'd sailed with on his first voyage and his last. It was not Samuel that said his name, because Samuel's voice was brighter, and besides, he was dead. Someone was saying his name.

'Edward. The ice. Look.' It was David Wilkinson. Edward's vision and mind at last opened out, letting in the light and becoming aware again of the constant ache he had become.

'Is it blood?' the doctor was asking.

Blood. The colour of the ice restored the word's meaning to him. The ice all about them was stained, in patches, a bright russet, as if some massacre had been committed there, arteries slit, his nightmares splashed all over the whiteness. Edward was glad that the doctor had pointed to it, so that he did not have to believe his own eyes.

231

He glanced behind him – Compton-Hill was safely sleeping.

'It looks like blood, Doctor. But you're the expert on that account.' How natural and measured his own voice sounded.

'Let's draw closer.'

They edged the kayak alongside a floe. He could hear Nordahl calling behind them. He pulled off one foul, stiffened glove with some difficulty, stretched out a hand and touched the surface. The red patches were raised and rough, and came off on his fingers. To the doctor's alarm, Edward brought his hand to his mouth and put his tongue out to it, a bizarre pink protrusion from the black mask of his face.

'Edward?'

Edward struggled to master himself, feeling foolish tears rising.

'It's lichen. It grows here in the summer. We can eat it. And it means we're near land.'

'Captain!' called Nordahl, breathless, drawing close.

'I know, Lars. We'll stop and gather some.'

Edward knew the stuff could sicken them, but it was edible nonetheless, and he would take his chances. They paused for an hour to take their fill, and moved off with their shrunken bellies stretched by this paltry feast, and the strength of renewed hope. He was sure, this time, he heard a bird's cry on the wind.

★　★　★

Within a day their hope was rewarded, and almost thwarted again. A ridge of black basalt burst from the ocean to the south-east, its contours so sharp in the clear air that it could not be a vision. The water roiled around its base as if it had only moments before been raised from the seabed by some wizard, wicked or kind; its crags and columns resembled nothing so much as a long, turreted and forbidding rampart. A tattered cheer went up from the kayaks; Hugh, clutching at Edward's sleeve, was whispering, 'A castle, Captain, do you see it?'

'We'll reach it in a few hours, Hugh, at this rate!' exclaimed the doctor; Edward kept silent. The air was too clear to judge distance; he knew it was twice as far off as it seemed, a deception of the cruel light. And he could see no way to breach those walls. As they drew close they were at risk of being wrecked against them. And again, he kept his despair to himself, but while they rallied and devised a route he took the time to record the moment: 'We are in sight of land; I have been unable to identify the shape of the coast from this vantage, and cannot tell what land it is we are nearing, if indeed it is known. I hope we may rest if we reach it.'

LAND

Two days pass before the next entry; it is a stoical Edward that next sets pen to paper, a man who has learned through hard lessons to be glad of small comforts. So he begins:

I am eating an omelette. Sitting on solid ground, with even a little green about me; I am almost dry, in the sunshine, and eating an omelette and sipping tea, and wondering when I shall be brought my morning paper. The tea is tar-black with nothing to sweeten it, of course, and the eggs are eiders', fried in seal oil, but I am not ungrateful nor ever shall be again.

Fighting the currents that would have smashed the kayaks against the very island they were striving to land on, they had spent long gruelling hours seeking refuge; the ice packed thicker close to the land and it, too, could easily destroy them. The crash of the waves could not quite drown out Hugh's constant, useless whimper, so that Edward was sorely tempted to tip the boy over the side, knowing his crime would not be condemned in this company, and for ever go unpunished. He told himself later he couldn't bring himself to do it; although perhaps in truth he simply couldn't risk upsetting the craft and taking the others down with him. In either case they somehow ignored him and pushed on, shouting across to the other boat through the squall, drenched and exhausted, until at last Edward sighted a low outcrop in the lee of a short promontory, which he thought they might reach with the Devil's luck – 'and we are all black as devils after all'. They brought the kayaks round and tacked slowly, painfully, into the foaming current that streamed from the sharp tip of the jutting rock, until they pushed through it into the relative calm of the tiny bay and reached the miraculous shore, a ledge barely five feet wide and four up. Nordahl heaved himself out as they came alongside; Andreev secured ropes to the kayak, tossed them up, and clambered onto the rocks, and together they lifted the craft from the water, cracking the beams horribly as they drew it up and knowing they would struggle to make her seaworthy again. Then they helped Edward, Wilkinson and Compton-Hill through the same process; Hugh refused to stand up in the unstable craft and had to be dragged by both wrists up the rock face ('squealing as he skinned his knees', Edward notes unkindly, all patience and pretence gone). As they hauled at the second kayak, they felt the damp wind that had been threatening pick up. All at once, it seemed, the sky and the water darkened, swirling suddenly below them, dizzying; a rope snapped and the kayak crashed back into the sea, shattering as it fell.

They sat on their little ledge, too breathless and tired to speak or to care, or even to think of the earth beneath them at last. And it was barely a perch, besides, which the angering waters threatened to sweep them from. They must ascend. They secured the last of their precious possessions within the well of the remaining, half-ruined kayak, lashing them in like a strange papoose, found a crevice running up the side of the cliff face, and with every muscle a painful knot they winched themselves into it one by one and inched up, their legs braced in the gap and their backs pressed hard against the black rock, each of them praying that the man above would not slip and take the rest in his fall. It might have been half an hour or more before they reached the top and, without a pause to tend their bruised spines or rest their thighs, turned immediately to hoist the kayak up, every smack of its side an anguish, until at last it was safe, the precious bundles intact, even if the hull was hopelessly broken.

And then they paused. The sun had again broken through while they toiled and was warm through the rags they were clothed in; no hard bright ice shone back to blind them, but a scrubby brown earth covered in sparse furzy growth, through which, incredibly, tiny flowers grew. And they could hear birds, the same that they had heard in the distance a day ago, just catching the sound above the crash of the ocean. High above the churning sea, a flight of eider ducks passed, oblivious to suffering and to the joy they brought the starving, ragged men below them. They cast themselves down on the ground on their backs and felt the certainty of soil below them for the first time in over two years, watching the clouds twist and furl above them, each in his own private retreat – a meadow, a lakeside, a father's farmland, a garden.

The omelette was a luxury he allowed them only for that first meal, until they could be sure of a source of fuel. They were not yet saved; far from it. It was almost September. Aside from the blessing of the eggs, they had barely enough provisions to feed them for two weeks unless there was more hunting to be done; and there were precious few rounds left for the rifle. Edward didn't dare waste one to see if it would fire at all, after weeks of drenching in salt water. And they would need shelter and stores if they were to last the winter here. He walked the coastline; the telescope revealed, to the east, what he took to be a smaller island, and another to the north-east which he thought was separate from their own, although a thick frozen channel seemed to cement them together. At the southern end of their long, thin island, a greenish glacier carved out a path and ended in a sheer wall of ice to the sea. He could not find its likeness on any map; he still could not say if they were at the edge of the archipelago, far to the west, or on the western edge of the northern group.

If they could attempt to repair the kayak, they might scout the outlying islands. But without wood and tar, barely any tools, and only their own ruined and essential clothing to act as canvas, he doubted it would be possible. And if the party was to be split, how could he split them? He would need Nordahl's strength and know-how; but could he leave the silent Russian and the stupefied boy in the doctor's care? The island had saved them, and now they were trapped. They would have to wait out the winter, make what repairs and preparations they could, and set out on the ice again on foot, as soon as it would bear them in the spring.

So he reasoned it out as he wandered the clifftops, his telescope fixed on the hopeless horizon, a king made captive in his own castle.

I have picked you a bunch of yellow flowers, my love. They are flimsy, frail and sullied by my hands, but I know you would see their beauty. Emily, if you were here would you absolve me? I have led these men on a fool's errand, and can only hope to preserve them through the months to come, and fulfil at least part of my promise and come back to you. I beg your forgiveness that I am delayed here, but hope that our meeting will be the sweeter for our longer parting.

In England, Emily's hope was fading as the leaves turned brown; she saw the willow yellow and pall and resign, by scraps and tatters, its glory. She knew, as the first frosts came, that he would not return that year; the gunpowder crispness of the autumn air that she had always relished had no joy in it, for though the bonfires burned and the fireworks burst and dazzled, she knew that he would not return until the earth turned green again. The north wind that reached her in England, blowing the sky clear so that the stars shone brighter with the chill of it, had on its breath the ice that now must be closing about him, and at night she left her window open to feel it on her skin. He must by now be snug in his cabin below decks, and would have to wait all winter, storing up his triumph to tell her when he returned (yes, his triumph, because he could not have failed to reach it). So, he would not come this year, he had been detained by the sea; but he would be free of it in the spring and come back to her, and she had waited this long, she would wait. She could not allow herself to believe anything otherwise; for all his black mouth gaped at her in her dreams, it had no words to tell her that she would care to hear.

They spent the first day choosing a campsite, then set about salvaging the remains of what they carried. With oil and a knife, like Romans bathing, they scraped their skins of blackness as much as they could, laughing at the stripes of white left behind by the blade. Cleaner than they had been in months, with tea and the most delectable brown, rubbery omelettes they had ever tasted, they stretched themselves out on the hard, solid earth and toasted the discovery of Mackley's Land. Edward raised his tin cup to their tribute and inwardly prayed that the island was already named, because if this Utopia was truly a new-found no-place, he might never know where it lay or find his way back from it, and it would remain for ever unmarked on the map.

In the days that followed, they began to build a rough stone shelter, tipping raw eggs down their throats whenever they felt hungry. The eiders' nests were to be found in every crevice, their long white eggs abundant. Edward tested the rifle on a roosting hen he came upon while egg-hunting; it worked. He would not risk trying to shoot them out of the air (despite Nordahl's well-meant jibes – 'You call yourself an English gent, Captain? Are you waiting for the season?'), but when he found such easy shooting he took what he could. Twice he came upon a mother carrying her brood one at a time to the water in her beak, while the others waited patiently for their turn; it needed only one shot, for it was easy to wring the little ones' helpless necks when they were left undefended, for all they pecked and flapped. They skinned and dried his kills and rendered the fat, salivating, scrimping out small portions of fresh meat, knowing they must lay away provisions; and in the meantime threw another egg down their gullets, garnished for breakfast and supper with the red lichen that clung to the rock. After such privation, the glut was too much for them; they could not control their glee, feeling the dark yellow yolks slip down like oysters. Within a few days, this diet had its inevitable effect.

> Andreev complains terribly of his stomach and is beginning to stink to high heaven, as I fear we all are. He says it is the eggs but what else have we to eat? The duck meat must keep, and he will not take what else there is. High heaven indeed; we are so high now upon the world and there is no heaven here in sight. But still, the little yellow flowers, and solid land, are perhaps a poor man's paradise.

Dr Wilkinson did his best to stave off treating their condition with laudanum, the panacea of the age; he feared wasting their only anaesthetic, he said, although he hoped they would not have need of it. But as the men grew daily weaker, Edward at last insisted that he open the chest and dose them, to soothe their suffering guts. The doctor hesitated, relented, fetched the case from the shelter. 'Very well, Captain,' he said, and without taking his eyes from Edward's he unlatched his store, and lifted out first one then another empty jar, and another half full, which he handed to Edward. There was a single full one left in the case. A pitiful wail drew Andreev and Nordahl from their work to see their captain and the doctor, eyes locked in understanding, and, a little way off, Compton-Hill crouched on the ground clutching his knees, his gaze wide and watery, chewing and chewing at his dirty nails.

'I see.'

'He must have been taking the key while I slept. I should have seen it. I thought he was merely exhausted, and frightened. I didn't think to check the chest until two days ago and . . . Look at him. It's a shame, that's all, a damn shame. I thought to keep it from his father. I'm sorry, Edward.'

Edward turned to the boy, whose eyes remarkably widened further, and welled with tears.

'Yes, I see. Thank you, Doctor. Hugh, fetch yourself a blanket, I think you will need it. We will watch over you until it's out of your system; if you can't stand it, you will have to learn to do so. And, so help me, you had better pray that none of us has greater need of what you've taken.'

Ignoring the grizzling, penitent heap at his feet, he turned to the others. 'Anton, you suffer worst; ask the doctor to give you a drop. For the rest, we must be more careful, and curb our greed.'

They pegged out a smaller shelter to the side of their stone hut for Hugh to sweat and shiver in, so that their own already troubled rest might not be further disturbed. Edward heard him moaning, bleating, sometimes shouting in his fever; Wilkinson tended him with water and the cleanest cloth they could muster, under strict instruction

242

to feel no pity. His bowels, so long stopped by the remedy the others needed, were let loose, and although his appetite did not recover he was fed only on precious bouillon, unable to digest anything more substantial, taking mournful choking sips from the spoon the doctor held for him between whining apologies. Edward knew the disgust the others felt; but when Nordahl came to him to ask why the boy should have this privilege while Anton must endure, he could only reply, 'Would you let him die, Lars?' He did not press for an answer, uncertain of his own.

With every passing midnight the skies began to grow perceptibly darker. Soon, twilight was upon them. The eiders' eggs grew scant within two weeks of their landing, and one evening, as they settled for the night, Hugh called out to them in a voice so measured and sane that they were drawn outside to find him gazing at the pale purple sky, against which the sad silhouette of hundreds upon hundreds of birds on the wing was cast. Wherever this island was, the five men were left alone upon it; unable to take flight so easily for warmer climes, they must make it their home for the winter.

High over the house, a flock passes, wings spread and rising on an updraught. Julia watches as they vanish into the depthless blue, with a soar of sadness, knowing that homesick pull of the heart.

THE END

The weeks passed. They struggled to keep a fire burning with the little fuel they could scavenge, and knew that the darkness would grow ever colder; they stayed huddled together for twenty hours in the day, having brought a chastened and haggard Hugh back into the fold. They covered the floor with what grasses they could crop; the interior of the hut, windowless but for a small hole for a chimney, was dank and reeking despite the cold, the oil that they burned giving off a greasy black smoke which still could not cover the stink of their own effluence. There was nothing to hunt for; the winter sea was barren, the nests empty, disintegrating and finally covered with snow. The sea froze again, ice clinging to the coast and spreading outwards over the open water like a creeping bloom on fruit skin, flowering in patches until all around was whiteness, under the dark and flashing sky. Edward's record becomes largely diagrammatic, numerical: he lists their ever-decreasing supplies; the angle of the lowering sun, and the moon when it makes its appearance in September; his few active hours

spent mapping and mapping the unknown coastline. When he can bear to write in words, he can
only offer despair: 'How impatient I was to leave
our safe, warm ship for this. If any of us live they
will say I was a fool, and rightly. Your foolish
husband again bids you goodnight, for it seems
the sun has set.'

Late evening, the sun long since vanished now: in
her mind Julia inks in the contours of an unknown
vista, a silhouette against the snow.

Edward gazed out over the frozen sea. The sky
shivered gold and rose above him, silver cords
winding across it. The lights no longer seemed to
blaze the fire of his own ambition; they were
remote, aloof, teasing his vanity with their impossible insubstantial beauty. He was half blind with
hunger. Then something moved, out on the ice: a
fox, now as motionless as one of John's mounts,
paw raised to run. His sight sharpened; he watched
her with a clarity akin to hallucination. He could
see her skinny flanks shudder. He could see the rime
of her breath on the air. She could smell the stink
of him. Her black eyes met his. He fired.

The faces of his companions appeared at the door
to the shelter, alerted by the blast in the silence. It
echoed about their heads, as hollow as the night.
Edward had reached his kill; they watched as he lifted
her, scrambling up a ramp of rock and ice until he
reached the top and fell to his knees, laying her down
so that he could support himself with both hands,

light-headed, laughing. He struggled to his feet. He could barely carry her; he brought the body to them, holding her aloft by the scruff of her scrawny neck.

'A pity to let this one pass me by.' It was as close as he could come to a joke in this misery.

And so they fell upon that last feast, the last fresh blood they would taste. They retreated to the shelter, hunkering in together, pulling the lice from their rags and slipping them between their lips, just to feel the crunch between the teeth. They did not speak unless it was to speak of dying; none believed they would be saved in death.

Julia puts a hand to her mouth, forces herself past it, past the place she has so often stopped. Having followed him so far, all through his journey, she cannot now abandon him.

> Anton lost his left hand today; the right is but a thumb. He has lost, too, his English; I do not think he knows where he is, or what. He does not return a man's gaze, but seems to search our faces as we feed him, as if he cannot quite make something out. As if to say, politely, 'Forgive me but I don't quite follow.' Like those happy drunks and madmen one sees on the city street. With his bland smile, dribbling, he is returned to infancy, and I am glad for him. He would not wish to know himself as he is.

Two days later, by Edward's reckoning, Andreev died.

Dr Wilkinson began to fade, as quietly as he had lived; Hugh, distraught at the loss of the man who had pitied him, fussed around him with futile, frostbitten hands, swabbing at his face with a dirty cloth. In the half-sleeping fug of the shelter, Edward became aware of a muttering, low and unceasing for hours, stopped only by the precious pieces of freshwater ice that Hugh placed on his patient's tongue. In what should have been the morning, the murmur of the doctor's mind at last ran down. Hugh, who had let his head drop exhausted in the man's lap, was woken by the silence, filling it with a wail when he saw the dead eyes, the jaw agape. He was alone with the corpse; he could hear outside the striking of metal against earth like iron; Edward and Nordahl were digging a grave in the hard ground.

It was some hours before they returned for the doctor's body, exhausted, to find their labour doubled; for the boy lay prone, spittle still foaming at the corners of his cracked mouth, his pupils flooding his eyes black, wide with terror at whatever he had last gazed upon. They had to prise the drained glass phial from the clutch of his dead hand.

This, at least, is Edward's tale; and there is no other to contradict him, so we must trust with

Julia that this is how the boy met his end. 'Hugh is dead, and the last of the tincture gone. For Lars and I there will be no last escape into oblivion. Perhaps I cannot blame him; perhaps I envy him. But now at least there is not the temptation; we will not be unmanned but go sober to our end if it comes.'

He was calmed by the moonlight but terribly, desperately lonely, a loneliness that was so hopeless it became one with the feeling of calm. No panic now; no fear or trembling, but for the cold. 'The human spirit, Emily,' he writes, 'has reserves of fortitude that I had never wished to imagine, and that I hope you must never plumb the depths of; for they are what I call upon in the quiet emptiness of this desolation.'

And Edward is right: these weeks of darkness and ending are far beyond the safety of today's sunshine; he does not have the liberty of simply setting the book down. To Julia, this above all is hardest to conceive of, this period of nothing but survival, of sleep and half waiting for the ease of death, and imagining sometimes, waking to darkness, that it is already come. But Emily, who lived and waited in comfort while he was starved and frozen, still knew in her way what it was to feel quiet and empty, and desolate.

The night drew on, day after day, without lightening; they waited for the sun. Their brief hours of daily toil were divided between exhausting ventures upon the floe, for freshwater ice to melt for drinking; salvaging what they could of sleds and snowshoes; and digging a last grave, so that one at least might be decently buried if such a time came. Edward does not reflect on this morbid labour, perhaps to the last resisting total despair; he insists on his belief in the spring. 'We can do nothing but wait for the first light, and hope to last so long; wait for the birds to return and then I will walk back to you, if I have to crawl.'

Pages of diagrams follow, transcribing the tricks of the moon and tracing what seem to be routes through the archipelago, with Mackley's Land transposed upon other islands or the open sea. In one, it becomes an additional Orkney – 'so close we are, my love'; in another it sprouts a vast tail, becomes a whale that will swim them to safety on her back. Every entry in the diary is dated, but Edward is often unsure if he has slept for one hour or thirteen, eight or twenty. He might have slept through the year, even, or ten, and still the night was unchanging. On what he takes to be Christmas Day they savour one of the choicer last morsels of chewy meat, and share an omelette of surely rotten egg, and take a hard ship's biscuit each. As they choose to welcome the New Year they sing in cracked voices the songs that Lars, long ago in a distant city, had taught the captain and his new wife. And on what he believes to be

20 January 1902, he writes five final pages in a hand barely strong enough to mark the paper. What is not illegible is often nonsensical.

He is nearing the end. No hope of the sun rising; the darkness has entered his eyes and his mind, so that even by the lit fire he sees only dimly. But he is close, he is close to it, he writes; he tries to write it down for her, what he can see now in the darkness. An Arctic map, he writes, is a map of concepts. Edgeless, shifting – no fixed centre, but I would have known it, had I walked upon it and felt the world turn. I set out now upon the ice in my mind and draw near it, now, my mind is as wide and clear as the white plain before me. Boundless, edgeless. The still point will come to meet me. Grace, all around me. I am nearing it. Circling. It is beautiful yet, this terrible place, the senseless lovely lights across the sky. It is dark now, I cannot see. A shard of ice has splintered my eye and she will come to carry me north to the still point. All about her is frozen but within her cloak it is warm, covered in her dark brass hair and warmed by a crimson blush . . .

These are the last faded ribbons of his tattered mind, which Helen did her best to unravel and reweave for Emily to catch at; Julia now takes up their frayed endings. A last fragment of clarity, and then the pages are nothing but white: 'I am sorry that I did not reach it and that you waited in vain; if I find that there is a place beyond this then I shall wait for you there in turn. I cannot go on with it, I fear; I cannot go on.'

So it ends for Edward. It's over, again. The old lament: 'I cannot go on.' Julia, too, cannot. And in another hand, the echo, 'I cannot go on without . . .' She lets the book fall upon her chest; she lets her eyes close.

In 1959 a Soviet scientific expedition found evidence of a makeshift shelter on a minor island in the north of Franz Josef Land, containing the petrified corpse of what had once been an unusually tall, broad-shouldered man, his red hair still clinging in strands to his skull; close by, four tin crosses marked a row of shallow graves. Upon exhumation, the fourth on the right gave up the body of Edward Mackley, skin stretched taut over his handsome cheeks, eyes milk-white, white teeth protruding under the straggle of moustache that hung from his shrunken black lips; when they tried to move him, they found his back was firmly glued into a solid block of ice filling the base of the coffin. The grave was rudely raided by the party that found it, in the hope of identifying the man whose name was unknown to them, so that his last effects were taken from him. To avoid upsetting the strained international relations of the time, after their government's inspection confirmed that there was nothing untoward, their findings were handed over to the Royal Navy. So his diary and the photograph he held as he was dying were returned to England, along with the remnants of the camp, which included an old tin telescope and a broken silver watch.

Emily was eighty-one years old, the heat of her youth and the loss of her maidenhood long since forgotten. She took care herself not to recall it, and was rarely troubled in those days by dreams. After sixty years of waiting, she looked down at her twenty-year-old self, the flush of her cheeks in the picture quite faded just as she herself had paled into old age, and wept. It was little more than the spilling over of an old woman's watery eyes.

But I was waiting

In the afternoon sun that streams through the attic, a hundred years after Edward Mackley died, the words that his wife heard at last at the end of her life now rest against Julia's heart. She exhales, exhausted, half sleeping. 'I cannot go on with it.'

But I waited

The words whisper about the house and into garden and out, a sigh caught on the breeze and borne across the sea to the north, stretching ever north, the longing scribed indelibly in memory's invisible ink. Julia is lost in the snow.

Waiting all that time, outstretched at the still point, I did not weep. I waited and he did not come, and I could not go on without

But she did, patient Emily, she went on without him, and when at last she knew he was gone, she let him go.

When Edward's body was at last found buried on a small island in the Franz Josef Land archipelago, Emily Mackley sighed the long, deep sigh that breathes through these rooms still, and went to bed until she died. She had lived patiently alone in her husband's brother's house so that he would know where to find her if he found his way back; she had lived through two world wars, seen three kings die and another abandon his crown for a wife, and seen a woman once again take the throne; she had suffered, and seen suffering, and done what she could to aid those that suffered; and all the time Edward had been resting, far from bombs and all the horrors and the wonders and triumphs of the century he'd seen only the cusp of, out in the snow. And now it was her turn to rest, and she lay down and rested. A little less than a year later, she died. They said she'd finally allowed her patient heart to break. The truth was less romantic, but it may have been that her liver was holding out for her heart's sake, just long enough to be sure at last. At the age of eighty-two she had had, they said, a good innings. She kept her figure, and her looks, well into old age;

she enjoyed a drink, and why shouldn't she? A well-preserved old lady, pickled in gin, they said, with the affection families have for their harmless alcoholics.

The last of the staff had departed some years since, but she had no need of a nursemaid as she neared the end; Helen was on hand, watching as she slept a little more each day. She brought her trays, plying her scant appetite with crackers, smoked salmon, sometimes a boiled egg; sweet tea in the morning with whole milk; thick, dark hot chocolate at night, a shared ritual that Helen had brought back from Milan; and, in between, gin and stories. They drank slowly and steadily, sipping away at a slow cocktail hour that began after lunchtime and, after a brief hiatus for Emily's afternoon nap, resumed and lingered until the sun had fully set.

PART V

Listen:

.   .   .   .   .

Five o'clock is happening all over the house, at intervals. It started five minutes ago, in the drawing room, the clack of the clock so decisive that there's no sense arguing, although it is mistaken. Then the silent steel hands of the kitchen clock slid into place. They have been counting the hours unobtrusively since 1973, with occasional pauses of sometimes days at a time before anyone notices the battery has gone, and often even then a week or more might pass before someone takes the trouble to drag a kitchen stool to the doorway and clamber up to change it and reset the hands to whatever their own possibly erroneous timepiece deems it to be. (Simon could reach it effortlessly from the ground, but it was Julia who spotted the poor thing stuck at the sad downturned angle of twenty-five to six last May. Dark so early? she'd thought at first, then realized the truth was two and a half hours later at least.)

Five o'clock, then, as set in accordance with some other inaccurate dial, has passed in the kitchen. The lamb should go into the oven soon, but Julia is not here, and even Tess has given up her vigil; she is curled up quite illegally on the rug in the bedroom, just beside the head which has been left attached to the empty fur. It is a favourite spot, forbidden to her, but the door was left open and Tess is hardly a stickler for the rules; and Simon, who she knows would lift her and drop her without ceremony in the corridor, isn't around.

Julia's wristwatch has not been sought since it was laid out carefully on the dressing table last night; neglected as ever by her gaze, it lights delicately upon the hour (a tiny silver line is all that marks it, covered by the slender silver hand entirely). One minute and thirteen seconds later, the red digits of the radio alarm follow suit.

In an office overlooking the plane trees lining the Thames, at precisely the moment the bedside clock changes, five o'clock occurs, reverberating to Big Ben's assertive bong. There is no drawn-out process of anticipation and catch-up here; the display on Simon's computer, on the mobile phone he's still ignoring, and on his watch are all in soundless but assured synchrony.

As the distinctive clonk of the grandfather clock in the hallway triggers the ratchet of the lead weight, and the chiming of the hour commences with a thud (only eighty-four seconds late), Julia wakes with a start in the attic.

A VISITOR

It is hard to say if it is clonk, ratchet, thud or chime that stirs Julia's snooze, or if it is the imminence of this sequence, like a sleeper who is so accustomed to the minute of their daily waking that they always anticipate their alarm clock by a second. For while she does not habitually wake at this hour, she had planned to prepare herself at five for her guest, and the soft thudding of the clock is constant in her, her heart keeping time with the house. She does not even hear it in bed, as Simon does; it is just a part of the sound of the night.

So, here is Julia, waking with a start at the striking of the hour. Her neck is stiff; the rose-coloured bolster has become squashed down into the crevice between the seat cushion and the arm of the chaise so that the ridge of her skull is now jammed against hard upholstered wood. Her hair is damp at the nape with day-sleep sweat; when she stands up (rolling as if to the floor and then suddenly upright), she finds her dress is stuck to her back, her knickers uncomfortably wedged, her skin tacky with sweat and dust. She catches

259

at an echo in the air, five chimes hanging in the silence:

Five chimes after the thud; why should I wake with a start? What is it I should be starting?

The sun has passed over the apex now, and the dimmed attic is thick with a viscid brown heat. Only a few faint motes dance in the deep yellow light. She looks down at the detritus of her morning's work: telescope, rifle, snow goggles, paper everywhere. Her notebook open on the desk with doodles of a fox in the margin, a double moon, a dog baring horrible teeth, a set of snow-shoed footprints disappearing off the edge of the page. A bundle of letters now retied with black ribbon. A photograph in faded silver of a young woman laughing, her eyes still bright, skis just visible below a skirt to the ankles

Setting out upon the snow to meet him. Too hot for snow. Too hot, I'm too hot.

She stands for a moment longer, uncomfortable in her sticky skin, lifting her hair away from her neck with one hand, snapping at her underwear's elastic to straighten it with the other. She ruffles the hair at the crown, matting it, then scratches the top of her head with her nails in an uncon-scious cartoon gesture of puzzlement that Simon used to find hilarious. The shock of her waking has left an empty sick-feeling pit in the wake of her stomach's lurch.

Hungry?

She looks up at the polar bear; it roars back, unhelpfully silent.

Polar bear posed with a roar, John taking the paw . . . John. John?

With a rush of clarity she remembers the lamb and, more urgently, the impending arrival of her cousin Jonathan, who is in London on business and dropping by for a visit before driving back to Sheffield, where he now lives, having left America two years ago; he got married, but she hasn't seen him since he was a boy, because he's busy with his job doing . . .

Something . . . And didn't come to Aunt Helen's funeral because . . .

But Julia has dashed from the attic down the stairs, the end of the thought suspended, having no time now for biography (and leaving the ship's clock in *Box 002* to make it to five in its own time). Barefoot, she does not clatter as she goes, and pads speedily along the corridor past John and his waltzing bear, and down the wider stairs to the first floor (creak, crack, no longer avoiding the tired wood of the centre), stripping off her dress as she crosses the bedroom. In the adjoining bathroom (airless, even hotter than it was at night, although the extractor fan whirrs noisily to life as she switches the light on), she takes the soft natural sponge from the shower, still floppy with damp and now clammy from the morning, and runs it under the cold tap and presses it over her skin. Her joints are surprisingly flexible; there is no place on her back she cannot reach with ease. Her shoulders, cramped in the chaise for too long, relish the stretch. A similar sponge, in its neatly labelled jar in the attic, bobs briefly to the surface of her mind:

Sponge in alcohol, old soak . . .

But all other thoughts are dispelled by the cool air from the window on her dampened skin as she returns to the bedroom. She drops her dress beside Tess on the rug on her way to the dressing table, noting out loud in passing, for the sake of appearances, that she is a bad cat. Tess glances up for a moment before curling back into yellow slit-eyed contentment in the fur, turning her head half upside down to expose the chin, in case anyone should feel inclined to stroke it. But Julia is at the mirror now, and Tess understands the need for preening.

Julia combs out her hair, pulling it free of the band which is valiantly clinging to a few last locks, and tugging first her hands and then a brush through it until it shines again. She sits on the padded stool in her underwear and pulls her cheeks down long with both long hands, exposing the inside lids under her eyes, and utters a little groan, which means

When I was a girl, my face was uncreased and wrinkles were something old people had, and make-up was excitingly bright pink and cheap purple and anyway forbidden and rouge was a word I longed for, and now I must struggle to attain what they call a natural look and there is nothing more unnatural or unfair than ageing.

Her mind is as creased as her skin from sleeping; she is groggy from the stifling heat in the attic and the half-dreams of Edward and Emily that linger about her, caught in the folds of thought, the shifting below her, the roll of the sea, the fall through the ice, the waiting, the horrible drawn-out death . . . She smoothes a cream with her hands about the contours of her face, across the forehead, which puckers briefly in annoyance at the small worry line between her brows; up the fine, high Mackley cheekbones that her mother admired; covering the darkness that has crept below her bronze-brown eyes, through which, following the line of their gaze as they meet themselves now in the mirror, we might still glimpse a remnant of the Arctic night, a deep, deep indigo lit by glittering stars. She frames them in kohl, smudging the edges gently so she doesn't look sharp, and brushes her lashes with black, and flutters briefly a butterfly kiss to her own reflection; *coquette*. The word prompts a whim, and she takes up a red lipstick that she knows Simon can't stand, and paints it on thick to receive her guest; her cousin will see how glamorous she is, how well the house fits about her beautiful life.

To match, she chooses a simple black dress and steps into it so as not to smudge the red, wriggles it up over her hips, zips and belts it, brushes her hair again, and runs down the stairs to the kitchen. The sun has shifted around, no longer pooling on the floor, so that she can feel only the residue of it on the tiles through her soles

Terra cotta, terra firma, better put some shoes on . . .

The kitchen is half submerged in the cool earth, and offers some respite from the heat. Nevertheless, by the time she has turned on the oven, stretched up to lift the lamb from the top of the fridge, foraged in the dusty wine cellar for a particular bottle she knows Simon likes, which of course is stowed in the most awkward possible corner, wrestled with the over-stuffed salad tray to pull out the beans and beetroot that have burrowed their way to the bottom and then forced everything back in so that she can close the fridge again, grappled with the clatter of the drawer full of obscure utensils to find the meat thermometer, speared the lamb with it and placed it in the oven, blowing out her cheeks as she opens the door as if hoping to push the blast of heat back in, and trodden in a carelessly abandoned chunk of fish by Tess's bowl – by the time all this has been accomplished, she is regretting her lack of planning and wishing she had come here first, before dressing. Her hair has reglued itself to the back of her neck, her hands feel grimy from the bottles of wine and the grease of the roasting pan, her foot presumably smells of tuna . . . She rushes back up the stairs (without pausing, this time, to admire the butterflies).

Too hot to wear black, you idiot, absorbing heat, white reflects like ice, like snow, oh to lie down now in the soft snow . . . I'll have to change, wear white, silk like snow like a wedding, no, not like a wedding, ridiculous, too much for a Thursday afternoon . . .

She flips through her wardrobe, each possibility dismissed with the satisfying metallic swoosh of a hanger on the rail. The wardrobe, which was Arabella's and once had to accommodate layer upon layer of lace and satin, is vast. In what Arabella thought of as the French style, it is as shiny-smooth as stretched skin, bulging at the sides as if it can barely contain the contents of its belly, although it somehow contrives to look gracious, tottering on its little feet and topped with

265

intricate twists and curls of foliage. Julia's more modest collection of skirts, shirts and dresses now hangs alongside a few remaining furs, including a sable stole which she coveted as a child and wouldn't dare to wear now that it is hers, although she sometimes brings it out to touch the soft, almost sickening crinkle of the edges of the skin. Her clothes had been crushed together in the small closet in their Balham flat; when she hung them here they shook themselves out, brushed themselves down and breathed a sigh of uncrumpled relief – only to be left in neglected piles on the floor as they always had been.

She selects, finally, a pale peach shift which she remembers wearing last week and discovers retreating under the bed. She checks her watch – it is almost half past – and, as an afterthought, clips it on. As she brushes her hair one last time and attempts to bind it neatly in a bun (it begins to slide as soon as her back is turned), she hears the doorbell, the old-fashioned ding-dong that has announced visitors since 1910. She once again descends the stairs, hopping on the landing with one hand on the banister to wipe at her foot with a tissue (the butterflies, implacable above their labels, rest in their rows), pulls on a pair of sandals she has fortuitously abandoned by the door, takes a moment to check herself in the hallway mirror and, meeting with the approval of the glass her ancestors passed through, turns to the dark form that looms without, a brown shadow through the amber glass.

So a stranger is about to intrude upon Julia's day, a real, living person to join the ghosts that she has woken and which swarm still about her. She is a little light-headed, a little giddy from her reverie, and she is still adjusting to the warm, solid world after hours following in Edward's path through the bright snow. She almost had him, today, she thinks. She could almost touch him, with Emily's hand. And she feels strangely nervous of opening the door, as if the spell of sanctuary she has cast about her will be broken. She puts the odd twist in her stomach down to the flurry of her waking. But it may presage something; she may be unwise to dismiss it. Who can say what a stranger will bring in his wake?

Julia opens the door and finds the frame filled by a man putting his hand out to be shaken. The handshake is firm and sure, not crushing, the kind of handshake she likes.

Jonathan Mackley is, like Julia, John's great-grandchild. His father was the son of John and Arabella's second son, Thomas, who was Aunt Helen's other brother. A little older than Julia, Jonathan is, then, some kind of cousin – she will work it out at some point, the removes. The surname has come to him through four generations; since Julia married, he is the last Mackley left to bear it, and has not yet passed it on. Names are borne like fruit, ripening on the old family tree, she thinks. He looks nothing like her, or like a Mackley; although as he clasps her hand and appraises her with his bright eye, she thinks she sees for a moment Edward's gaze, looking out of the portrait and far beyond, to the north and glory. Jonathan's very blue eyes are not black but they have that same stare about them. He is tall, not so tall as Simon, but broader, powerful and thick-set. His surprising orange hair (from Arabella's side) is beginning to fade and he has a pale blond neat beard and almost invisible eyebrows, lost against his ruddy face, and wears a very clean-looking white shirt, no tie, and little round glasses on a little pointed nose which give him the appearance of an intellectual, friendly, slightly overweight ferret. She notices that they are still shaking hands, and also that his eye has not left hers, and she wonders what he makes of her and feels suddenly very conscious of her red lips.

'This *must* be Julia,' he says warmly, and she feels pleasure flush her chest, knowing by his emphasis that he remembers her fondly, and admires what she has become.

'Yes, I suppose it must. How nice to see you, Jonathan.'

She leads him to the drawing room and asks if he would like a drink before they go upstairs, and adds hurriedly that most of the archive is housed in the attic if he'd like to see it while he's here, because she fears her question might have sounded salacious. Then she has to stop herself thinking about what it might be like to sleep with Jonathan Mackley, who is after all a cousin, albeit at some remove, and not an especially attractive one at that – or at least, she corrects herself, not to her taste; she doesn't wish to be cruel.

'A gin and tonic would hit the spot' is his response, not tea or coffee or even lemonade or water which was what Julia had imagined herself to be offering, on a weekday afternoon. But in the kitchen as she hears the ice clink into the glass, scents the sharp lime and the bitter spice of the spirit, she anticipates the tang and bite on her own tongue and wholeheartedly agrees – what an instinct for the apposite this cousin of hers displays. Look at him there with his ankle resting on his knee at such wonderful ease in his armchair, smiling at her as she comes in, without adjusting his pose; the way a man sits in a room alone will tell much, she thinks. She hands him the tall glass and he settles back, the redness visibly leaving his face as he lets out a long exaggerated sigh of contentment.

'That's just the ticket. I'm afraid London makes me thirsty; I can't take the heat on a day like today.' He speaks with a trace of an American accent; Great-uncle Thomas moved to Boston as a young man in the Twenties and this branch of the family have rarely been seen on this side of the ocean until Jonathan's return, although they have determinedly clung to their clipped English vowels through three generations. Under the influence of Jonathan's mid-Atlantic intonation, and in her soft peach slip and red lipstick and sipping her gin, Julia feels herself suddenly cast as some sparky Golden Age Hollywood heroine or sultry *femme*, in some noir or screwball, a feeling that could never fail to please her. She watches him, and remembers a midsummer-themed birthday party, an awkward, rather plump, older ginger boy too embarrassed by his accent to speak, looking longingly at the sweets; she remembers how she chose the nicest little cake and held it out to him on her hand.

Jonathan's broad face beams in the sun from the window.

'Ah, that's hit the spot, sure enough,' he smiles. He sips from his glass happily, strangely delicate in his big hands. His eye comes to rest on the Mackley family portrait on the wall opposite Edward and Emily, which is haunted by four dim spectres, the light reflecting on its dark, oily surface so that only the starkest contrasts are visible. Two gaunt and thin figures on the left, the smaller just taller than the other's knee; the pale amorphous mass of Arabella on the right, with a fat pallid blob of baby on her knee, his own grandfather-to-be.

'It's been a time since I was last here. Not since I was a boy,' he says, peering into the viscous depths; then, returning his gaze to Julia, remembers

270

something he had meant to say. 'I am sorry I couldn't come to Aunt Helen's funeral. I haven't been to this house since I was a boy,' he repeats, 'but it seems just yesterday that she sat where you sit now. Extraordinary woman.'

'Yes,' Julia smiles, in a way that does not include him, although she does not mean to be rude. There is a pause. Jonathan again casts about the room. He recalls a warm summer's day, a tableau of nymphs, of little well-behaved fairy-girls with narrow faces weaving flowers into each other's hair, sitting around his extraordinary aunt who wore . . . Did she wear a peach evening dress? Were her lips carmine? He remembers them whispering and laughing in a pretty, secret way and then fluttering off and alighting again on their butterfly wings, calling to each other, 'Peaseblossom!' 'Cobweb!' He thinks it was Julia that offered him one of their tiny cakes, peppermint-green and impossibly dainty with a pair of cake-wings settled on the cream, as if it might fly off teasing from his fat little hand. This scene has not occurred to him in many years; but here he is again in the very same room. Julia reclines in the wing-back chair, bare legs crossed and one shoe dangling, her arm resting on the chair's arm and the oak knob nestled in the hollow of her palm as if shaped by it, just as Aunt Helen sat. He looks around him; the brightness suspends what he sees in a shimmer of dust, as if this little pocket of time that seems to clack on with the clock was called

271

to a halt some decades ago, and the hands that move about the dial are an illusion only, always counting off the same hours. The rug is faded gold and blue. The walls are faded ochre. The faded curtains hide channels of rich sapphire in their folds; they are rarely drawn over the muslin drapes in summer. Jonathan senses that beneath every object, where surfaces have been hidden from the years, everything is vivid still; beneath the fade of time, the past still thrives. He wants to ask if it was indeed her who held out that tiny sugar-dusted treat on the palm of her hand. He sips his gin. He says:

'You don't think of redecorating?'

Julia, still smiling to herself, almost starts at this.

'Oh, you know. All the family things . . .'

Jonathan doesn't know, but makes a politely prompting noise in the hope of an explanation. He remembers, vaguely, that Julia is some kind of historian, an archivist. She is not at work. There was no question of her being at work when he asked if he might visit. Perhaps there is a connection.

'I'm trying to sort it all. It's all such a mess. And Aunt Emily's, too. So much has been left here. Valuable things. I should say Great-aunt, shouldn't I. No, Great-great-aunt, isn't she? Helen was Great-aunt. John was Great-grandfather, and Edward Great-great-uncle and the other Edward not great, just Grandfather. But your great-uncle, so he was great too I suppose. So much greatness.'

Julia is blushing now. She has quite lost her thread. But Jonathan laughs as if it is a joke she meant to make, which he finds most amusing.

'All these Mackley generations, half of us called the same thing. We all just collapse in on each other,' he says; he is so understanding, she thinks, so kind.

'As if he might walk in at any moment with the ice still on him,' she says gratefully, unexpectedly.

Jonathan looks surprised, but only for a moment. He is finding the conversation refreshingly free-wheeling after the stuffy boardroom. 'If only he had, I suppose. But then I might not be enjoying such delightful company this afternoon. Who knows how it might have gone, if he'd come back?'

Julia laughs. 'I should hope I would still be right here! With perhaps one or two more polar bears to keep me company.'

'Well, yes. Perhaps. But where would Edward be?'

'Edward?'

'Your grandfather, I mean. The son. Would he have come about, would he have been a different man? You know.' But Julia, in turn, does not know. There is that twist in her stomach again. Just the gin, she thinks.

'I'm not sure I . . .'

'I wonder if everyone's family is so fascinating.'

'Why would he not . . .'

'Just imagine, if he'd come back too late,' oblivious Jonathan plunges on.

'Too late?' falters Julia.

'If Edward had already been born. Would they have told him?'

She takes another sip; another nauseous twist. The ice cube she's munched and swallowed has become an unbearable lump of chill in her stomach suddenly. The freeze is spreading to her forehead. Far out on the edge of her awareness, Julia hears something massive groaning. A judder in the world that resounds in her chest. Something shifts and threatens to split.

Sometimes secrets are patient and will wait a century to be revealed; they seem solid enough to build upon; they will hold, perhaps; but perhaps there is some animal sense, something that tells us that they will eventually give way. So we should not be surprised by the freeze that is stealing upon Julia, a sensation akin to panic. She has waited for this, without knowing there was anything to know. If she'd looked closer, she might have seen it in her own eyes in the mirror, but why would she think to seek secrets there? What does that indigo at the centre hide, dark as the Arctic night?

'I'm sorry, Jonathan,' says Julia, rising to take his glass, mixing more drinks at the cabinet. There she stands with her back to the room, wondering if she should fetch more ice and lime from the kitchen and if there can possibly be any sense to what he's saying. Her narrow back, and hair just beginning to work itself free again, a runnel of cold sweat between her sharp shoulders, but quite composed and casual except for the rattle of the bottle on the rim of the glass as if she has the shakes, drinking on a hangover, what can you expect, she thinks, what can he possibly be saying? She is watching herself from a distance, watching herself moving and speaking like an ordinary person might, in a voice that sounds like it ought to if she were the ordinary slightly glamorous middle-class housewife she appears to be . . . 'Told him what? I'm afraid I'm being rather dense.'

Jonathan has been rolling a cigar back and forth between his fingers, wondering if they might take a stroll outside and waiting for an appropriate pause to suggest it, and only now registers the incomprehension his idle imaginings have met with. The strong strain of tactless inattention has survived all through Arabella's line, although it has been tempered in this man with kindness.

'Well, you know. About Emily and John.'

Julia looks politely blank.

'Did no one ever tell you?'

The creak and groan that sounded from afar grows more urgent, becomes a physical lurch beneath the feet. The frozen sea is roaring. What seemed solid will not remain so. The ice in their glasses has melted in the heat. She should certainly restore it.

'Let me get more ice and we'll go into the garden,' says Julia in her normal voice, seeing the cigar. Smoking seems like a good idea, a good, normal thing to do. She takes the glasses into the kitchen and yanks at the stuck freezer drawer and bangs the ice-cube tray on the counter so hard that the ice flies everywhere and she takes the pieces that fell on the floor and puts them in her own glass, its rim distinctly smeared with red, which seems the socially correct thing to do; then she slices two more wedges of lime, taking extra care not to cut herself, which she so often does, being so easily distracted. But now she is certainly concentrating on the knife, there was something Jonathan was saying, something rather important, but for now she is slicing a lime. He can explain it in the garden.

Here they are, walking in the garden. She tries not to hear the words whispering, I cannot go on with it, I cannot go on.

But I waited . . .

Jonathan, failing to register the seismic heave his words have triggered, seeing only Julia's apparent calm and enjoying his cigar in the sunshine, is telling the story. Julia is smoking her second cigarette of the day as she listens to his voice beside her, far off; she gave no thought to lighting it, she is barely aware of the thing in her hands or the smoke she takes in deep with every inhalation because what had seemed solid is slowly, slowly cracking beneath her, wider and slow

Wide and slow, a crevasse widens, a chasm, a chasm, a chasm . . .

She cannot think beyond this, she is falling into this empty echo. It is cruel perhaps to force the thought into the shape of words.

She is Emily's great-grandchild.

I cannot go on without . . .

Emily did not wait. She could wait no longer alone, in the cold. She could not go on without. So soon, she betrayed him. Julia herself exists because of this betrayal.

It is so hot this afternoon. The day is relentless, pressing up against the evening with a close threat as if on the point of drenching, although the sky is endlessly blue, a depthless ocean, a blue that looks black if you look up long enough to let it consume you. The sun has been too long on Julia's dark blonde head, soaking through, her mind all sun-stroked; she is dizzy with the gin and the nicotine, the heat and the glare. She is silent. They smoke together and admire the garden. The smoke will make the sheets smell, she thinks. She hasn't taken the washing in; she considers this. It doesn't seem to matter. The silence becomes awkward. And why after all should they have anything in common? Blithe, blundering, kind Jonathan; Julia, born of betrayal. Jonathan starts talking again, he is saying something about Edward and Thomas, something about death; about Aunt Helen, did Aunt Helen not know? Julia is overheated and frozen to the core; there is sweat on her brow and down her spine. She lights another cigarette and inhales deeply and flutters out over the chasm.

In the first damp chills of September, in 1902, four Norwegian survivors were found on Spitzbergen, and Emily Mackley ebbed away to her room where she was thought to be grieving, or whatever equivalent is left to the wives of the not dead but lost. But she emerged from her self-imposed confinement the following summer, fuller and quieter, and assured anyone who asked that she had not given up hope. A slip of the tongue and the truth is out: she was, indeed, confined, in the sense in which her contemporaries used the word. And no one knew; no one but John and Arabella, who had good reason to keep the secret hidden. Since winter, when the truth began to show, Arabella too had been concealed from the world. She lay upon her bed, reading romantic novels and stroking the spread flesh of her flat, if well-covered, stomach and hoping too, waiting . . . but of course they couldn't afford to be betrayed by a genuine swelling. John was courteous, and bent down each night to wish her sweet dreams with a kiss on her soft, plump cheek, but had a cot made up for him beside the big double bed, and Arabella's fingers, outstretched in the night, could just barely graze his quilt.

Jonathan explains all of this as if it were an interesting fragment of family history, an Edwardian oddity. Let us be clear, then: on 6 July 1903, Emily Mackley gave birth to a healthy boy, who was rapidly taken from her and christened Edward by her husband's brother and his wife, who had for the last seven months feigned a pregnancy of her own. The household staff could not have missed the deception, and could not have mistaken Emily's yells for their mistress in labour, but remained loyal and silent and the secret stayed bound within the walls of the house. And two weeks later Emily was wakened, perhaps by the cry of her own son in the nursery down the hall, or perhaps as usual by the birds in the willow; and rose and dressed in plain grey and came down to breakfast and said she would take some toast, and no, she had not given up hope. And so a scandal was avoided, and the legend of her patience remained intact. It is not certain whether Arabella, by all accounts a dull woman who hadn't the wit to keep a diary, or else had the good sense to destroy it, knew of the child's parentage. Emily, who had loved only one man in her life and betrayed him only once, of course knew. And so, we can assume, did John.

Edward Mackley the younger was raised, then, as John and Arabella's own, each day his likeness to the Mackley men remaining carefully unremarked upon by his parents and his supposed aunt. The three of them were plunged into a peculiar evasive embarrassment when visitors noted how like his father the boy was.

Arabella had a child of her own two years later. Thomas, stocky, large, florid, was every copious inch Arabella's son, but had nothing of the dark, lean quickness of the Mackleys. Helen followed, unexpected, in 1916. Arabella died quietly enough some time in 1934, and passed out of history with as little an eddy as her entry had stirred. John remained a profoundly liberal, compassionate man until his death early in 1937, thus spared by two years the dubious satisfaction of proving to have been right about Europe all along. The house was bequeathed quite legitimately to Edward, the older son; Thomas had already found his own path, which took him over the Atlantic.

By the time Edward inherited, he had been living, teaching and practising in London for more than ten years. He had married a graduate of University College, an unremarkably clever girl he had taught and fell in love with in his own restrained way. Neither Edward nor his young wife, who had been brought up in Highbury, had a use for the house or any desire to forgo the city; so they left it in Helen's care (and Emily along with it), returning occasionally for fleeting and oddly uncomfortable visits. In appearance, Edward was very like his father, and like his name-sake uncle also, but he lacked the long gaze that was to re-emerge incongruous in the blue eyes of Thomas's grandson (and which is even now shining upon Julia in the garden, casting a ruth-less light into previously dark corners). It was, in fact, the severity of Edward's short-sightedness that saved him from conscription in 1939. And perhaps it was also what had blinded him to his Aunt Emily's tears when he went up to Cambridge at the age of eighteen, and also when he returned to say goodbye for the last time forty years later, to find her more or less where he'd left her, in the modest room she'd slept in since she was a young deserted bride.

'She told him, on her deathbed. And he told his brother – my grandpa. They weren't close. I think he thought there might be legal implications. A cautious man, your grandfather, and honest too. But Grandpa, well, you know.'

No; again, Julia doesn't know. She's not sure she knows anything any more. He sees her looking at him blankly, as if lost. Lost in the snow.

'He's rich enough,' says Jonathan, by way of explanation. 'Not the type to start suing his own brother after all that time. Knew better than to take on his sister, too, and anyway wasn't about to uproot the ladies. What could it matter? So they let the sleeping dog lie.' As if stuffed. Posed into a contented nap and mounted to sleep that way for ever with its glass eyes shut.

Julia still doesn't say anything.

'I'm surprised Emily didn't tell Aunt Helen. Perhaps she was embarrassed; John was Helen's father too, after all.'

281

Embarrassed. *Embarazada*, indeed. How embarrassing, to have your husband's brother's baby. Only three years since she'd said goodbye and she betrayed him. Embarrassed or ashamed or disgusted with herself and trying to forget it. Or else she was too sad to think about any of it any more . . . but this sounds to Julia like an excuse, like forgiveness. She betrayed him, she did not wait. She could not go on without – without what? This is not, then, some romantic aporia.

It's just fucking. She could not go on without that.

Julia flushes, shocked at these words which come unbidden and do not belong with brave patient Emily, waiting. Her face is burning. It is so hot. Her head is full of the pound of hot blood, her ears feel stopped with it, her cheeks feel swollen, her mouth with its red slick of paint feels ridiculous. Here is a chair. She has sat down.

'Julia – are you all right? I'm sorry, have I upset you?' Jonathan perches his bulk upon the spindly iron-fretwork chair beside her.

'Oh, it's just so hot. No, I'm fine. I'm quite all right. Would you like another drink? I'll be fine, I just. Perhaps we should go inside.'

They return to the drawing room. Jonathan is solicitous, concerned. Julia is determined to be a good hostess, and presses another gin that he has refused upon him, bright and brittle and rattling the bottle against the glass.

THE LIKENESS

Close to the end of Emily's life, young Edward (almost sixty years old now) came to visit her, and found his sister Helen at her bedside in a bright and placid room, the two women exchanging half-sentences peacefully. He sat with them until Emily's head began to nod, and took Helen to one side.

'Is she drunk?'

'Probably.'

'Do you think it's a good idea, to let her drink?'

'Do you think it's a good idea to stop her? What harm can it do her now?'

'And you, drinking with her?'

Helen smiled at that. 'I'm a lost cause, Dr Mackley. You should know your sister by now.'

Edward left the following morning. He had always felt awkward in that house, although he was born there; he felt a little out of place everywhere he went, but, because the house should have been home to him, felt it there more keenly. Helen remembered the hush that preceded him into every room, in the days when he haunted her childhood with the pale glower of his adolescence.

He would always find the most difficult spot to halt at, neither in nor out, always somewhere between sitting and leaving so that conversation couldn't possibly continue. And, she thought, it pained him that he didn't know where he should sit.

That morning, he had brought Emily's breakfast tray to her: half a pink grapefruit, already segmented with a special knife designed for the purpose; two slices of toast cut very thin from a fresh loaf, as she liked it, with an apricot preserve that they had made last summer; and tea in a primrose-patterned teacup that is now gathering dust in the dresser, part of the china that Julia daren't use for fear of breakage.

Edward watched as she slurped each grapefruit segment. It was warm, August, she wore a high-necked sleeveless cotton nightgown, and he saw that her arms, once strong, had grown slack and thin. He remembered her lean and powerful, and now she was shrunken, her shoulders round and narrow, her gown stained with jam that she dabbed at absent-mindedly. He knew from the darkening of her skin, from her thickened white fingernails and the flowering blood vessels on the back of her hand, that her liver was failing; he remembered her always with a drink in her hand.

Of course, there was a time between girlhood and old age, for Emily; Julia knew this, of course. And she has heard the stories of an independent, strong-willed woman – a woman who took her honeymoon skiing in Norway, after all, and returned on a ship alone. Emily in middle age, always soberly dressed (even if she wasn't always sober, the family would chuckle), keeping up with modern poetry, going to the theatre, thrilled by cinema when it came to the town, a twentieth-century woman – but she was also, and always first and foremost for Julia, the Emily that waited for Edward, who did not remarry but longed for him always.

Here she is, in the drawing room; sitting on the sofa with a tall glass as the boy walks in, hesitating at the door.

'Come sit with your Aunt Emily, Edward. How like your uncle you are. Will you be a sailor, Edward? Or will you stay close to shore?'

Edward takes a wary seat at his aunt's side, smelling the lime on her hands as she holds his face in them.

'I shall be a doctor, I think, like Father, Aunty.'

'A doctor, a doctor, indeed. But ships need doctors, Edward; sailors do sicken, too.' He could never be sure if she was laughing at him.

'Now, Emily. Let the boy alone,' says John, not unkindly, indulgent even. 'Another?' he notes, eyebrow raised, as Emily pours herself a gin with a steady hand, squeezes another slice of lime.

'Oh, not another, naughty Aunt Emily! Too far north again, as we used to say. Do you know that

285

phrase? Like a drunken sailor, what shall we do with her?' She smiles, indulgent in turn and adding another splash. 'Citrus for scurvy, isn't it, Doctor?' And she flicks her front tooth, making Arabella, stitching quietly in the corner, wince. 'You won't catch a tooth falling from *my* head.' Arabella has been plagued since girlhood with cavities – which, she insists, can in no way be connected to her fondness for fondants. Emily is not a tactless woman, so this must be rare spite in the guise of tactlessness, sharpened by the spirit. 'And quinine for malarial fever. I am quite equipped, by the contents of this glass, for any ills our fine empire might throw at me, should I choose to venture out,' she triumphs, finishing the drink with tonic water and taking her seat again beside her nephew with a bounce. And little Edward, his brow ever drawn down in a determined frown, refuses to see her sadness or return the squeeze of her hand.

And many years later, he came to see her before she passed, and stood awkwardly at her bedside, trying not to watch the mess her old mouth made of her breakfast. When she had pushed away the second piece of toast half-eaten, she turned to him. He had been telling her about his son, twenty now and an undergraduate, a medical student like his father and his grandfather and all the first-born Mackleys (Miranda, of course, included). How proud he was.

'Have you a photograph?' asked Emily, suddenly eager.

'Of William? Certainly.'

He produced a picture from his wallet. It is the picture that is now framed on the bedside table, for Emily asked if she might keep it, and Julia, who had put it in a drawer in the embarrassment of early adolescence, retrieved it six years later and restored it to its place, when it was all that was left of him – because this, of course, is her father; so look carefully. An earnest, quiet man who would waste away before he was fifty. Here, a young man of nineteen, the hair which had barely begun to grey when he died is thick and dark and worn over his ears in a curiously wavy style which would in time lengthen to suit the decade that was beginning. In 1960, though, it is a wilfully Romantic decision, because in truth he is a sensitive soul who likes to remind himself that Keats, too, trained as a doctor. He has the black and searching eyes that bypassed his short-sighted father, the same eyes that penetrated John Mackley's patients and the same that Edward almost saw the Pole with.

Emily looked from the photograph to her son and back and then further back, into her own past.

'You are so like him, both of you.' With an effort to raise herself on her pillows, she reached up to remove Edward's thick glasses; he blinked, and she smiled. 'I wonder if he would have grown to look like you.' Her son was now twenty-five years older than her husband had been when she saw him last.

But this Edward's shoulders were not so broad; he was lean but a little bellyful of good living rested comfortably on his belt; and his eyes, unaided, could not see further than two feet beyond himself, let alone beyond the horizon. Still, he was like him; Emily put a hand to his cheek, and left it there cold and dry for a moment that felt longer and stranger than it should have for Edward.

With a sigh, she passed his glasses back to him. And then she told her secret, sad and calm. He thought how he had never much loved his mother and wondered if this was perhaps why; and understood why he had always felt awkward around his aunt – because she loved him more than she ought to. He said sorry, awkwardly, without knowing what or who he was sorry for. She offered no apology or tears. It seemed to both too late to recover anything now; it was long past and her life nearly over. A little later he left, managing to brush her papery cheek with a kiss. She lay for a long time looking at the photograph of William, the grandson she could never own. Then Helen came in, and took it gently from her hands.

'This is William?' she asked.

'So like him,' said Emily, quietly, tired. Edward's diary lay open on the bedside; Emily's eyes watered with frustration every time she tried to read it. Helen took it up, unasked, and read to her the gentle parts, of the sky, the lights, the star-sparkled ice, for an hour or more, watching her drowse and drift as she made her way over the snow towards him, back over the years to the time of their innocence, before he was lost, before she was.

When she seemed at peace, far beyond the world, Helen quietly closed the book; but then Emily started suddenly and grasped at her wrist, the jerk of her waking closely followed, as ever, by the perpetual disappointment of finding herself old; it was not snow that half blinded her after all, just age, just time, clouding over.

'Helen,' said Emily, recalling herself to the present with an unwilling effort.

'Yes, Aunt Emily? Can I fetch you something?'

'There's something, it's Edward, there's a secret I told him . . . I wonder, should I tell you . . .' Emily, in her later years, was prone to this kind of whimsical self-address, as if the person she really wanted to talk to was absent, even when there were others in the room. She sighed, sinking back; her grip loosed.

'You're tired, aren't you?' said Helen, whose voice was hoarse from reading and holding back tears, tired herself, truth be told, and now seeing her aunt's eyes film over again with snow.

'I'm tired, true enough. Yes, I'm tired, Helen.'

'What did you want to tell me?'

Emily breathed a long, shaking breath. 'I don't suppose . . . Does it matter, now? All these years waiting . . . perhaps it doesn't really matter now,' she said, dozing off.

Unless she woke to speak again to the one who had always walked invisible beside her, those were her last words, for when Helen brought her soup that lunchtime her white eyes were fixed wide open, unmoving, the pupils shrunk to a tiny point in the milky brown, as if flooded with light.

THE MIRROR

It is close to seven. The clock in the drawing room clacks loudly in the silence that has fallen between the two cousins. Jonathan is feeling a little woozy from the sun and three gins on an empty stomach. He can smell the hot fat and rosemary of the lamb. Julia seems distracted, gazing into the dust in the evening sunlight, so that it seems to shimmer over the surface of her eyes. He wonders if it is necessary to look at the archive or if he can escape without seeming rudely uninterested. But his pretty and highly strung cousin and the savoury, homely smell of the meat are making him think of the long journey back to his own wife; the dark portraits and the dust are becoming oppressive.

'When do you expect Simon home?' he asks. Julia looks at him blankly for a moment, as if trying to recall who he means. She glances at the clock: almost seven.

'I'm not sure. Any time now, I should think.' This is a small lie. He is usually home around half past, by eight at the latest. And besides, he said something about working later tonight, possibly.

She remembers him saying something of that sort, as he wiped up the last of his egg. But she wants this cousin of hers, with his bright blue eyes and his casual revelations, to go now. She wants to be left alone.

'Well, I must let you get on with whatever it is that smells so delicious; if I don't get on the road now I'll never get home.' Jonathan's stomach growls audibly, anticipating its plastic-wrapped service-station dinner. He hopes she doesn't think he is angling for an invitation; it crosses her mind but she cannot bring herself to ask him to stay. Their desires are in perfect accord. He stands, places his glass carefully upon the cabinet.

'I do hope I didn't upset you today. I really had no idea, my father told me so long ago it's become a sort of – you know, a family myth.' (Yes; this she knows.)

'Not at all; it was a surprise, that's all. Please don't worry. It's been so good to see you, we mustn't be such strangers. Any time you're in London just give me a call,' says Julia, standing too, pushing absent-mindedly at her hair and talking quickly now, and they are almost wedged together in the doorway in their hurry to leave the room.

'Give my love to Laura,' she says, hoping that she has remembered his wife's name; if she hasn't he is too polite to say so.

'And my regards to Simon. If you'd like to visit sunny Sheffield, we'd be glad to have you.'

'Oh that would be lovely. Let's do that.'

They have made it to the front door; the clock clunks and begins its whirr, winding the pendulum, and strikes. Get out now, please, seven times over.

'Thank you again, Julia, have a lovely evening.'

'Safe journey!' she cries, waving him off up the drive as he leans out of the open window, then he draws in his head, reverses through the gate, and he's gone. She closes the door as the clock lets its weight unwind gently and settles back into its sonorous rhythm, and the house is again becalmed.

Yes, families and myths.

Julia turns to herself in the mirror. She reaches to the back of her neck and unclasps the silver anchor, feels it hot in her hand from the skin of her chest. Bright bronze eyes flash back as if fevered. Her cheeks are crimson. She sees the resemblance and finds herself wanting. On an autumn day in 1902, Emily Mackley saw her sin burn thus. And here is her great-granddaughter, staring back now at those same eyes – and holding the gaze steady; she will not let her look away.

NORWEGIAN PARTY FOUND AT SPITZBERGEN reads the headline in Monday's *Times*, dated 29 September 1902. It is Emily's privilege to receive the papers first – it was not, then, placed by an unwitting butler on John's breakfast tray as we supposed, but here on the little round table by Emily's usual seat. John, often busy with patients

293

or otherwise occupied with his animals, will turn his attention briefly to the world at teatime, finding politics more palatable with a teacake in hand. So it was Emily, in fact, who first read this headline, cruelly hidden on the third page so that from the front the day's news seemed innocuous.

Emily sits in the morning room with the paper before her, the first page turned, until the clock has ticked its way through almost an hour and a half. She stares at the faces of the men who had sailed with her husband, who she must have met during that first leg of the journey she joined him on; they are unrecognizable now, gaunt and bearded; and it seems so long ago. These men had watched him set out upon the ice; and what was she doing on that day, she wonders, what was she doing on 1 March last year when her husband set out upon the ice?

(She was moping. The weather was dismal, she longed to walk outside but couldn't bear explaining herself to her nosy maid when she came back damp and muddy-shoed to change for dinner. So she spent the afternoon half reading and looking out at the grey garden. As she sat down to her soup that evening, feeling oppressed by the day spent indoors and the dulling sky, Edward was enjoying his first meal upon the ice, toasting his companions and the Pole with champagne and thinking of his wife at home, wondering what she was doing, seeing the time and knowing that she must be just sitting down to the soup.)

She reads the dates over and over; and the phrase 'after one hundred days, they had not returned'. Edward had set out with provisions for one hundred days. He believed they would reach the Pole in forty, and take as many again to return; they could not carry the load of any greater contingency. He had planned his course and hoped to reach the camp at Cape Flora around eighty days after setting out, where they would find enough provisions to sustain them until they were collected. *Persephone* was to make her way to that point, if possible, as soon as the ice released her. It loosened in May and they managed to navigate a course, breaking through when there was no open water, and reached the island ninety-four days after bidding their captain farewell, expecting to find him there. A week after their arrival, the party had still not returned. *Persephone* was at risk of being trapped for the winter if they waited too long; they had agreed with Edward that they would not endanger her by doing so. Still they held out a further twenty days, dissolving in and out of the fog (they did not know it, and so Emily could not either, but that same fog was blanketing the captain and his team in their lonely struggling kayaks less than two hundred miles away). A hundred and twenty days after Edward and his party had left the ship, the crew of the *Persephone* set sail, telling themselves that he would surely have the wherewithal to winter over, and that they would return the following spring. They would arrive at the log cabin and find the six of them, feasting on seal meat around a roaring fire. 'What took you so long?' they would cry from the shore; 'We've no flags to wave for you, we've left them at the Pole!' And a great 'Hurrah' would sound out across the water.

After fifteen days' sailing the ship was again enveloped in the thick fog, and they could not get their bearings; when it cleared they found they had been carried far out to the north-west, beyond the archipelago. Then the ice began to close in. When the sun set for the long winter they were once again trapped and drifting; in the violent packing of the early spring, they heard for the first time the ship's timbers groan and crack. It was a deep freeze that year, they were still far to the north, and the ice failed to release them as the summer drew on; provisions and morale were low. The English surrogate captain was dead. Seeing no alternative, not trusting the ship to last out another winter, the remaining crew of twelve brave men struck south upon the ice as soon as it was passable, hoping to reach Spitzbergen before the long night fell. They struggled for six weeks towards salvation. Eight men died. Four survived. The Russian whaler that took them in a week after they reached land had no news of the *Persephone* or its captain.

Half past twelve twitters past and Arabella, whose rumbling stomach has been softly disturbing the

296

quiet for the last half-hour, glances up to say, 'I wonder what can be keeping lunch'; but she gets no further than 'I won . . .' (an empty victory) because she sees that Emily has not passed the third page of the paper and appears to be weeping over a picture of four fur-hatted men (one of their wind-burned faces on the yellowed page in the attic is indeed blurred out by her tears).

'My dear . . .' she says, at which John enters the room, his expression grave, delivering her from the need for compassion by asking that they might be excused. Arabella gathers up her silks, the question on her face unanswered, and goes in to lunch alone.

Perhaps we needn't pry into what passed between her husband and their sister-in-law while she enjoyed an extra serving of each course; perhaps it is unnecessary, unkind. But Julia will not allow them to get away with it so easily, will not let them off the hook although history has done so. She knows full well that two bodies meeting in defiance of death are not always tender. She sees Emily go to him – yes, she would go to him first, right there in the morning room where Julia first made love to her own husband, not knowing the place was sullied, and the love she had imagined all spoiled. Emily goes to him and weeps against his chest and he, barely knowing what he is doing, kisses her hair and smoothes it back from her face, kisses her forehead, her weeping eyes, stroking her head as if to soothe a

child, and she stretches up to meet his lips and
he resists, at first, but her mouth wet with tears
is too much for him, and he clasps her and returns
her kiss, and they clutch at each other, they wrestle
together with her stays and stockings, frantic now,
he tears at them with his big doctor's hands and
grasps at her thighs, lifting her onto him, both
crying, and it is over in seconds; so Julia imagines them, spending their rage and grief upon each
other in a burst of frenzy until there is nothing
but the fingerprint bruises on her skin and silence
and guilt between them. And then she straightens
her skirts over her shame, thinks how she will have
to hide the torn evidence from the maid,
straightens her bodice and leaves him there in his
damp shirt-tails, trousers round his ankles. And in
the hallway on her way to her room, she meets
her own eye in the mirror, sees the red flush of her
cheeks and her eyes bright. But how, thinks Julia,
could she have looked herself in the eye then?

And nine months and seven days after that
fateful article appeared in *The Times*, Edward
Mackley was born, quietly, and passed to his
father's wife. And Emily, taking her seat at the
breakfast table, said she would go on waiting.

Julia retreats numbly to the morning room and
lies down upon the rug; but it gives no comfort.
The Arctic hero, the wife bidding farewell,
waiting . . . It is all spoiled.

Laid out on bearskin, desolate. Poor Edward in the night, the snow and the darkness for miles around him and the north wind, struggling, nearing the still point where she should be waiting, unable to go on, unable without . . . I cannot fill this want, this lack . . . I want Simon.

Simon; yes, she wants to speak to Simon. A feeling of physical want gaping suddenly so wide and empty that it shocks her, it has been so long since she felt it; but it should not surprise us or her. True, there is much that they have not confided in the last few years – there are longings and fears and losses festering – but she could not go on alone now as she was before he found her, before he followed her over the threshold. She wants her husband; there is nothing strange in that. She wants to tell him – she's not sure what. She wants to ask for forgiveness; she's not sure what for.

She reaches for the phone, grasping blind with one hand above her on the table by her head. It gives a faint ting as she hooks a finger under the rest for the handset and brings the old thing down to her, resting it on her stomach. She insisted on keeping it, and it pleases her every time she uses it; so she stretched out here as a girl, twisting the cord about her fingers as she chatted, back when her worries were so pressing, exciting and short-lived; before life started taking everyone from her. Apart from Simon. Now without thinking she rings each impatient digit round the dial, barely

299

letting it wheel back before catching it and spinning the next number round, and listens for the clicks of connection and hears it start to ring, somewhere in London; after eight rings, nine, ten, Joanne answers, a little breathless; she was just stepping out the door, she says, no he left ten minutes ago; Julia's normal voice thanks her and says she'll try his mobile, hangs up, again flicks each number with quick, nervous fingers, and hears it ring. And somewhere in London, Simon's phone rings on unanswered.

WHISKY, ALE AND WINE

Julia would never betray her husband. The very thought of betrayal is anathema to everything she believes in, the whole fragmenting edifice she has staked her identity on. But, unknown to her, infidelity has been hovering at the edges of this day, disturbing sleep and lending the morning its oddly affectionate cast. It is a possibility only, an opportunity, somewhere in London, about to be offered.

Julia will never be unfaithful to her husband. She is not the nearly guilty party.

The afternoon has dragged past inevitably, but painfully slowly, for Simon. He has been laying foundations on paper while Julia's have crumbled; while Julia's world has splintered and split, Simon has been making new structures solid. But he himself, he knows, cannot stand so firm. Seven o'clock has at last bonged out across Westminster, and he has been forced to forgo the refuge of work and face consequences. Now he is pushing his way through the ever-present horde outside Parliament. The Gothic immensity of it is so familiar that he doesn't even glance up at the towers and spindles, golden in the evening sun, which have mesmerized the gaping tourists that crowd the pavement, striking them dumb. In every sense of the word, Simon grumbles to himself, as he narrowly escapes the back-stepping trainer of a photographer moving out for a wider angle without thinking to look behind her. Simon is rushing for an appointment he has serious misgivings about attending at all. He checked his phone before setting out, hoping that he might somehow have missed a call or message to cancel, knowing he hadn't. 19.06. If he hurried, he could have a drink before she got there.

Simon reaches the pub and orders the only single malt he can spot. He has arrived ten minutes early. This is not like him. He is, as you might expect, a punctual man. This means that he likes to arrive at any destination precisely on time, so that no time is wasted in the place before the minute of the assignation. Yet here he is, ordering himself a whisky at the bar, having deliberately allowed himself this time alone. Could it be that a spot of Dutch courage is called for? It would seem so. He doesn't want to seem on edge. No, he doesn't want to seem anything, suave or indifferent or boyish or . . . A clean break, just as he has already decided. Several times over. He fidgets with the glass, in the measured way that passes for a fidget in Simon's fingers, rotating it round and around.

Staring into its amber depths, thinking of his wife's eyes, thinking of her sleepy, surprising smile – the first notes of the concerto creep into his mind, and he recalls that she didn't get to hear them, that the alarm barged in right at the end of the piece, without regard for the careful layering of intensity, the suggestion building to insistence that precedes the final culmination; he has remembered too late what he forgot at the bathroom mirror, and resolves to find the CD for her when he gets home – and he will be home soon, just as soon as . . .

Here she is. He has stationed himself cleverly so that he is far from the door and partly hidden by the pillars of the long bar, but with a clear view of anyone entering. She is early, too. The old man further along the bar turns to look lasciviously – or so Simon imagines the look to be, with a prick of indignation that he quells before he can acknowledge it. He picks up the whisky and swallows it down, while she scopes the gloom, sunglasses incongruous on the top of her head. Simon had thought this place neutral, and wonders now if it is possibly bordering on the insulting, a grubby run-of-the-mill pub among a wealth of more pleasant options. Or if otherwise, to a certain turn of mind, there might be some sort of romance about the place. Some sort of run-down post-war glamour. He isn't sure which would be preferable. He wishes he had another whisky (his father's drink. He is not a big drinker.

He is not like him. Certainly he'd never known his father to be nervous). Too late, she has seen him and he hurriedly puts the empty glass away from him and stands to greet her with a decorous kiss on the cheek, which she repeats on the other unexpectedly, awkwardly, and he shrivels inside. He orders an ale that he really doesn't want and a white wine for her – 'Oh, anything, medium dry,' she says, and he feels an automatic inward sneer that he is, at least, ashamed of. He motions her to a table in the middle of the room so that they are quite exposed, avoiding the cosy booths around the edges, although he can see her speculating. Imagining the accidental brush of an ankle. Craven, he knows he is craven.

'Oh, it's just too hot for shopping today!' she says, dropping carrier bags, fanning herself and sitting in the chair emphatically. She pouts her underlip to blow away a hair; it remains stuck to her forehead. Her cleavage is beaded with sweat and the red lipstick she wears is blurring her mouth at the edges. In the airless gloom, the grimy windows filtering the sun and casting a sickly light upon all within, she looks a little older than he'd remembered.

'Buy anything nice?' asks Simon politely.

He is relentlessly polite throughout the half-hour conversation that follows, politely evading any attempt at flirtation. She tries harder. She puts her hand on the table close to his and, without meaning to, he pulls away sharply. He notices her

304

nails are now immaculate, newly manicured. For his benefit. He puts his hand on hers. His last chance: he might, then, have given into the crackle now coursing up his arm from his palm; offered a compliment; he might have smiled bashfully and suggested that they walk along the river, perhaps. But his hand is on hers out of kindness, his hand on hers has forced the moment to its crisis, so that there is nothing left to do but say:

'I think I should apologize for my behaviour. It was inexcusable.'

Watching his lips make the words, Sandra's own quiver just a little before she clamps them firm, a tightness at the corners the only hint of instability. She withdraws her hand delicately to lift her wine. She nods, understanding. A brief, murmured conversation follows; the words are the same as ever. My wife deserves better and so do you; in different circumstances, he implies, in another life, he lies . . .

But other lives are not our business. It is over, before it began. It might have gone differently, had it not been for the pheasant, for that shiver and the tenderness that followed; the unexpected smile and Rachmaninov and the eggs for breakfast, the accident on the road, the awful client and his squalid stories about his mistress. If the steak had been a better excuse for good wine, which might have induced him to drink more, and made the afternoon irrational. If the day hadn't been so hot; in short, had it not been today. There are any number of factors, some of which we have surely missed or cannot know, that compel Simon to stand now and leave her with another peck on the cheek (this time she makes no attempt at symmetry). She holds her smile until he's out of the door, and she's left with a large glass of white wine that has no savour. It is an unpleasant yellow that makes her think of a man's piss. She drinks it anyway, quietly despising everything, including herself, staring at the table between acrid sips and not letting go of the stem. Then she dumps her over-stuffed handbag on the table and roots around for her lipstick.

She is almost relieved. She never meant to be a home-wrecker. She has been lonely since she left her husband. She'd like to make friends. She'd like a lover. She's not sure which she wants more. She wants to wear scruffy summer dresses and still look beautiful, like her neighbour. She wants to stand in the dawn sun naked and not be ashamed. She doesn't think a vicious kiss in the conservatory to be much of a triumph, in the face of that unassailable easy loveliness. A kiss like that has no hope in it. Thoughtful, she takes out her compact and carefully reapplies lipstick and powder although she's quite aware that her make-up will soon be ruined anyway, the moment she gets in the door if she can keep herself together for the whole of the train journey home, because she cries all the bloody time, these days, and it's making her eyes puffy.

Simon, meanwhile, is making purposeful strides for the Tube. He feels his mobile vibrate in his pocket and remembers thinking he felt it before, on his way to the pub; this time, he draws it out and sees that it's Julia. When she calls him, her face fills the screen, her lips pouting for a kiss. This is her doing; she likes to surprise him with such things. When he first saw it, he shook his head and smiled. Now he quickly slips it back into his pocket, hiding her wide, trusting eyes. He feels sick. He drank the pint far too quickly, on top of the whisky too, so desperate was he to abandon Sandra with her near-full glass of wine; his stomach turns and turns again. The vibrating stops, and starts again almost immediately. He told her he'd be back late, he thinks, with a surge of irritation, was she listening to him? He is doing his best to get home to her now, he's rushing for the Tube, he can't answer or he'll miss the train, what more does she want of him? She'll just have to wait until he gets back.

This spell of self-vindication lasts for precisely fifteen seconds, which is how long it takes for his voicemail to kick in, at which point he knows she will ring off – she hates leaving messages. As he feels it stop, he imagines her cutting him off in mid-sentence, 'You've reached Si—', lying on the rug with the phone on her belly and the handset still to her ear, listening to the dial tone, letting it fill her head with its lonely sound, because she hasn't reached him at all, she has reached out to him and he hasn't answered and he knows how sad such things make her, sad out of all proportion, and he wills her to dial again but she doesn't, she's given up on him. He is, he thinks, disgusting. But he has reached the entrance to the Tube and will soon be out of range; as he descends into the foetid depths of the tail end of rush hour, he thinks at least he will be home when he said he would be, and hopes she was listening when he told her he'd be late. He will be home by nine, at the latest. He thinks of her pulling that silly big-eyed bug-face, her impression of a butterfly puckering up; he thinks of the other woman's full fleshy mouth leaving lipstick on his neck; the beer and the whisky and the coffee and the foolishness of what he's almost done slosh about in his stomach as he jogs to the platform, and to a chorus of tuts he presses himself into the crowded carriage, into the stink of perfume and sweat and after-work booze and thinks he's no better than the rest of them and his stomach turns as they set off with a lurch into the tunnel.

TELEPHONE

Julia lies on the rug listening to the dial tone, deciding whether or not to try once more. He either hasn't heard his phone or is ignoring her. Why would he ignore her? If he'd just left the office as Joanne said, he would have been heading for the Tube the first time she tried (so he wasn't working late, after all); she gave him half an hour, waiting impatiently, scrunching the fur with her fingers and bare feet and feeling it heat up under her back; remembering lying there with him and trying now to regain that tenderness, trying to feel anything other than this awful disappointment, this want, this lack. When half an hour at last had elapsed, she tried calling again; he should be on the train home by now. She let it ring on, hung up when she heard his business voice telling her she'd reached him when she hadn't. She tried again, cut him off again. Now she is listening to the dial tone. She holds the handset to her ear until the sound cuts out to a constant monotone which seems such an empty hopeless sound that it makes her want to cry. Is he ignoring her? She tries one more time. This time it doesn't ring; his

309

voice answers immediately, straight to voicemail. Underground? Strange, she thinks, sighs, and replaces the handset. She lies there for a while longer. She tries to take comfort:

Laid out on bearskins, skin against the snow . . .

but she cannot find it. The dream which has been so vivid all day to her has vanished; the lights no longer flash unbidden across the sky, the expanse of snow no longer rolls out beyond her. She looks up at the dark red ceiling, at the swirls of the glass lampshade; she knows every whorl. She wonders when he'll be home, makes plans without consciously hearing herself do it –

Glaze the carrots, let the lamb rest, thicken the sauce . . . should I change into something pretty? No, I've changed already. Have I changed? Does this change me? Wipe off the red he hates it.

She lies there longer still, unable to exert the will to raise herself although her back is now uncomfortably hot against the rug. At last she lifts the phone off her stomach and sits up, leaving a sweltered patch of flattened fur behind her; she sits cross-legged with the phone in front of her and taps her top lip with her fingertips. Then she reaches again for the handset and dials another number.

★ ★ ★

Miranda is in the locker room at work; she just has time for a cup of tea before starting her shift. She opens her locker and is about to throw her handbag in when she hears her phone ringing, digs it out just in time. Her sister.

'Hi, Julia, what's up?'

'Hello. Nothing really, I just thought I'd call. Well, it's just that . . .' Miranda's colleague clatters the door of his locker, greeting her loudly as he does so before turning and silencing himself with that mouth-pursed hand-flat gesture which means 'Oh, sorry, I didn't see you're on the phone.' Julia picks up the noise in the background.

'Are you at work? Sorry, I didn't think.'

'Start in ten minutes, it's fine. Was it important?'

'No, not really. It doesn't matter. I can call you tomorrow or . . .'

Miranda by now has heard the slight quiver in her sister's voice which means that it does matter, it is important. She tries not to audibly sigh.

'Come on, something's up. What's happened?'

'It's . . . Jonathan came to see me today.'

'Who?'

'Our cousin, Jonathan Mackley.'

'Really? The little ginger boy? And?'

'He told me that . . . Oh, it's just so weird. I feel so strange. I don't know, he didn't seem to think it was at all important, maybe it isn't but I think it is, and Simon's not answering his phone and I thought I should tell you too.'

Miranda is struggling not to betray her impatience;

311

she is also struggling to make her much-needed cup of tea without betraying the sound of her doing so.

'Julia, tell me what?'

'It's about Emily. She had a . . . well, Edward . . . he was her son.'

Miranda takes the milk from the door of the fridge and bumps it closed with her hip. 'Edward was . . . what? Whose son, Emily's? That seems unlikely, not to say biologically impossible. Wasn't she younger than him?'

'No, no, the other Edward. Our grandfather Edward.'

Miranda is quiet. This is, indeed, very strange news. She is attempting to absorb it while also concentrating on unscrewing the top of the milk with one hand.

'Miranda?'

'Yes, I'm here, yes. So, hang on. So you're saying Grandpa was Emily's son? Julia, where are you getting this from?'

'Jonathan told me. He says she told him when she was dying and he told his grandfather but she didn't tell anyone else and neither did he, but they all know about it and he thought we must too.'

'I'm confused; who's he, and she, and we?' says Miranda, laughing; but Julia, she realizes, is not in the mood to laugh at her own rambling. She is sounding quite unsteady now. Letting out a soundless nasal sigh, Miranda sits down with her mug and listens. Her shift can wait two minutes; her sister is upset.

'Sorry. Start from the beginning. Emily told Edward that he was her son.'

'And John's. She slept with John.'

'John who? Our great-grandfather, John?'

'Yes. It's so . . . her husband's brother. It's so horrible.'

Miranda and Julia were always close, even as children, both quiet girls who enjoyed mainly their own and each other's company; they survived together their father's dying and their mother's grief, each drawing upon the other's strength, which they reserved for each other when they could not find their own. They know each other's nuances as if they were their own; they share gestures and habits unknowingly; if one yawns, covering her mouth with the back of a splayed hand, the other catches the yawn in sympathy, at the other end of the country, and splays a hand to stop it. Sometimes, one of them will turn to the other with a nudge or a giggle, to share something hilarious that she has just remembered, and then she realizes that they are four hundred miles apart and they miss each other terribly.

They forget to call each other. They don't speak sometimes for weeks on end. They rarely visit; Miranda's schedule is tough, she has children to take care of, Julia suspects that she dislikes Simon. Miranda knows full well that Julia dislikes Matthew. But lately they have been more lax than usual and although Julia doesn't know it Miranda has been putting off a call, because she doesn't like to keep things from her sister but for the last two months she has been seeing a radiographer who works some of the same shifts, and she knows that Julia, who has never been Matthew's champion, still would not understand.

So Miranda's response is not what Julia expected.

'God, yes, it is. It's so . . . it's so sad. Poor Emily.'

'. . . Really?'

'Just think, all those years pretending. Were they having an affair? Do you think she loved him?'

'John? No, I think she thought her husband was dead and he thought it was a good opportunity for a mercy fuck.'

'Julia.'

'What? It was when those Norwegians turned up, it was in the paper. That day. And afterwards she went to bed for months and pretended to be grieving.'

'Maybe she was.'

'She was pregnant with her husband's brother's baby.'

'That doesn't mean she couldn't be grieving too, does it?'

'But how could she? It's so . . . it's just so sordid.'

'Julia.'

'She said she'd wait.'

Miranda checks her watch (a sensible, easily read dial with a leather strap, which she always wears).

It's gone eight. She's late to report for her shift. She is growing exasperated now with her sister, the hopeless romantic. For whom love has always been this perfect unrealized thing, free of the complications of real life, of annoying piles of laundry and dishes and kids yelling and crying and not getting any help, of trying to make breakfast for them all and trying to make your face look less of a train wreck at the same time, of wanting someone just to want you and not necessarily loving them but yes, sometimes just wanting to fuck as if there isn't this mess of toys and puréed turnip and mortgages and obligations at home, just wanting to get away from it for just a little while and just fuck someone who just wants you, and not everyone's perfect but some of us will just have to make do.

There is silence on the other end of the line. 'Oh. Um . . .' says Julia, at which point Miranda realizes that she has said some version of all this out loud. Her voice softens.

'I'm sorry. I didn't mean that. Well, yes I did, some of it. Look, Julia. We can't ever know how it happened. She was lonely. People do strange things when they're sad. It sounds like it was a one-off. And then, think about it, she had to pay for it the rest of her life, living in that house with her son, and who knows, maybe she was in love with John, she knew him a lot longer than she did her husband, but if she did she couldn't do anything about it. I feel sorry for them. I know

315

you want the grand romance but really it's just a woman getting old on her own. Not waiting, just having no choice.' She hears a small sniff on the other end of the line, and feels the old familiar mix of frustration and tenderness and guilt, she can picture her sitting there on the rug, not crying, her lips clamped, refusing to look up, all confused and sad so that you feel as though you've slapped her for no reason or trodden on a kitten.

'Julia?'

'Yes?'

'Are you okay?'

'Yes.'

'Look, I'm late for my shift. I didn't mean to upset you. Sorry. I didn't mean what I said, about having kids, and all that. And Emily . . . I don't know. I don't know what to think about it. It was a long time ago. I wonder what Dad would have made of it . . . Well, at least now we know where you got your lovely eyes from.'

Sniff.

'It doesn't change who she was, not really. I still think she was pretty amazing. We should be proud to be her granddaughters.'

Sniff. Silence. 'Great-granddaughters.' Julia, in some things, has a strain of pedantry to rival Simon's.

'Ah, there you are. Thought I'd lost you. Okay, go and have a cup of tea or a glass of wine or something and think of your poor sister up to her elbows in guts all night. We'll chat tomorrow, okay?'

'Okay. Thanks, Miranda. You're probably right.'

'I'm always right.'

'Miranda, what you said about . . . Are you all right? Is something going on?'

She'd hoped to have got away with that. Her sister isn't quite as hare-brained as she seems, sometimes.

'I'll call you tomorrow. I'm fine. Goodnight, sis.'

'Night. Enjoy your . . . enjoy the guts.'

And with that, they are cut off. Miranda taps her top lip slowly with her fingertips for a moment, then shakes her head, drains her tea, rubs her face with her hands, repins her sensibly bobbed hair, and leaves the locker room to start her night's work.

And Julia? Julia is thinking. She was so sure she was angry, she was hurt, betrayed, on Edward's behalf; she was sure she was in the right. But now, she looks at her watch and it's ten past eight, and Simon should be home around now but then he didn't answer her call, he had no reception half an hour ago and she can't work it out, and she thinks:

What if he just never comes home?

EMILY'S ROOM

T here are rooms in this house that they rarely go into. The second floor, for example, where the ceilings once lowered upon lowlier occupants, is now largely a repository for the junk and detritus of the last three generations – some of Julia and Simon's old furniture has been stashed here among the serviceable old servants' beds and wardrobes. The largest room, the nursery, is a dust-sheeted wasteland, as if long-fallen snow had drifted upon the vague oblong forms just visible in the curtained permanent twilight; the kind of landscape that to an adult seems desolate, and that would delight a child, and needs only a little explorer to bring it glistening to life. The last children to spend their days here were Edward, Thomas and Helen, almost a century ago; the house has since been childless, as each generation forsook it while those that remained were barren. There are still some boxes of books and toys that Julia and Miranda were allowed to play with, carefully, and which Julia imagined she would show to her own children in turn; and although she has not allowed herself to imagine such things lately, sometimes a little wooden white fox, once a neglected gift from Emily to her son, wheels itself quietly into a corner of her mind, catching her off-guard.

Immediately below the nursery, in an unobtrusive corner of the first floor, a rarely opened door has been left ajar. Peering around the frame, we will find a pale-green-painted interior, ample enough for a single bed, a slender wardrobe, a walnut desk beneath the window, inlaid with lighter wood patterning on the fronts of the drawers – one of these drawers has been pulled out and gapes empty, exposing its now scentless liner. Perhaps not quite scentless; if we were to lean right in, sniff at the faded paper roses printed on it, we might just catch the tang of soured hope and sadness. The curtains are open, the windows wide; the evening is filled with the final blaze of the setting sun. The last of the yellow light is trapped in the willow that shushes and rustles outside, every bright leaf folded upon its own narrow, soft shadow.

Julia peeks in quietly, pushing the door and creeping in as if she fears to disturb something. She returns a bundle of letters to the open drawer and, turning to the dressing table, she sits before the mirror. In this same seat, she watched her face become more her own each year, more the person she imagined herself to be; her skin cleared, her cheekbones sharpened, her eyes became, she saw, possibly beautiful. It seems strange to see that same face now, in this room which felt like her own and which she now so rarely enters, this room in which she outgrew her girlhood. She would take up the necklace of Aunt Helen's that she most coveted, three strands of pearls fattening to the centre, milky, coral and periwinkle-blue. The three strands diminished evenly to the prettiest part, where the tiny seed pearls were gathered by a flat silver clasp, etched with an intricate and winding oak-leaf design. Julia liked the knowledge of it at the back of her neck, hidden by the mass of hair that she brushed over and over with a shell-backed brush; a thrill would trickle down her spine from the point where it rested, as she imagined a hand pushing aside her hair to find it there; the new word 'lover' tickled her skin. The thought of that necklace makes her chest tighten with nostalgia for that time of anticipation, for the woman she thought she would become, the home she thought she would have. That home was always modelled on this house, although in those days Julia never thought she would own it; and now here she is, and yet her chest almost hurts with longing for it.

The mirror has a hinged base in which the sisters still store their inherited treasures, once closely guarded. It contains a jumble of Emily's and Aunt Helen's jewellery, precious stones tangled with costume tat. As children, they would race to put them all on at once. Julia would make them laugh by plucking a long strand between two long fingers, holding it away from her body and swinging it gently; with her sharp shoulders and boy's backward slouch she was every inch the flapper, said Aunt Helen. Now she wears only the silver anchor, or did until she unclasped it tonight, set adrift, no longer sure of the meaning of John's gift.

Julia thinks for a moment she can smell Miranda, tobacco and deodorant (those cheap shiny cans they used to buy, Julia the green one, Miranda the purple); but Miranda is far away and of course has switched brands, to a reliable roll-on that will last her the shift. It is possible, thinks Julia, that the room still smells of cigarettes – in the later years of their visits, Miranda would come tapping at the door and the girls would sit and smoke here. Chain-smoking Aunt Helen, enemy of hypocrites, champion of choice, allowed this and even provided an ashtray, a painted pottery dish she'd brought back from Lisbon. This has disappeared from the bedside and resides now on Miranda's coffee table. First thing in the morning or in the early evening, before she leaves for the hospital, she can be found staring into it at the ash-smeared blue bull in the bowl. She sits with her elbows on her knees, back flat and tipped forward, fag hand dangling over the rim. She is always intent; sometimes, she is thinking of the summers she spent flicking ash at it; most often, most likely, she is thinking of the shift ahead, or perhaps, in recent weeks, of her lover. The ashtray is the only object that Miranda has taken from the house.

★　　★　　★

In the days following their father's funeral, the girls sat dazed in their rooms or in the conservatory, delaying the question of a return to their studies. They sat side by side, sometimes talking, sometimes quiet, sharing cigarettes; in the evenings they ate with their mother and Aunt Helen and poured out memories along with bottles of white wine. After four days of this, they went to the pub along the road before dinner; although they didn't admit it even to each other, they were stifling in the nearness of their mother's grief. They got talking to a local boy, home for the weekend from college. Julia felt awkward and shy and underage, although no one out here in the country seemed to care; Miranda let him buy them one vodka and orange after another, and told him all about the Mackleys. Her bright nails, painted just before they left the house in defiance of mourning and death – Julia can see them now, *magenta* and *fuchsia*, so many words for pink there were in those days, *cerise* – her nails clashing with the orange in the glass, and touching the boy's leg lightly so that Julia looked away embarrassed and wished she hadn't come. 'You should see the place, it's like a museum,' said Miranda, as if it was only a lot of old junk. The boy said he'd love to see the polar bears and came home with them for dinner. If Aunt Helen and their mother were aware of him leaving in the early hours of the morning, neither one said a word, tacitly agreeing that Miranda too was grieving, she was nineteen years old, after all, and deserved to take her comfort where she found it.

Julia remembers how she'd heard him pass her door and minutes later heard Miranda's creeping tread creak on the landing. She knocked gently and came in without waiting to be asked, sat down on the side of the bed and lit a cigarette. Her eyes were wet; they reflected the flame, shining in the near-darkness.

'He freaked out,' said Miranda.

'What happened?'

'I started crying. After. He thought it was my first time and started being all manly about it so I told him it wasn't that, and that my dad was dead. Then I really started crying.'

Julia remembers herself sitting up in bed, the cool early morning, remembers Miranda's damp forehead under her fingers as she brushed at her fringe.

'And he left?'

'Yeah. He did say sorry.'

'Well that's all right then. God, Miranda.'

'It's okay. These beds are tiny anyway.'

'True. Want to get in? We're only small.'

They slept side by side that night, as they had when they were younger and Miranda still lived at home, when she would come in from friends' house parties and forbidden clubs and climb in beside her little sister smelling of cheap drinks and perfume, to tell her the secrets of the evening. That night they slept soundly, although it was not a bed for two people to sleep in. It was the bed that Emily Mackley came back to, the guest bed that she should have only rested in for a spell, before her husband came home to lay her down on their marriage quilt.

Laid out here with the space beside her. The endless cold white sheet. The snow. A foot of space which should have been wider, which couldn't have been emptier, which should have been filled with him. Warm, soft like snow her skin. Waiting.

The white curtains stir in the air from the open window, fluttering out into the room.

Wind in the sails pushing her homeward. The white sail billows. She will soon be ashore. Assured of his love, of his courage. She would wait for her husband the hero who would not fail. She could not have him fail. Even now he is striding, his footprints track a path in the snow to victory. He will come back to find her waiting. He will lay her down on the whiteness and she will warm him. She waited for the day, watching the horizon, laid out waiting, and he did not come.

A snowflake-patterned bedspread covers the bed. This thread has come loose: tug at it gently and it will pull free. Where the stitching has taken it below the surface, the pale sea green remains unfaded. Arabella Mackley made it for her sister-in-law, to keep her warm; it is embroidered with a design of her own devising, each flake as in nature unique. It is hard to know what Arabella meant by this quilt over which she laboured, this masterwork of envy and restraint. It may have been nothing more than a tribute to the snows that Emily longed for; a lapse in tact, possibly, to bury her too under ice, but not necessarily a cruel or stupid act. Emily kept the window open all through the year so that she could feel the cold sky on her skin, dreaming under her blanket of snow just as her husband lay under his (although she did not know then that he was buried, and no longer dreaming).

Lying there alone, night after night, it may have been that she wanted only a husband, not a hero. It may have been that she did not care if his heart was with her always, that the weak charm of his words lost their power to warm after months upon months, after a year, after three. Yearning hopelessly after him, night after night, the memory of him physically, actually present fading inevitably even as she grasped after it, until she could no longer recall his actual pulse beating against her palm.

Emily, lying prone on her bed, is far out to sea in a boat, alone. The sides nudge against icebergs, drifting all about her as she floats on the cold, black sea; she does not feel the chill through the boards under her back. No, she cannot feel a thing.

Four Norwegians have been found on Spitzbergen. After a hundred days, Edward and his men had not returned. She can see the words still, the photograph, their four gaunt faces that she cannot recognize, her own tears falling upon them. Mourning the hope that was torn from her when she turned that page.

She had sat as always in the morning room; the needle punctured and pulled; she turned the page. She stared at it for half an hour or more before complacent Arabella noticed a different pitch to the silence and looked up, saying, for something to say (although it was not yet twelve), 'I don't know why it is, but I'm quite ravenous today. I do hope lunch isn't late. I wonder if cook has coped with the *soufflé*.' She liked to say the word with an especially sophisticated French emphasis, and would very much have liked to share her concern with *someone* about Mrs MacLaverty's inability to conjure an acceptably fluffy rise – barely half an inch last time, she'd reckoned – and John seemed so indifferent to these matters ('Shall I fetch my steel rule, dear?' he had said, rather drily she'd thought; she coloured at the memory). But the hope of a *confidante* was deflated as she looked up, because Emily was bent over the paper which she'd barely turned since sitting down to it, her hands and forearms flat on the table, her nose not six inches from the third page, over which she was weeping quietly.

'I do hope . . . my dear. Are you unwell?' At

which Emily stood up abruptly, and asked to be excused, and hurried out of the room as fast as her skirts would allow her, without seeming even to hear Arabella ask if she would be coming down to join them, or should they have a tray sent up?

Emily is far out on the icy sea, alone. Thinking of nothing. This is the lie she is telling herself. Nothing, nothing. No more tears. A bleak and empty, freezing sea. She must think of nothing. After one hundred and twenty days, the ship set sail; they had not returned. The Norwegians brought no news. Nothing, nothing. She stretches out north and cannot find him. No news from the north. A barren frozen sea. He is lost to the frozen sea.

There is a knock. She can attach no meaning to the sound. Another, more persistent, a man saying her name softly. Ah, he has come back to her after all! How like him to surprise her. But no, she cannot deceive herself thus for longer than one fond moment. Gingerly she sits up, as if by moving quickly she might wake herself, and knowing that to be awake, to be aware, would be calamitous. She must stay afloat. It is all a strange dream, in which she is floating out in a little boat, alone, and cannot reach him . . .

'Come in,' says a woman's voice, her own but hollow and even.

John pushes the door gently. He takes a step into the room, but his other foot is reluctant to cross the threshold, leaving him with a foolish feeling spreading from his intruding knee to his chest, which he suddenly feels to be puffed, pompous, hopelessly inadequate to this task.

'Emily . . . Arabella told me . . .'

'Would you tell her that I'd rather not take lunch today, thank you. I am not feeling myself.' Or anything, she assures herself, I am not feeling anything, I am not anyone, as empty as the sea. Nothing, nothing.

'Emily. I saw the paper. I am very sorry. I . . . You mustn't despair. We mustn't.' His voice catches. 'I am sure Edward is safe; he will find his way home.'

Emily looks up and sees what John is withholding, what she, as a woman and a wife, can be permitted (although she will not permit it, she will not weep). She remembers that her husband is also John's brother, and sees that he, too, could not bear to lose him. She puts a hand out to him and his black eyes fill with ink; he will not allow them to spill.

Then he steps forward, closing the door behind him, and takes her hand. They cannot think now of propriety, which should halt him there at the threshold. He means only to sit beside her, with her hand in his. They each need only understanding, which they find in this grasp. He sits beside her, her long hand in his large one. He turns it and strokes the palm with his thumb. Then, although the foolishness has spread now across his shoulders and down his arms, and he is red with embarrassment and unsure of what he does, he raises it and kisses the centre, and presses it to his cheek, and then puts his to hers. They sit that way, each barely touching the other, for a long time. They hear the bell for lunch and do not stir. Their palms are wet with each other's tears. Eight men have died. Her husband, his brother, has not returned from the north.

Then, with tremendous care, keeping the keel steady, he unlaces her and lays her down on the bed, on the floor of the boat, with the indifferent sea all around them, rocked by it, and clinging tightly . . . She could allow him this, once only, the smallest space, opening for him to slide into

. . .

And then they are two bodies in the English sun, streaming through the window, and she weeps, and weeps, and he strokes her hair at the temple and she wonders if she can ever stop waiting, if she could permit herself or be permitted, what purpose it would serve to only stand and wait. She listens to his breathing even out beside her before she opens her eyes to see that his eyelids, still wet, are dark like Edward's. She kisses each one like a sister; she knows their lips will not meet again.

Nine months and seven days later, Edward Mackley was born with the briefest of cries, and passed quietly into Arabella's arms. Emily sat down at the breakfast table and said yes, she had hope still; yes, she would wait.

So this was where she sat, and watched herself fill out, grow round, and then age and slacken. Julia sees herself in the mirror now, the faint lines about her eyes that she earlier despaired of; when Emily was her age she hadn't been touched for ten years. She watched her son grow up; she played with him as an aunt ought to; at first her breasts ached and leaked to feed him but she did not. She was grateful, perhaps, that they took him, that they let her stay, that she could be near him. Where else could she go? She watched as his face took the shape of Edward's – and, of course, John's – his brow, his nose, the angle of the head upon the neck.

Like the Snow Queen's chambers, the chambers of Emily's heart grew vast, empty and cold. They cracked and ached with ice in the night. She would wake and find her fingers clutching and frozen. Only young Edward could melt her, but he was brought up to be sensible, with none of his namesake's fire; a rather chilly little boy with a pedant's brow and a serious purse to his lips. John taught him morals, Arabella taught him manners, and Emily could rarely persuade him to make mischief. Once she lifted him to ride the snow leopard, treasuring his giggling delight as she cried, 'Faster! Oh, Edward, the bears are coming, we must go faster!' Hearing his father descend the stairs, they froze, forming a brief tableau with the animals, suspended in motion as if they had never been animate (but moments before, how the leopard had run!). She put a hand on his mouth and lifted him gently down so that John found them quite innocently examining the baby bear's paws. He paused to ask distractedly 'what on earth the pair of them were up to' before passing through the hallway with a bemused smile. In truth, he was uneasy around his son, and more so around Emily; he was comfortable only with those he could gently condescend to, his patients, his wife.

Emily, too, felt embarrassed by young Edward's presence, and by his adoptive mother's indifference to it; the more so when little Thomas arrived, a robust, sanguine boy, instantly (and naturally) his mother's favourite, forever upsetting whatever delicate project his brother was occupied by, and clamouring for Emily's attention with a child's intuition that she loved his brother better. Even though his mother doted on him so and was not awkward with him as she was with Edward, even though his father withheld something from his older brother that he himself did not want for, even though, indeed, he wanted for nothing, still this preference on his aunt's part seemed to Thomas unfair. But Arabella praised him lavishly, for his strength and his appetite and his lovely bright hair, especially in Emily's presence. When the boys were led in to visit them in the afternoon, before they all sat down to tea, she would heave him onto her knee – 'Such a big boy!' – and jiggle him while Edward and Emily sat separately, alone, each intent on a book, and if Arabella meant to prove by this that she was the victor, then Emily could not hope to dispute it.

The children, of course, spent most of their time in the nursery, which later became the schoolroom. Emily would drop in on them occasionally, longing to interrupt and take over a poetry lesson but knowing she had no right, no place there. Her days were spent for the most part, as ever, with Arabella; Arabella with her pudgy face, her nose as pointed as a pin, her rounded shoulders, her surprisingly small and clever hands, sitting when she remembered with her back straight and slowly sagging until the call for lunch revived her. They could offer each other no comfort. Was it for her sister-in-law's sake that Emily surrendered the remainder of her youth to drabness, that she wore dark blue and grey, that her hair was pulled into a sober bun, that she was calm and placid with company and no longer allowed her dark gold skin to flush crimson? Was it out of tact or penance that she transformed herself into her son's maiden aunt? Or did she fear the consequences of allowing her eyes to flare in John's presence?

Very little of Arabella survives in the house. All that remains of her is a drift of cloths and cushions and coverlets; of the doilies that each heirloom is placed on. Always in the corner of conversations, she lived by needle and hoop and hook, turning a crocheted circle around and about or puncturing linen and pulling the silk through, silent, possibly bitter or jealous or only sad. History can be cruel; she was only an ordinary woman, washed out by the dazzle of the remarkable family she married into, for ever on the edges of the Mackleys. In photographs, the light seems never quite to reach her, an indistinct human mass by John's side, expanding as the years roll on.

It had always seemed to Julia that it was Arabella who was pushed to the edges; but she sees now that in life she was triumphant, even if the record doesn't bear this out, even if it is Emily who is remembered. In the early pictures, that brief period when Edward and his young bride are captured together, they seem somehow to radiate distinction and brilliance through the faded half-tones of sepia or silver, as if the plate can only hint at what they shone with. Beside Edward, John is the lankier, older, more conventional brother, but still together they are a handsome pair; and Arabella, to her husband's side, does not quite fit with this trio of striking individuals. In later pictures Edward has vanished, but whenever Emily makes an appearance, although she is reduced, thinner, wilfully plain, alone, always it is to her that the gaze is drawn.

It was usually John – one of the last true

Victorian dilettantes, a keen amateur in this as in so many things – who set up the shot. It is easy to imagine that the blurred white-pink mass of Arabella, swathed in lace and satin, was as overlooked in life as she was by the photographer's composition. But perhaps it was not that Arabella was inherently nebulous; perhaps the focus of the lens betrayed John's eye, which in life he would never again have allowed to wander, having more than learned his lesson. In the family portrait in the drawing room his gaze is turned indulgently upon his wife, as it should be. But there is an unsettling oddity in the otherwise orthodox arrangement of the painting, a dark gap between the elder son at his father's side and the mother with babe in arms. As if there is a figure missing, who has no right to be there.

Emily went on living in her husband's family's house, having no other option. Taking tea in primrose-patterned cups, spreading toast with the pale yellow shells of butter that were pared off daily with a silver butter-curler. Receiving guests and answering politely their questions about her husband. 'Well, he may yet be found,' they would say, scraping butter on toast complacently, the same phrase every time gaining in absurdity as the years passed. Eventually, it was clear that they could only be referring to his body, and yet it was said in the same way. And 'Yes, we may hope,' Emily would reply politely, in the same way every time, as they crunched, crunched, scraped and crunched. It was never suggested that she should do otherwise, that she should cease to hope, that she should consider forgoing the childless dignity of the widow. So she lived with her secret son and her nephew and a man who painfully resembled the one she fell in love with, so that it was difficult sometimes to recall the details in which his features differed.

It was impossible now to imagine the marriage that never was. He could not have tolerated the life she had been compelled to lead in this house, and she could not now imagine another; he would have grown more restless and dissatisfied with every scrape and crunch. They would scrape and stifle thus until he went away again, sooner or later, on another adventure, and if he came back he would have left again, and again, and their life would be always this parting and waiting and each reunion would diminish in joy as the years went on, perhaps, and she grew each time noticeably older and thicker in his absence and weighed down with nothing but waiting; and the romance of that must surely pall. Because what was she expected to do but wait?

If Emily gave in to such bitterness sometimes then she smoothed it, in the evenings and sometimes in the afternoons, with a glass of gin and reminiscence. Having nothing else to hold on to, she remembered herself as she had been and resurrected nightly the man she had loved, carefully preserved just as his corpse was, although she didn't know it. She remembered skiing and playing in the snow, and the mist clearing from the fjords in the morning, and the brief months of what seemed now to her a perpetual consummation, of tenderness and laughter and passion. She read the ship's log that the Norwegians brought to England and laughed aloud to herself, saying, 'How like him, how like him,' willing herself to remember him, to hear his voice and almost believing she heard it. At first she would read parts out loud until she realized, from the inattentive smiles of her listeners, that she had read this part before perhaps; she found it hard to recall. Edward out on the snow; shooting the fox; the ice, the sky. She told the children the stories. She was saddened by little Edward's polite boredom, as if he wished to distance himself from the name he'd been given; Thomas, in whom she had little interest, was anyway too restive to sit and listen for long; so when Helen was born, she found a welcome and unexpected ally. The girl would ask her to tell the same stories over and over, reviving them with her questions – what did she wear on this occasion, on that? Was her corset awfully tight? Was Dr Nansen very brilliant, did she speak to him? How did Edward look, how did he stand, with his arm on the mantel and the fire of ambition burning? Did he really shoot the bear, right through the eye? What did he say when they met, when they parted? Did she really love to ski, did she fall in the snow? Were the Norwegians terrible and huge like Vikings? What colours flashed across the sky? – so that new details emerged, new vibrancy and life, and it became difficult to extract what was true from the tales she had embellished for the child. By then, she was over forty. If she had ever hoped for another life she had made no mention of it; and now it was too late.

Each evening she rose and made her way, at times a little unsteadily, to her room, bidding the polar bears goodnight. She climbed the stairs and tried not to notice how it grew harder as the years drew on, how her knees grew stiff; she closed the door to her room behind her and undressed and quickly pulled on her plain brushed-cotton night-dress so as not to touch her own breasts or her belly, rounding and sagging gently from her skinny frame; she unpinned her hair and took care not to see the fade of its lustre, took care not to meet her own eye in the mirror, preferring to sit in half-darkness with only the bedside lamp lit; then she would climb into bed to read, and if the letters swam it was probably only the gin, not her sight failing, and never tears.

She waited sixty years to hear the end of the story, read to her in this same bedroom that she had slept alone in for so long. One day in January 1902, Edward had slipped from the world without her knowing, and now she could not say if she had dreamed of him that night, even. His body was preserved by the ice, they said; only his skin had blackened and contracted, his dark eyes like hers pearled over. How long it had been since she dreamed of him. Helen read the tale, all the way to the end, trying to follow his maps, to trace a route through the rambling torment of his dying – always pushed on by Emily, who wanted to know. She would answer, sometimes – 'No, they do not call you a fool, dear' – as if he were beside her and in need of reassurance; 'There is nothing to forgive, Edward, if you can ever forgive me'; 'Yes, goodnight, sleep well, goodnight' as if she stretched out beside him where he lay, transformed by the frozen sea: 'Those are pearls that were his eyes, now, Helen. Look!'

When at last she gave up her secret to his namesake, there was nothing more to tell.

Laid out on the cold white sheet, on the snow, with the vast deep sky above and the ice deep below, the beat of her heart escalating, coruscating, high and skating across the sky, dying as he came to meet her across the snow.

PART VI

Deep evening.

Outside, the last of the gold has dripped from the leaves of the willow, leaving them burnished copper-green. The sky has softened into violet. The air is still balmy from the day's heat, but it is not so fierce now; the curtains flutter in the cooling air, the room grows dim, the glass darkens. It no longer returns any gaze, for we are alone now with Emily's fading ghost; the room is settling into emptiness. Julia, who was moments ago reflected in the gathering shadows, has left this thought trailing behind her:

The white sail billows . . . white sheets in the wind . . . Damn, the laundry.

Following the trail of it through the dark house, we will find her once more in the garden; how different now in the twilight, no longer scorched by the sun. Pause now with her on the lawn and breathe in; listen to the insects and the rustle of plants, leaves furling, the fluff and settle of feathers, earth shifting under tiny paws and turned by pallid grubs and worms; the garden easing into the blue darkness. Night flowers open cautiously, quietly, the warmth of the day transformed into deep sweet perfume. More vibrant blooms are dimmed without the sun to brighten them, and give up their glory to the pale, fragrant flowers of the dusk. The night-scented stock, innocuous by daylight, releases its essence. Honeysuckle, cupping its hands to hold nectar for the moths to sup. The scent of the garden, the tiny white blossoms like stars fallen on the lawn, and her bare feet white against the grass, and the white sheets; and the moths, intoxicated.

CLEAN SHEETS

Out in the darkening garden the sheets are indeed still aflutter. She washed and hung them out this morning after last night's crumpled rest; the bedlinen has for two weeks tangled nightly about their too-hot limbs, and she'd forgotten to launder the spare set. And daily comforts must be served even as the world turns through its more momentous changes, and if Julia is unsettled then there is at least the certainty of cool, clean linen to lie down on. If she leaves them to flap on the line they will be dew-soaked by morning, and will disturb the darkness of tonight's garden. Simon will be distracted by them, as he is by all that is misplaced, and she will sense him struggling with himself all through the dinner she has planned (which she needs to attend to, because he must surely be home soon?). She will sense his distraction as he appears to listen, to enjoy, to praise her cooking and savour the wine that she has chosen specially, but he may not even notice the choice she has made because he will be resolutely keeping his eyes away from the sheets while deciding whether to mention it (which would irritate her and so spoil the evening) or discreetly take them in himself once they are finished (in which case his rising from the table at the first opportunity will spoil the evening with disappointment), so it is vital, yes, it is a matter of preserving the life of their undernourished marriage, it is a matter of this frail thing's survival that she take in the sheets.

Shadowed wings flutter about her, drawn to the brightness and the sweet air, creamy with scent:

Honeysuckle is his favourite smell, he said, furred creatures suckling sweetness; he laid out the sheet on the ground and lit the lamp and they came flying. One after another, winged things all about us and the smell overwhelming, the scent of the flowers and the dust from their wings. Flying at the light until they were senseless and the sheet was covered with winged little lives that fell at our feet, and I chose one for his jar and he killed it, but tenderly, with dark eyes admiring, so I did not think him cruel but beautiful.

The sheets spread in the night have reminded Julia of this, years ago, not long after they were married and visiting Aunt Helen; of how Simon had hesitantly asked her if he could set out a trap in the garden, if she would like to join him. It was a moths' paradise, he said, that garden. He named the flowers that grew there that would draw them and she was surprised to learn he knew these words, surprised by his love of honeysuckle, did not know then of the nights he'd spent wrapped in the smell of it and the silence, the whisper of dusky wings, patient by the lamp alone and glad of his father's absence (who was interested only in brazen butterflies).

She loved him for it. She loved him, then, for his careful labels, for his delicate hands, which she watched in fascination as he drove the pin in and laid tape across the wings to set them, for his patience –

'What now?' she'd said when the catch was all covered, the one she'd chosen that he said he'd set for her.

'Now we wait,' he'd smiled.

'For how long?'

'Two weeks.'

'Two weeks!'

'You have to learn to enjoy anticipation.'

'Oh' (sigh). 'Well, what else now?'

'For a start, turn the lamp off and take in the sheet. And get it washed before Aunt Helen sees we've covered it in wing-dust.'

Later, on a different, clean sheet, she'd lain out cruciform –

'Would you like to set and pin me?'

'But you are so lovely in flight.'

Yes, she loved him for this, for all of this, which she hasn't thought of in so long. She unpegs and bundles the sheets into the basket, and checks her watch, and could it be wrong? It is almost nine now. Where is Simon? When will he be home?

Simon is on his way, he is stuck on a busy train, which all the force of his will could not move faster. He had emerged from the underground into the station with minutes to spare, only to find that his usual train was arbitrarily cancelled. He found an angry crowd around the announcements board, and joined the chorus of watch-checking sighs, tuts and muttering. He called home but the line was engaged, and, upon realizing that he was relieved at this, felt a fresh twist of the horrible guilt that he had allowed to be subdued by the press of strangers on the Tube. He pushed his way onto the first service available, glad of the advantage his height gave him and trying to justify his urgency as he turned to face out, nose almost squashed into the glass, to see those left behind, a woman close to tears, laden with shopping, a couple in evening dress, an old man. How could he have helped them? Every man for himself . . . how he loathed himself.

He breathed his own hot breath back off the pane for the next four stops; then, as ever, the exodus freed him and he was left to a half-empty carriage, pushing on into the night, escaping from under the city's orange sky. He found a seat on his own. This was worse. There is nothing like the crushing proximity of others, the putrid commute of a summer's night, to clear the mind of everything but desperate and immediate disgust. Now he sits, cooled by the air from the open window rushing, and despair begins to close upon him, a narrowing chasm.

The beer is making him drowsy; he can feel his senses dulling as if he is wrapped in a thick layer of glass (or ice); sounds are muted, the bright carriage interior falls away. Narrowing, crushing. How tightly she held him last night, how silent she was, how innocent of his sin, still crying and gripping him to her, her eyes tight closed as ever, and he felt her heart against him, a spasm, soundless, tightening around him . . .

and then she falls away from him, dissolving, beyond his reach, impossibly distant, retracting to a point in the centre of a vast white plain. Then he is on a boat sailing into a narrow gully, crushing, the fingers he feels gripping his skin are red-nailed, tearing his skin and leaving scratches to show she owns him, and biting at his neck and shoulders, a fleshy, powerful body beneath him, on top of him now, a big brutal bright mouth and she keeps her eyes wide open, a chasm, and he is crushed, crushed from all sides, with a groan, and he wakes with a guilty start as the train squeals into the station, halting just beyond the platform and easing in slowly enough to let his blood ebb. He is shamefully engorged, like a boy on the school bus, he thinks; but by the time he must stand it has subsided, although the shame remains, thick and red.

The train spits Simon on to the platform and trundles off with a wheeze to the coast, where it could fall off the end of the country into the ocean for all he cares. He checks his watch – two minutes past nine. He is late. He told her he'd be late. No cause for suspicion or alarm.

He gets into his car and sits for a minute, for two, for three at the wheel, his hands resting on it, staring at himself in the windscreen, projected out onto the darkening night. His head drops; he sits with head bowed for a moment, for two, then raises it, pushes his glasses back on to his nose, turns the key and sets off for home, hoping the road is clear.

Julia is in the bedroom; in the kitchen, the lamb is resting, ready to carve, the broad beans are steaming, the beetroot is roasted and tossed in dressing, the wine is breathing quietly, steadily, letting the warm air soften its cherry-rich savours. She has upended the laundry basket and is folding towels, her stomach a little grip of hunger and nerves; where is he? She strips the bed, pulling off the sheets and cases, and dumps the dirty linen in one pile, the naked duvet and the pillows in another, surrounded by the familiar pleasing crump of duck feather and down. She checks her watch; ten past nine. She matches the corners of the duvet to the inside-out corners of the fresh cover, thinking as always as she grips through the linen of a little mittened hand, the little fingers lost in padding. She glances at the bedside clock – 21:06. Well, her watch is a little fast. But even if it is four minutes earlier than she thought, he is still late. She is amazed to feel the back of her throat strain and catch, the tightness of starting tears through her nose and jaw. Hormones, she thinks, almost time again, again, the remorseless flow.

The child that Julia and Simon didn't have would be four years old now. Its fifth birthday would be soon, today even, if it had arrived a little early. If it had arrived only a little early rather than much, much earlier, far too early. Julia doesn't like to think of the child as 'it' but it was too soon to tell. In fact, Julia doesn't like to think of it at all. Only sometimes, like now, as she straightens and tidies haphazardly, the fingers of her left hand graze the place where that bump had just begun to grow. It is flat and soft now, that place, tight with nothing but fore-boding, but her fingers remember the tautening skin.

Calm down, idiot, don't cry. Hush. A lullaby. I don't know any lullabies, I haven't the words for lulling, I would have learned them if

She flumps the just-filled pillows and slaps at the sheets of the bed to smooth them, then straightens the duvet on top.

Lulled by waves, by water, I was always; the sea that I love, salt water. We went to the beach and I lay there letting the waves lap at my happy belly, buoyed, my boy maybe, before it

She folds a towel with an uncharacteristic, smart flick to straighten it. But the hand, when the towel is stowed on the pile, wanders back.

Lullabelly lullaby, sleep don't cry, hush little hush don't cry

Stupid, don't cry

It may or may not please her if she knew it was, indeed, a boy.

They do not speak of it. She was not even three months' gone; no one had noticed the bump, but she could feel it. She put Simon's hand on it. His face, intent upon her skin, rounding and dipping, his warm gentle palm curved below her navel; she can't bear to recall his face, then, the sincerity of his awe. They have not tried again. Julia is frightened. The first was an accident, they didn't plan it; a happy accident, they agreed at the time, but have never spoken of another. It is perhaps a conversation they should have. The words that Simon can't find in the silence:

'I am sorry that I cannot find a way to make you happy, I am frightened that you will never be happy, I am frightened of your sadness. I will not leave you alone, you should not be alone, I do not think that we should be alone.'

And she:

'I am so frightened of death. I am scared of growing old and of not growing old, and dying. I am frightened that all my babies will die, that you will die, and of dying.'

The things they do not say only grow louder with time, no matter how neatly the towels are stacked, how clean the sheets. But the bed is made now, and Julia closes her ears to the words that have gone unspoken and tells herself the clutching emptiness in her belly is just hunger. And it's true, she is hungry; it's getting late. The smell of herbs drifting up from the kitchen reminds her.

Rosemary, for remembrance. Just hungry, just hormones.

She sits at the dressing table and carefully wipes off the last traces of her red mouth; she brushes her hair; Tess lands lightly on her lap, taking care not to catch the dress on a claw, and starts to turn and settle, but is lifted before she can make even one exploratory revolution, and carried out of the room. Julia flicks the switch and closes the door just in time to miss the searchlight sweep of Simon's car pulling into the driveway.

The house is dark as he approaches. Bedroom, drawing room, attic windows and all in between unlit, as if sleeping or abandoned. He cannot remember seeing it so, aside from the night they moved in, and as he makes his way up the gravel drive the sound of his own footsteps seems detached from his own tread, as if in a dream, displaced.

Edward Mackley followed this dreaming path many times over; he dreamed of coming home, and knew with the certainty of nightmares that all the rooms were dark and empty; that they were occupied by others who would not know him, and would not allow him in; that his own family, his wife, would not know him, and would scream at his blackened skin; that all within were slaughtered, somehow by his hand. But always he woke before the door could open, and could recall only how close he had come, how he had almost reached the end of his long journey home, and cursed himself for waking.

Now Simon approaches the house and sees, in that space of a few crunching gravelled steps, visions of Julia at the centre of the darkness, waiting for him, knowing somehow what he has done and unable to forgive him for a single kiss, for even contemplating betrayal for an instant; sitting waiting in the darkness submerged in cold black water. He does not know if he will tell her the truth, if it would hurt her irreparably to do so and who he would in truth be sparing if he spared her that. He does not know if the truth is always necessary, if it is sometimes better to conceal, or if that is merely selfishness, and if selfishness is inherently wrong. He knows only that he does not want to lose her, and also that he cannot go on with it as it is. He cannot go on failing to fulfil what she lacks, aching to fill the emptiness she won't acknowledge, whatever it is that she is without.

He has reached the door, keys in hand; he opens it cautiously (9.18). Creeping inside, he can just make out the dying flowers, the mirror (he avoids the spectral version of himself therein, the pale face and guilt-darkened eyes); he calls her name. There is no answer. He smells lamb cooking, knows she wants to please him and hopes it isn't spoiled. But he told her he would be late home.

He must slam the door to close it; the reverberation shudders the air into a thousand pairs of fluttering wings, clamouring about him in a panic and settling back into dusty slumber. He calls her name again, 'Julia?', gently, as if she is already beside him, invisible; as if he wishes to summon just this one of the spirits without agitating the rest.

In the drawing room, the ladies' white forms in the portraits are brilliant in the darkness, a full moon opposite a crescent; Edward's and John's shadowed eyes, across from each other, watch their living likeness pass between as Simon runs the gauntlet of her ancestors without turning the light on. He moves into the dining room. The crystal and glass catch facets of yellow light; the doors to

353

the conservatory are open to reveal a table set with silver, candle-lit, and beyond, looking out to the garden, is Julia.

There she stands: facing out to the night, her back to him, her loose hair flickering bronze. Strange how peaceful she looks, framed by the square panes of the open French doors, as if part of a painting in which the artist has imposed the same muted blue upon the stillness of the garden beyond and the unwitting sitter's repose. She does not move as he watches from the darkness at the back of her. Nothing stirs; the night is silent. It would be possible now to creep behind her, slip off shoes and pad across the rug and step out onto the warm tiled floor, and sweep her hair forward from her neck and blow upon it gently, or kiss the sharp nub of her spine just below the nape, just where the fine fronds curl and wisp, put a hand to her waist and let her head fall against the breast-bone behind her . . .

Simon watches. He finds that he is holding his breath, and lets it out very gently, soundless. Then he steals out into the corridor, and down the short flight of steps to the kitchen, turning no lights on; it is hot, the oven has been on for hours and, he sees from its orange glow, is keeping dinner warm; but still he unlatches the door, at which Tess has been idly scratching, so that she streaks out into the night before him. He makes his way up the path, like pale stepping stones over water, tiny icebergs, white on black. He does not look back at the house, so that they can both pretend she hasn't seen him; when he reaches the shed and sneaks a glance back to the conservatory, she is gone.

But she has not gone. She has merely taken a step back into the darkness, as we will discern if we take a moment to discover the gleam of her eyes. She has retreated so that, if he were to look back, he won't know she's seen him. A few moments ago, she thought he was behind her, thought she felt the darkness shift to accommodate another form; she thought she felt him approach and waited, hoping, almost feeling his fingers brush the nape of her neck, but when she turned the room was empty and when she turned again, she saw him on the path in the moonlight. He did not come to find her. He does not want to find her. She wants to go to him but finds she cannot. Did he savour the scent of the meat, at least? She stares into the flame and at the moths that hover about it. She cannot go on without.

PIANO

Simon is sitting at his desk in his shed. This shed, his own, is at the far end of the garden, behind the one that belongs to the house, which is full of old gardening tools and predictable cobwebs, clutter and dust, a confusion of worn wood and prongs and paint tins. Simon's shed is tidy and clean; it smells of pine and cedar and the coal-tar pong of naphthalene – mothballs, to the layman, to protect dead wings from the living. Behind him, on the wall, a series of Brimstones, caught when he was fourteen, have settled above their names, which he wrote out proudly with a fountain pen – his first mounts, simple, delicate, greenish-white.

A set of wide, shallow drawers occupies most of the far wall. Simon sits on a straight-backed chair, from which he tends to hunch forward. In front of him is a window onto the garden, with a blackout blind. Sitting at the desk in the evenings, with the angle-poise lamp beaming bright into the garden, Simon had too many times been startled by the smack of a moth upon the pane. Although he cannot credit them with a sense of irony, still he found this pelting of furry death distasteful, in light of his occupation behind the glass. So the blind was installed to insulate him from the night.

Tonight, Simon is very still, and for once sitting straight; there is nothing before him on the desk to hunch over; the blind is open, the lamp is not lit. His expression is hard to discern in the dimness; the little light from the moon reflects on his glasses; his eyes may be open or shut. His long hands rest on the desk.

He has left Julia behind in the house, she has not seen him; he has escaped into the blue garden, warm and still, full of insect clicks and piping, heavy with the honeysuckle that for weeks he has forgotten to come out and relish the scent of. What is he doing here while she waits inside? He sat down at his desk here and found he could not turn the lamp on, he could not open the drawer or take up his tools to set a catch which should be dry now in its jar, and ready to mount; he is not sure this was ever his intention. His hand instead raised the blind, left closed to keep the space cool, and then came to rest two feet away from the other on the desk, and he has been sitting for perhaps four minutes now in this position. He doesn't quite know what he's doing here, while she waits inside. He does not check his watch.

He tries to steady and gather himself in the darkness, but he cannot pursue any single thought; he is at the mercy of his own memories, flitting and battering about his head, and he is powerless to drive them away. Every bitter disappointment, every grate of shame, every time he's wished for something different from himself or someone else.

His mother, washing up at the kitchen sink, leaves soap suds on her face from the hand she swipes her cheek with so he will not see her crying. He leans against her hip, pressing his face into her, and receives a damp hard squeeze of the shoulder, quickly withdrawn with a sigh. 'What do you *want*, Simon?'

He tugs at his father's sleeve one too many times; his father's hand slips, botches the pin, pulls away angrily. '*What*, Simon?'

They can't afford a piano, they tell him; he will have to practise at school, he will have to practise there to be the best. He plays at the concert. He gets the most applause. They say well done then praise at length the choir and Rebecca Jones who read a poem. Simon would not dare to speak or sing. He did not dare to hold the last chord quite long enough. This means that he played the last chord wrong. He mentions it, hesitant, in the car on the way home. His mother says, to comfort him, 'I'm sure no one cared.'

Julia is surprised, delighted, to find him sitting one evening at the old piano in the drawing room. She has been out with a friend but has come home early, he did not expect her. They have known each other for ten years, they have been married for eight. She didn't know he could play the piano. How is it possible that she didn't know? She pleads with him to play for her. He hasn't played for years, he says. He won't remember. He wasn't very good. Go on, she says. He doesn't want to. He won't. He shuts the lid; he doesn't mean to bang it. She winces. Her voice is very quiet. 'I just didn't know you could play.'

The tips of his fingers are pressing against the wood of the desk, the rhythm of the first notes she missed this morning. His eyes are closed. He takes off his glasses without opening his eyes, pinches his nose, presses forefinger and thumb hard into the corners of the deep sockets until blue lights flash across the dark maroon; he opens them and feels the resurgent blood spread across the bridge of his nose and up across his scalp. Carefully, he sets his glasses down, stands and ventures out, closing the door softly behind him, and picks his path step by round pale step back to the house through the scented garden.

Standing at the top of the stone stair to the kitchen, he sees that the countertop light is now switched on. In the dark of the house, Julia has cast this single circle of electricity about herself. She moves beyond it and then he sees her face brightened again in the glow from the oven as she opens the door to lift out plates and dishes, blowing out her cheeks as she does so, as she always does. It is a gesture so familiar that he could not recall now the first time he saw it (it was scones, on his fifth visit – he'd remember the scones, if he were reminded. If reminded, he would recall the decadence of clotted cream, the home-made jam, the contrast with the dense, claggy, margarine-spread treats of his childhood). She places the plates in the pooled light on the countertop, then presses her hands to the foil-wrapped meat, checking it hasn't gone cold he supposes, then moves back to the hob; she is just barely lit now, a warm sheen on her skin. She stirs a pan in her ponderous way, staring into it as if she is divining something in the sauce, and lifts the wooden spoon, stretching her head towards it instead of bringing it close so as not to spill it (so that her lovely neck emerges from the mass of her hair); she puts her lips to it gingerly, holding the spoon lifted for a second after sipping, reaching for the salt and changing her mind, resuming her slow stirring with a satisfied smile which is very close to sadness. And all of this together, the fine downy arm that stirs, stirs, the peer into the pan, her long neck, the sound of that tiny sip and her sad smile, sets off a ripple in Simon which swells into a wave of tenderness, building, building, so powerful that he fears he will be drowned, which he wishes he could unleash in a great cascade down the steps before him, but he cannot unleash it and he feels something in him reaching, but still he does not know how to reach her.

Julia stirs, stirs. At the centre of the rich wine-brown sauce, a circle of glutinous bubbles bulges and pops like a swamp, satisfying to watch. Should she go out to him in the garden, tap on the door of the shed? It's getting late. But there is an unspoken rule, that he would never ask of her, and which she yet obeys, that she does not disturb him there. But it's getting late. But he did not come to find her; she heard the door slam and half heard him call, but only once (he only half wanted her to hear him). And then he was out in the moonlight alone, and doesn't want her to follow. She stirs. Tastes –

No, perfect, it needs nothing. Except someone else to taste it.

Resignedly, she resumes stirring. She hears, in the garden, a purring mmrrr-iaow of pleasure which means that someone has stroked Tess's fur backwards. She looks up, startled by the sound so near to her when she thought herself unseen in her little lit circle.

'Julia . . .'

'You scared me! I thought I heard the door . . .'

'I'm so sorry I'm so late.' He comes down the stairs now and into her circle of light. 'I told you I had that meeting – but then the train was cancelled. I called when I came in but you didn't answer so I thought you must be upstairs.' (Although, he thinks, there were no lights on, which he couldn't fail to have noticed, so he cannot believe his own lie; but she seems to, she doesn't know that he noticed, she has no reason to doubt him. He cannot explain to her that he saw her standing in the darkness, and wanted to go to her but couldn't.) She is still stirring, so that he cannot encompass her entirely as he'd like to. Instead he touches her elbow and kisses the top of her head, just as if this were any other day.

'I was worried – I called the office and Joanne said you'd left about seven. Then I tried to phone and you didn't answer.' She is trying to keep the reproach out of her voice.

'I had to meet a client for a drink. Awful man. I thought I'd told you, sorry.' Simon knows full well that he kept the details as vague as possible; but he is relying on her inattentive morning manner and knows she will, again, believe him. And this is anyway not quite a lie, but a conflation and omission of truths – which still feels as nasty and spineless as a lie. 'I tried to call you back but the line was engaged.'

'Oh, I was speaking to Miranda maybe – I'm sure you did tell me. It doesn't matter, you're home now. How was your day?'

'Hm, you know. The usual. How's Miranda?'

'She's fine, she . . . I had a bit of an odd day, actually. With Jonathan.'

'Ah, I'd forgotten.'

Julia has put down her spoon now. She turns to him with a strange soft sad look about her, which he can't remember seeing before. 'Simon . . .' A hand, hesitant, on his chest; then her head laid gently beside it. He holds it to his breastbone and strokes the small of her back with his thumb, and kisses again, more tenderly this time, the top of her head. He thinks she may be crying but when he takes her shoulders and holds her away, forcing himself to meet her eyes, he sees only that same softness, as if she is trying to say something. For a moment longer they stay there, wordless, as if about to speak.

And then, because it all happened a hundred years ago, and now it's late on a Thursday, and she has opened a good bottle of wine, she gives herself a little shake and says:

'Hungry?'

'Absolutely. I hope I'm not too late.'

'Well, a minute later and it would have been Tess's lucky day – but you know her table manners are appalling. I'd much rather eat with you.'

'Why don't you serve up and I'll go and put some music on,' he says, with a last squeeze of her elbow.

Tess, who has followed Simon down to the kitchen, has for the duration of this exchange been noisily licking up the last of her fish, the plastic bowl scraping on the tiles; having heard her name mentioned and seen them looking down at her, she has taken this as an invitation and is now attentively, affectionately curling about Julia's ankles, in the hope of a scrap of fresh-cut meat. Julia is somehow able to move freely, uncon-strained by this furry figure of eight; she takes a shred of the meat's crust and drops it into the waiting maw. Tess carries her morsel to a corner, pins it carefully with a paw and gnaws at it contentedly.

Julia carves the lamb onto warmed plates, perfectly tender and not spoiled at all. A sequence of notes creeps up on her from the drawing room. The theme is familiar, but she cannot place it. She wonders what he has chosen; it is not their habit to listen to music together, it is one of his secret provinces. He is making her an offering, she thinks. She has to strain to hear; has it stopped? No, there again; the same sequence a little stronger this time, it seems to loop into itself, this tune; whatever it is, she likes it. It halts and trips and goes on; a wrong note? What would she know – but yes, there again, a pause and corrective repeat. This is not a recording. Someone is playing the piano.

On quiet evenings, when the Mackleys were not entertaining, the family retired to the drawing room to play cards, to converse, to read, to smoke. These were the days when leisure was an organized affair, when the hours before bedtime were structured and edifying, before the century slumped into passivity. Every large house then had its piano; the Mackleys' was largely neglected aside from social occasions, upon which Jane Whitstable (or some such) would warble her way through a repertoire of pastoral ditties and German folk song, to the plodding accompaniment of whichever young man most hopelessly admired her. John would occasionally strike up at Christmas; Arabella had no ear. It was brushed far more often by a maid's duster than by a musician's touch.

But John came in from town one afternoon in the early spring of 1901 to hear, as he handed over his coat and hat in the hallway, the sound of a favourite sonata played with simple elegance and passion – so much of the latter that Emily did not hear him greeted at the door – and of course in those days the wood had not yet swelled and there was no slam to alert her. He came into the room to find his sister-in-law seated there, eyes closed as her long quick fingers found the keys, unerring; her thumb finished a phrase with the barest depression of the ivory, sliding off as her foot held the pedal for a moment longer, and as her foot lifted she lifted her head too and saw him, and the blush of her fervour darkened to its deepest crimson.

'I'm sorry, I have disturbed you. I couldn't resist listening.'

From then on, their evenings were filled more often than not with music and John's enthusiasm, the clack of the clock and the ponk of Arabella's ever-industrious needles drowned out by Bach, Beethoven, Chopin; Emily rapt and John enraptured, leafing through papers or some weighty volume that could not possibly interest him more than the back of her neck and her quick clever fingers, caught in the corner of his eye.

Then four Norwegians were found on Spitzbergen, the last presumed survivors of the *Persephone*, the ship abandoned to the ice to be forced down into the underworld for ever; and Emily took to her bed, and his wife too was resting, and after little Edward was born there was no more music heard in that house. When Helen asked, many years later, if Emily could play, she replied that she had fallen out of the habit, somehow, and had probably forgotten, and she blushed a dark red that had not burned her cheeks for a long time, for too long. And John said, 'Don't pester your aunt, Helen,' and the subject was not raised again. And so the piano went largely unplayed. For a century it was touched only roughly, by overexcited guests and children, or with the mechanical delicacy of an occasional tuner whom Aunt Helen brought in on the off-chance someone might take pity on the poor old thing and play properly, she said. She would be pleased to see Simon sitting there now, to know her efforts were not wasted; for when he came into the room this evening, thinking he would finally recover that CD for Julia, and found himself instead lifting the lid off the keyboard and making a tentative approach to those first creeping phrases, he found that, just as it had been last April when he had refused to play on, it was almost perfectly in tune. A few years of neglect had only slightly flattened the low notes; he recalled the ugly pale yellow instrument he had been compelled to play at school, and forgave the deep mahogany timbre of the Mackleys' piano for this minor fault.

Julia creeps through the dining room into the conservatory, so as not to disturb him, and sets out the plates and dishes on the table, and pours the wine and takes a deep red sip and breathes in the quiet evening and the music that suffuses it.

Then she carries both glasses through to the drawing room, where Simon, in deference to her, has lit only the small lamp on top of the piano, not wishing to shatter the darkness with harsh crystal light. She leans shyly in the open doorway, watching him. He is intent upon the keys, frowning, but not angrily; he slows and quickens as his fingers trace the path down years of forgetting; he picks the melody out and the chords follow with a rightness that beguiles her. A phrase loops upon itself, another loop, more gentle, and a diminuendo upon the last variation; a pause, a half-bar's rest which seems to suspend the air, to contain the day and the night, so that all is held within and turns upon it. Then his resting fingers come to sudden, fluttering life, as fast and subtle as the wings he's caught so many times between them, and there is a flurry of notes doubling back and pushing on, higher, some sure and strong and others barely a shiver, as if his hands are cupped about her heart and it beats in time with this hectic crescendo, an overspilling of something that can't be contained in one single simple rhythm but seems to burst free of its bars . . . She can hear that some of the notes are wrong, but he does not stop or slow down, his long hand graceful even in error, trailing down and rushing up the keys until a last, tragic chord . . . which he allows to briefly linger before letting the pedal go with a bang, so that their eyes meet in an abrupt silence. Then he laughs.

'Something like that, anyway.'

She laughs too, delighted, and remembers that she can't applaud because she's still holding the glasses, and rushes to him to hand him his with a kiss on the cheek and then claps wildly with the ends of her fingers against the inside of her wrist, splashing her wine on the rug – it's seen worse and they ignore it.

'Bravo!'

'Rachmaninov – I wanted to find it for you. The opening is wonderful. Like this,' he says, and sets down the glass and plays again, more surely now, the sequence that she heard from the kitchen which has haunted him all day. He does not need to look at the keys, he looks into her face as he plays, his elbow cramped into his side, his head dipped between his shoulders, really Simon your posture is appalling his piano teacher would tell him but Julia, seeing that boyish stoop, his concentration and the appeal in his eyes, says:

'Ah! You're right, it's lovely. I love you.'

MIDNIGHT

The day is almost over. They sit at last at the table, with only a candle to see by. Her hands circle, the silver knife glinting as she gestures, like a signal in the darkness; Simon cuts and compiles neat forkfuls with a little of everything, attentive to her voice and her hands and the flare and flicker of the lights in her eyes caught by the candle, dancing; she tells him the story of her day, which we, having witnessed, need not strain to hear in detail. He watches and listens and swallows this full-bodied, berry-scented wine which he knows, without checking the bottle, she has chosen for him; he lets it fill his mouth with deep simple luxury and watches her hands circle, her eyes wide.

They eat slowly, with pleasure, in no hurry to finish the evening. At last Simon lays down his cutlery; first the knife, then the fork, at a perfect right angle to himself, the careful gesture which Julia now observes with affection, and finds her own hands repeating. They take up their glasses and sit, side by side, on the wicker divan.

★　　★　　★

In the evergreen bushes that grow thickly not far from the conservatory, a curious night-lurker might find an opportune spot to observe from. From here it would once have been possible to witness the flowering of a famous romance; a bloom out of season, for, this being a fine October evening in 1897, there were then no roses in the garden. None but the dark red blossom on the cheeks of a young woman, not yet twenty, flushed as if she had just come in from the snowy landscape that the man beside her is describing. The northern lights crackle between them in the air, invisible. He takes her hand in his, nervous as a boy now, and she is bold for all her blushes, and clasping her fingers about his, draws his palm up to her mouth, to kiss it. The grass is already glistening with the frost that has sharpened the stars. On the cold north wind we might catch a promise, forged in this first sudden passion and never forgotten: 'I will reach it'; 'I will wait.'

Well, so began the Mackley romance; she shivered, they went in, to the relief of the hidden watcher, because October can be bitterly cold as well as beautifully frost-clear in England. But the couple that recline on the wicker divan tonight are not so straight-backed and perching, with neither whalebone nor an exaggerated sense of propriety to hold them rigid.

Fragments are all that can reach us in the darkening garden, where we may relish the night's warm splendour, in these last minutes before midnight. 'It's strange, I think I dreamed last night about Edward; about the Arctic anyway; huge bones in the water; the crushing ice; it woke me and I couldn't sleep. Formaldehyde.' 'Cheese before bedtime.' 'James and his peerless Stilton . . .' (She laughs.) 'Ice on every side, grinding and crushing.' 'Have you read, do you remember? The way he describes it' (far in the distance, the deep heart-boom).

'I didn't know what to do, I wanted to tell you . . . but then Miranda said . . .' 'Hm. It is sad. Very sad. Poor Emily.' 'I keep thinking what she wrote – it must have been after, but how long after? "I cannot go on without," she wrote – but she did, she went on without anything.' 'All those years, pretending.' 'Never saying a word.' 'Watching her son grow without knowing.' 'But at least able to watch him. Not quite alone.'

They quiet to a murmur now; it is hard to catch the sense of what they are saying. An apology? An admission of guilt? No, he will not tell her; perhaps another day. There is no need for that now; Sandra Mitchell cannot touch them, they have closed upon themselves and we, too, must struggle to draw near. But still, 'Sorry; I'm sorry . . .' A memory; a moth flitters. Do you remember? she says; and Do you?; the pond in the park; honeysuckle, aniseed . . . a street café in Paris, drinking pastis (but no, it was kir, she says); I wanted to buy you flowers today, and remembered . . .

remembered how I wished I had brought you flowers. When I came empty-handed and could not speak or reach you. I'm sorry. And hesitant, a promise whispered: there will be a better time to buy you flowers.

When I was a girl I cut holes in the world, and I've slipped through somehow and now I live alongside you, stranded in a different air, and I am fighting now to come back to you and breathe your breath again, in when you breathe out, skin against skin.

They are almost soundless now. Sometimes their lips move but the words are all but lost.

Skin against snow and the sky all around us, the sky and the snow, stars vast all around as you lie down beside me to watch the gold and rose across the sky, snow rounding and dipping like skin, soft like skin against skin, at a still point . . .

She slips down to rest her head on his chest and he puts his mouth to her hair, and they stay there for a long time in a silence no longer restrained. The clock whirrs and strikes twelve, but they do not hear it; the clock in the morning room, which has been waiting for midnight, marks it in silence.

At last they rise; he takes her by the hand; the wine has weighted their limbs with languor. He cups a hand about the flame, breathes, and they are enfolded by the darkness; we might imagine the tiniest fizz as he pinches the smouldering wick with wet fingers. She leads him out, a wisp in the milk-moonlight; she knows her way through the house in the dark.

She leads him through the drawing room; the chandelier is not lit. Dr Nansen's icy slide-show has left no trace upon the wall; we will strain to hear the remnant chatter of voices here. The piano is closed, humming to itself with the barest vibration of pleasure at the recent memory of being touched again. In the hallway the mirror hangs in darkness, all its reflections now melted to silver.

The butterflies hover pearl-white in the stairwell. Upstairs, in the master bedroom, Arabella slumbers one hundred years ago; her husband turns restless on the cot beside her, always recoiling at the precipice of dreaming. But they must forgo their places, cede them to a later generation; Julia and Simon undress in the darkness and lie down on top of the sheets, still fresh from the garden air. It is another warm night, perhaps not so heavy as the last; the window has been open since Simon pulled it up all those hours ago, and as they lie here the long, strange day shifts and settles over their skin. Without speaking, they reach for each other; in the faint streetlight he sees the bronze flash in her eyes, and when she lets herself fall, pupils wide and filled with an indigo sky, she falls into the black gaze that holds hers in the dark without pause, without elision.

★ ★ ★

In the attic, the light from the window gleams off tooth and claw, shining in the glass of eyes that are also unblinking. Those same creatures are all that remain of the dreams of two little boys in the night nursery: two mismatched forms, one narrow and dark, one round and red, lost in their respectively solemn and boisterous fantasies. Beneath them, in the bed where Julia later settled into the dip of the mattress that had shaped itself around Emily Mackley, Emily herself lies beneath a snowflake-patterned counterpane as the century turns, outstretched upon the snow, waiting, feeling her belly grow bigger, feeling it slacken as all but memory fades and her boy cries out above her.

Tess slips out into the garden; after a long day of drowsing and idle, half-hearted play, the night's hunt can at last begin. In the dark, in her element, she is longer, sleeker, stripes silvered in the moon. She slinks under a hole in the fence and is gone, lost to a rodent-rustling wilderness that the human inhabitants of the road would never guess at.

Little Jenny next door rocked herself to sleep hours ago, feeling the pull and rush of the swing still beneath her. Two doors down, over the road, Sandra Mitchell can be seen through her curtains by the light of an unwatched documentary; she has fallen asleep on the sofa, and will no doubt wake through the night sickly with white wine and shame and disappointment; but she is the sort who will pick herself up again, tomorrow. Further up the road, the old man who admired Julia as she passed now sleeps exhausted from his day in the garden, in the sun, and finds his wife waiting for him, in a sundress she never owned. The grocer dreams on a bed of lettuce. The baker's head is pillowed on a soft white roll.

In London, a man of the world bids goodnight to his mistress and sets off home to his unsuspecting spouse, pleased with his day's efforts; free lunch, good wine, good whisky, his new development shaping up, a diverting evening, you *can* have it all he thinks (he will come home to find a house half empty and a cursory note signed *Your estranged wife, Susan*).

In a town two hundred miles away, Julia's cousin of some remove is talking in the darkness to Laura, a woman who has no role in the story he is telling her about the Mackleys and the house he hasn't visited since he was a boy. She may not belong to this story but this woman, his wife, is at the centre of Jonathan's world; she thinks she may be pregnant and she is right; between them another life is readying itself, another Mackley will be born.

And pushing north, through hills and towns and dales and moors, past the silver city where Miranda is washing her hands again and thinking of a man she isn't married to, and of the children sleeping innocent, and of her sister and her father and her mother; through lowlands and highlands and on to the sea; past islands and over a half-frozen black ocean, on to the ice, north, north, leaving the night behind us, into the endless day, here is Edward Mackley, sleeping still under the snow, under the bright Arctic sun; and push a little further and here at last is the Pole, and the world turning beneath us.

Julia's eyes trace the curls of the ceiling; Simon's are closed, his dark lids sheened. Emily Mackley's great-granddaughter turns to face her sleeping husband:

Simon. Pure as the driven . . .

She feels her mind widening in a slow spiral, and she gives herself to sleep, turning her back to him. A few minutes later, he does the same. Their breathing falls into a rhythm with a harmony of its own, a syncopated sighing that cannot be transcribed. But listen: it is peaceful. The symmetry of them, naked above the sheets, the shape of an urn. His knees are drawn up higher so that if they were to move their feet backwards . . . but look: the soles of their feet are already touching, her toes curled hot under his.